LAND SHARKS

LAND SHARKS

A Sage Adair Historical Mystery
of the Pacific Northwest

S. L. Stoner

Yamhill Press
P.O. Box 42348
Portland, OR 97242

Land Sharks

A Yamhill Press Book
All rights reserved

Copyright © 2011 by S. L. Stoner

Cover Design by Alec Icky Dunn/Blackoutprint.com
Interior Design by Josh MacPhee/Justseeds.org

Edition ISBNs

ISBN	13: 978-0-9823184-4-7	(softcover)
ISBN	10: 0-9823184-4-8	(softcover)
ISBN	13: 978-0-9823184-5-4	(ebook)
ISBN	10: 0-9823184-5-6	(ebook)

Publisher's Cataloging in Publication
Stoner, S.L., 1949 –

Land Sharks: A Sage Adair Historical Mystery of the Pacific NW/S.L. Stoner.
p.cm. – (A Sage Adair historical mystery)

1. Northwest, Pacific–History–20th century–Fiction. 2. Shanghai-ing–History–20th Century– Fiction. 3. Labor unions–Fiction. 4. Detective and mystery stories. 5. Martial arts–Fiction. 6. Historical fiction. 7. Adventure fiction. I. Title   II. Series: Sage Adair historical mystery.

12 11 10 09 08 07 06 05 04 03 02

PS3619.T6857L362011   813'.6   QB110-600115

This Book is Dedicated to

Chad Michael Mather
(April 2, 1970 – May 13, 2010)

*A kind, generous, thoughtful, and funny champion
of working people who will be sorely missed.*

ONE

August 15, 1902, The Columbia River opposite Astoria, Oregon

SPLINTERS JABBED INTO HIS cheek so he rolled onto his back. Much better. His matted hair cushioned his head. Movement. Why were the wood planks shifting? They'd not done that before.

He opened his eyes. For the first time, there was dim light. It showed beneath that door at the end of his feet. As he twisted his head sideways, the too familiar swoop of nausea forced his eyes shut—but not before he saw tiers of planked bunks attached to walls that angled inward. When he cautiously opened his eyes again, he saw men lying on the bunks, a few of them groaning, others as still as death.

When he turned his head the other direction, he saw a metal crossbeam less than a foot above his face. Beneath him, the planks vibrated and bucked as if skittering atop an uneven surface. The air reeked of unwashed men and burning coal, same as when they'd crowded around the plant's furnace to warm their hands last winter. A jolt of realization hit him, stiffening his body. A ship. He was below deck on a coal-burning ship.

He slid off the bunk, his hand jabbing into an unconscious body as he fell to the deck. He struggled upright, pain knifing through his bare, swollen feet. His fumbling hand found, then turned, a cold metal knob. When he pulled the door open, he stood at the head of a narrow passageway lit by a string of dim electric bulbs. Still, it was more light than he'd seen for days.

He lifted one foot across the threshold, then the other. His shoulders twitched, anticipating a clawing hand reaching to jerk him backward into the darkness. Nothing happened. So he staggered forward, the pain in his feet, the residue of drugs, the roll of the deck and weakness combined to spin his body first against the left wall and then the right.

At the passageway's end, yet another door opened at his touch. The air that hit his face was cold and so clean it smelled like snow. Clutching the door frame, he breathed its sweetness in through his mouth because dust still clogged his nose.

He stepped out onto the jittering deck, its metal surface cool under his aching feet. One step from the door he froze at the sight of two men coiling a heavy rope onto the deck, their dark figures nearly invisible against the moonless night. Terror swept the confusion from his mind sending his eyes frantically searching for a hiding place. A few steps away a small boat hung next to the railing. A lifeboat. He hobbled around it, squeezing his body between it and a waist-high railing. He held his breath, listening. There was no cry of alarm, no feet running toward him.

His back braced against the lifeboat, he took stock of his surroundings. Ropes swooped overhead like giant spider webs. Rigging and the coal smell meant he was on a steam sailing ship. He looked across the railing and water towards a dark mass that stood silhouetted against the star-studded sky. There faint points of light flickered. Kerosene lamps. Homes. Land.

Leaning out over the railing, his eyes searched ahead of the ship. Farther along the shoreline, lights were clustered, some of them the brighter electric lights. A town. Beyond the town the black ridge of land sloped down until it flattened into nothing. Leaning further out over the water, he saw the faintest band of silver tracing the length of the horizon–day's last light sinking beyond the ocean's rim.

"Noooo . . . " The wail was soft, too low to reach the ears of the men coiling the rope. He collapsed against the lifeboat, his face lifted upward, his tears cold on his face in the breeze that blew from the west. There was no time to waste. Stepping to the rail, he stared down at the rolling swells of ink-black water against the ship's hull.

Climbing over the low railing, he felt the rushing air lift his matted hair. There he stood, hands clutching the solid metal rail, holding on until the ship drew abreast of the town lights. Gulping air, he used his aching feet to launch off and away from the ship.

"Grace." He breathed her name as a prayer as he plunged toward the water.

The ship rode low, so the fall was shorter than he'd expected. Too soon he hit water so cold that he gasped and swallowed. Coughing and sputtering he broke the surface to see the lethal black hull close, too close. He flailed away toward the shore. After a moment of breathless panic he saw that he'd cleared the danger. He'd made it. Escaped.

Downriver, the ship's wake was a pale white froth. Treading water, he watched for a moment before he realized he was shivering. He twisted in the water until he faced the twinkling lights on the dark shore. They seemed farther off, probably because he was no longer high up on the ship's deck. He started stroking toward the distant lights. At least his feet no longer burned from the infection. They were so cold he couldn't feel them. If the water weren't so icy, this swim might feel good. He'd always liked to swim. Back home, the water was brown and bathtub warm. Nothing like this.

Time had seemed endless when he'd been so thirsty. They'd sometimes begged for a sip of the foul tasting water even though they knew it would send them back into the world of nightmares. Now, water surrounded him. His tongue lapped at it. Sweet, yet cold, so cold. Lifting his head, he again sighted on the shore lights. They weren't any brighter or bigger. How could that be?

His teeth began to chatter so hard that he was afraid they'd crack. God, his arms felt heavy. He relaxed, let his mind drift with his body. Grace liked to slide her hands down his arms, smiling, half admiration, half tease–her hands featherlike, her face moving closer.

Was the water warmer? Had he reached the shallows? That made sense. The sun warmed shallow water during the day, and now he was floating in that warmer water. Yes, it was definitely warmer, just like the water in their Saturday-night hip bath, Grace so beautiful, glistening water drops on satin skin. How she blushed rosy whenever she caught him staring.

He lifted his head. The shore lights remained tiny pinpoints. His arms ached, his legs moved like logs too heavy to lift. And he was so sleepy. Now that the water was warmer, maybe he could float on his back, rest a bit. No hurry, now that he was free.

He rolled in the water until he faced the sky. He'd always liked to float staring into the deep blue prairie sky. Still, he'd never lain back just to look at the stars. Look Grace, that group over there is the Big Dipper. And that low red one? That's Mars, I think. Never seen the stars this bright. Could almost read by them, couldn't we, Grace? Some folks claim the stars are suns, so maybe that's why they're so bright. Watch me reach my hand up and touch one of them. Funny, my arm is so weak it doesn't want to move—maybe because they hardly ever fed us. No matter.

Grace. Sometimes, I say your name softly, just to myself. I've never told you that. I should have. I can picture your face, bright just like a candle. Oh, how it's going to light up when I walk in the door. I'm so tired. I'll just sleep a bit in the warmth of all these suns. After that, I'll come home. I promise.

TWO

August 16, 1902, Portland, Oregon

LIKE DRAGGING A ROTTEN FISH across a bear trail. Sage smiled, watching as the Chinaman, two woven shoulder baskets draped across his hunched back, shuffled past the drunks leaning against the Tex saloon's front wall. "Hey there 'Mister Pig-tail,' you scurrying back to the hive? It'll be dark soon," one of them shouted.

The derisive whoops and hollers heaped upon the passing Chinese man were no surprise. It was a common enough occurrence on Portland's streets. Especially outside saloons in the North End. The Tex, in particular, attracted disreputable layabouts, men who lacked anything better to do with their time. Despite the drunks' noisy attention, the Chinese man kept his face averted, well-shadowed beneath the wide brim of his conical straw hat. What he couldn't conceal, however, was the wide band of gold encircling each wrist. As he reached up to adjust the yoke, his loose cotton sleeves dropped to his elbows, exposing his wealth to the sunlight. The sight quelled the rowdiness and hissed speculation took over.

One of the lounging men, who'd remained separate from the others and their antics, straightened to his full height of at least six four. Probably tipped the scales at two hundred and seventy pounds, Sage estimated. Not fat, though. Nothing in his physique suggested that. He looked like a man fond of spending his idle hours heaving boulders. The man snarled at the others. They stepped away from him, their merriment disappearing quick as water down a drain. With a laugh and dismissive wave of his huge hand, he strode off in the direction taken by the Chinese man. Murmuring broke out among the wastrels, a few shaking their heads in disgust, some sending hostile looks at the departing man's back before turning away. Sage chose to assign a positive interpretation to their general reaction. While they might think it fine sport to verbally abuse a Chinaman, anything worse was more than they could stomach.

From the other side of the street, Sage tracked the giant's progress, turning aside to peer into dusty shop windows whenever he thought the big man might look behind. There was no need to bother. The man appeared oblivious to everything except the progress of his prey.

Half a block ahead, the Chinese man slipped into a dark alley. The big man sped up by lengthening his stride. The man was so intent that he failed to notice Sage crossing the street and quickening his pace in an effort to catch up. Seconds later, the big man also disappeared into the alley's dark mouth.

When he reached the opening, Sage saw that there'd been no need to hurry. Fong was already in his fighting stance, the yoked baskets and straw hat tossed to one side. The lack of fear and readiness of the much smaller man seemed to give the big man pause. He hesitated. Then laughed, with all the contempt of a man twice the size of his victim.

Sage shook his head and pulled a bandana from his pocket. Tying it across the lower part of his face, he made sure it fit snug. Although many a man roaming Portland's North End streets sported a droopy mustache, there was no point in risking future recognition.

In front of him, the brute spread his arms and waded forward, looking as if he intended to sweep the smaller man into a crushing bear hug. That was a mistake.

With an audible snap, the slipper-clad foot flashed out, connecting with the big man's midriff hard, knocking a resounding "oomph" out of him. That first blow was followed by a tornado of feet, legs, hands and maybe even a forehead slamming into the man's chin. Sage wasn't too sure about the forehead, it happened so fast. Fong's final whirlwind blows, whether from fist, feet or other body parts, had left the big man lying on the ground, curled around his middle like a pill bug.

Sage stepped forward and leaned down close to the big man's ear. "My friend there can kill you with a single kick. Do you believe me?"

A whimper was his answer.

Sage kept his voice low and spoke slowly, "Listen carefully, Budnick. You have jackrolled your last old man in this town. I don't know what manure pile you climbed out of, but you be aboard the southbound train that leaves in exactly one hour. Otherwise, my friend and I will shove you under the nearest rock with more broken bones than you gave those old men you like to hurt. You hear me?"

The big man groaned. Sage nudged his work boot into the man's kidney. Budnick shrieked, "Okay, one hour. I'll be on that train in one hour."

"See that you are. We'll be watching."

One hour later, Sage lounged on a polished wooden bench in the middle of the Union Station's cavernous waiting room. He was watching Budnick hobble across the platform and gingerly mount the metal steps onto the San Francisco bound train. A stuffed valise dangled from one hand while his other hand pressed against his ribs.

Minutes later, Sage and Fong met up in the alder woods at the southern end of the rail yard. The departing train's chuff and toot drifted back to them through the summer twilight. The train wouldn't stop until it hit Salem, fifty miles south. It was a ride much more comfortable than the jackroller Budnick deserved. But, at least he was gone.

"He go?" asked the Chinese man.

"He gone," Sage responded with a smile.

"Where now?" Fong asked, smiling back.

"Need to head on down to Nelly June's boarding house. Oscar took Timmy O'Shea there after Budnick beat him up. We'll tell them what happened. That way, Oscar will stay at home and take care of Timmy."

Timmy had received a bad beating from Budnick. Yet, he was a tough old buzzard, already on the way to recovery. It was Oscar's reaction, more than Timmy's beating, that had spurred them into action. The fire in the frail old man's eyes left no doubt, Oscar intended to revenge the hurt dealt to his lifelong companion. The two geezers were a matched pair, North End regulars who'd regale anyone willing to listen with colorful stories of bygone days. It wasn't just Timmy and Oscar. Budnick had stepped way beyond his welcome in Portland town. He'd left a trail of penniless and hurt old men in his wake, always careful to pick on those too enfeebled or small, to hurt him back. Sage and Fong agreed the time had come to step in and take care of Budnick once and for all.

"Nothing more than a sniveling coward running around in a Goliath body," Sage observed.

Beside him, Fong said nothing. No doubt reliving and critiquing his fight with Budnick. Correction. His split second "trouncing" of Budnick. That had been a one-sided demonstration of incredible skill. No "fight" to it.

"Hurt side of hand. Should hold it like this, instead of this," Fong explained as he slightly altered the angle of his hand.

Sage wasn't certain he saw a difference. To him, Fong's every move looked like flowing perfection. "Mr. Fong, I thought you were magnificent. I hope someday to have your skill at the 'snake and crane'," Sage said.

"Time and much practice decide such things. You are young enough. Maybe can still happen," the other man responded before asking, "After we visit Miss Nelly June's and tell old men Budnick gone what we do next? Weed roof top flower garden?" Fong's voice lacked enthusiasm. Sage wasn't the only one getting bored with the inactivity.

"Darned if I know." They'd used up a few days tracking Budnick down and deciding how to bushwhack him. That accomplished, they were at loose ends once again. "I keep wishing for a letter from St. Alban. Cleaning out the town's jackrollers isn't my idea of how to effect serious political change." Sage's voice was glum.

"All action political," Fong intoned. Sage couldn't tell from his companion's blank face whether Fong was serious or employing deliberate parody.

The heavy dirt pressing down on his chest forced him to gasp for air. A fallen boulder trapped his arm. Even though he strained to see, it remained blacker than coal tar. Unable to move, he was going die here.

"Sage, Sage, wake up, son!" Her urgent voice pierced the blackness. It wasn't a boulder on his arm, it was his mother's hand. Strong, firm, and alive. She was shaking him.

He opened his eyes, looking up into her worried face that was lit by the sputtering candle she held in her other hand. She placed the candle on the bedside table, kissed his forehead and smoothed back his black hair with its shock of white at the temple. "That's what happens when you and Fong lark about stirring up trouble," she said, without a hint of compassion. She straightened and headed toward the door.

"You're just jealous," he mumbled to her departing back.

"Humph," she responded as the door closed behind her.

Two hours later, they sat eating in silence at the small alcove table Sage kept in his third floor room. He held his Sunday *Daily Journal* upright although his sleepy thoughts meandered, like the dust motes in the breeze that poured through the alcove's open window. Aside from those flitting bits of dust, his combination bedsitting room, with its red Turkish carpet, four-poster bed, walnut bureau, beveled mirror armoire, two easy chairs and lace curtains, was immaculate and even–here, his conscience twinged–luxurious. Still, if any stranger glanced into the room, nothing here would belie Sage's public persona of wealthy and attractively shallow restaurant owner. Unless they looked under the bed.

Across from him, his mother sipped her coffee and munched a biscuit while paging through the latest issue of *Collier's*. Under her breath, she either clucked at extravagance or thoughtfully hmm'd when something interesting caught her eye. He studied her face with its high cheekbones. The morning light exposed faint lines around her eyes and vertical grooves that bracketed her wide mouth. Otherwise, her skin was still smooth and her chin firm. In her mid-fifties, Mae Clemens was a striking woman. Not head turning but a woman whose beauty grew more apparent the more often you looked at her. Only her rough, big-knuckled hands betrayed years of eking out a living in the coal field towns of Pennsylvania. He knew that those had been years of extreme poverty, endless work and unbearable loneliness. Yet, they hadn't broken her.

"You're doing it again," she remarked, her eyes still on the magazine, her tone a tad irritated.

He tossed the paper onto the table. "I think I am entitled to look at you. After all, I didn't see your face for almost twenty years. That's a lot of time to make up."

She looked at him, her dark blue eyes exactly like his. "Sage, I don't mind you watching me, but leave go of those regrets. They darken the day like a low hanging cloud."

An old conflict. Yes, now they both lived in improved circumstances. Life was good. She was here, living in their third-floor rooms at the top of a building he owned, thanks to his Klondike gold. They operated the elite Mozart's Table, a restaurant second only to the Portland Hotel's elegant dining room. And, best of all, they worked as partners in a secret mission. It was a mission that gave meaning and purpose to both their lives.

Still, playing the urbane restaurant proprietor, John Sagacity Adair, was trying at times. From his twelve years as the rich mine owner's foster child, Sage knew what to say and wear. He also knew how to insert himself into a group of wealthy men and win their confidence. His mirror told him why their wives seemed to like him; his six-foot height, even features, jet black hair with its dash of white at the temple, and his luxuriant waxed mustache always drew favorable attention from their direction.

But all of that was the public John S. Adair. Few in Portland knew of Sage Adair or his many itinerant worker personas. Also hidden was an internal toughness. One forged during the lonely years when he'd lived with the cold-hearted mine owner and later, in the Klondike, where that toughness saved his life in situations where most men died.

He counted on the fact that Portland's wealthy elites were so taken up with their showy excesses that they failed to see beneath John Adair's well-groomed exterior. They had to remain oblivious to his purpose, a purpose as unyielding as the hard rock coal he'd mined as a child. He intended to make sure that economic justice triumphed over their selfish greed.

Sage shook off his reverie. "I keep waiting for St. Alban to write. I'm ready for some excitement," he said, his fingers absently drumming on the table top.

"Do tell," Mae responded, slapping the magazine shut. She tossed it on the table, "You might say that today. As I recall, a few weeks ago, you were singing a different tune entirely. Fact is, I recollect you telling me you'd reconsidered your adventuring life while you rode in that boxcar, all trussed up like a Christmas goose."

Her jab sent him back to that boxcar ride. It had been a very close call. Only Fong's remarkable fighting skills prevented the killers from bashing Sage in the head and dropping his body off a railroad bridge into the river.

He smiled wryly. "You know how it is, Mother. Memory fades. Besides, next time I'll be more careful. Think things through before I act," he assured her.

"Ha! John Sagacity Adair, rashness is your trait and always will be. You flirt with risk like a moth 'round a candle," she sputtered before seeing his wide grin. "Here, eat some of these," she said, nudging a plate of jelly-filled pastries toward him, "Ida baked them this morning, just for you. That poor woman is tiring herself out cooking up all these tokens of gratitude."

Sage patted his flat stomach. As part of his boxcar escapade, Sage had also saved Ida's nephew, Matthew, from being hung as a murderer. He hoped the restaurant's cook would reach the bottom of her gratitude bucket while he could still button his trousers.

He held up his hand. "Can't eat now, Mother. I'm heading up to the attic. It's time for my lesson with Mr. Fong. He says that I'll get sick if I eat beforehand. And as you know, Mr. Fong is always right."

Her eyebrow arched. "Humph! Nobody is always right unless he can walk on water. And I haven't seen our Mr. Fong perform that particular little feat yet."

Sage smirked. He knew she relied on the Chinese man's insights as much as he did. Although they'd been working together less than two years, it was hard to envision any of their St. Alban missions succeeding without Mr. Fong Kam Tong's assistance. "Yup," he thought with satisfaction, "The three of us form a team as sturdy as a well-built, three-legged stool."

A soft tap sounded on the door. It swung open just wide enough for the red-haired Matthew to poke first his head, then half his body, into the room.

"Excuse me, Mr. Adair. A messenger," he cleared his throat and continued, "I brought a letter for Mrs. Clemens from her cousin in Telluride, Colorado, and I thought that maybe she'd want it right away, leastways that's what Aunt Ida thought, so I hoped it was okay if I disturbed you . . . I will come back later if you'd rather . . ." Matthew had already started edging backward, even as his words continued pouring forward.

Sage raised his hand to gesture the boy forward into the room. "No, no, you're fine, Matthew. Mrs. Clemens does want the letter. You did right to bring it up. Thank you."

A blush flooded the boy's freckles as he shambled awkwardly forward, ducking his head politely to Mae Clemens. After handing over the letter, the boy hastily backed out of the room but not before first planting the door's edge squarely into his back. Face now scarlet, the boy scooted into the hallway, shutting the door with a bang.

"Good Lord, that poor boy is as bad as his aunt when it comes to worshiping you. I think if it were possible to hide in your pocket, he'd climb right in." Mae shook her head but a smile tweaked the corners of her mouth. She handed the unopened letter to Sage. There was no "cousin" in Telluride. The letter was from St. Alban.

Sage thought about the boy as he slit open the envelope. Matthew was indeed showing a marked tendency to get underfoot. Not good if it required continually dodging the boy. "Well, Matthew's still unsettled from his brother's murder and his own time in jail. He'll get his feet back under him. He'll get over it." Sage said, unfolding the single sheet of stiff paper. "Besides I'm thinking to buy him one of those bicycles. That'll take his mind off what . . ."

Sage looked up, a surge of excitement sweeping through him and into a wide grin. "It is from the Saint. He's assigned us another job!" he said.

THREE

A DUSKY PINK ROSE stood in a sapphire blue vase, its velvet petals glistening in the sunlight streaming through the skylight. Fong sat before it, cross-legged on the polished pine floor. His half-closed eyes seemed focused on the flower, his long face a serene mask. Sage dropped into a similar cross-legged position. He wanted to confer with Fong about the new mission but Fong was strict when it came to their training regimen. No talking until it was completed. Sage chaffed over the delay but it was useless to try to push.

As they sat in silence, the sound of wagon wheels rattling on the wood block paving four stories below mingled with the sound of the pigeons' burbled cooing in their rooftop coop. As the sunlight heated the room, a sweet rose fragrance began layering the air.

Cramps began to tighten in Sage's legs. He shifted and hoped that Fong was nearing the end of his meditation—not that the older man would allow anything as insignificant as leg cramps to intrude upon his internal quest. Not only could Fong sit cross-legged for hours, but when done, he uncoiled lithe as a snake.

Fong's eyes opened and he looked at Sage. His smile was gentle; his voice quiet as he observed, "This flower you placed in vase is most beautiful. One day your flowers will grow this beautiful."

Heat traveled up Sage's neck into his face. His recent

rooftop gardening efforts were another outcome of that terrifying train ride. He marveled at the contentment he felt puttering around his sprouting plants.

"This flower," Sage said, touching a petal with his finger, "came from the garden of an elderly woman up near City Park. She gave me this rose and a small cutting when she caught me standing on her lawn admiring it."

"Ah," Fong said. "A gift, more precious." He rose to his feet in a single fluid motion. "Come, we begin."

"Before we begin, Mr. Fong, there's news from St. Alban," Sage said, lurching to his feet, one leg numb from holding in one position for too long.

Fong raised a hand to halt Sage's speech. "First, we exercise. After, we talk."

As sunlight slowly traversed across the floor, they moved through the snake and crane exercise. After the final movement, the raising and lowering of parallel hands, they immediately faced off to practice the attack-and-defend fighting style Fong called "push hands." At last, Fong halted their workout after he'd effortlessly flipped Sage to the floor five times in quick succession.

"Not good today. You too distracted. Like riverbank fish. Sucking air and swimming at same time. No good." Fong tossed him a towel.

Sage caught the towel and laughed. "There's no such thing as a riverbank fish."

"You never fish river, so how you know?"

"Anyway, it's your fault, Mr. Fong. I wanted to tell you the news but you made me hold it in until we'd finished. My mind wouldn't let go of it. I tried."

"Hah," said Fong, his face momentarily splitting into a smile. "That is point! Always there is distraction. Distraction is another enemy in battle. To defeat, focus on firm ball in center of belly. Let distraction flow in and out without sticking, like ocean wave on beach. When thought stick, relax and release it."

Sage shook his head ruefully. "Another one of your lessons within a lesson, Mr. Fong?"

"Of course," Fong said. He turned and climbed the ladder that led to the roof.

Exasperated at yet another delay, Sage looked around the attic. Acknowledging that there was no one with whom to commiserate, he shrugged and followed Fong up the ladder.

The late summer morning was heating up and the rosebush leaves drooped. Sage crossed to the rain barrel and used a tin can to dip up water. He watered the dirt around the plants that grew in the four wooden boxes he'd recently installed on the rooftop, careful not to wet their leaves. That task completed, he joined Fong on a south-facing rough bench that was also a new addition to the roof. To the east, just beyond the waterfront warehouses and the naked spars of sailing ships, the sun glinted on the Willamette River. Directly across the street, to the west, a six-story building obstructed their view of the Vista Ridge hills. The air smelled of roof tar, pigeon coop straw, and the warming dirt in the garden boxes.

Sage marshaled his thoughts, eager to talk about Kincaid and the other missing organizer. Yet again, Fong forestalled him by saying, "This garden is both peaceful and always changing. Like the snake and crane way of life we Chinese call 'tai chi.' Many hundreds of years old. Means all things must be in balance and done with moderation."

"Yes, I know. I think I've learned part of that lesson the last few months." Sage waved a hand at the flower boxes. "That's the reason why there's now a garden up here on this roof. It's me trying to create a little balance in my life."

To cut off the subject, Sage plunged in, determined to begin discussing St. Alban's problem of the missing union organizers. "Right now, let me tell you what St. Alban has asked us to do. He wants us to discover what has happened to two union organizers. He says that they were helping plywood workers form a union in their factory. Now both organizers are missing. The first man was unmarried. One day, about six months ago, he didn't show up for work at the factory. Didn't say a word to anyone. St. Alban thought maybe he'd just gotten discouraged by his slow progress and abandoned the job.

"Problem is, about two weeks ago, the same thing happened again. Only this time, the missing organizer is a married man—with a wife and baby. That made St. Alban think that maybe these men didn't leave on their own. He's afraid they're dead. He wants us to find out what happened to them and stop it from happening to the next guy he sends."

Fong squinted across the rooftop toward the river. Sage waited patiently. The other man was a full partner in their missions for St. Alban—ever since that night a few years ago when he'd rescued Sage from a beating and learned of Sage and Mae's secret life. Fong had asked to join their efforts, explaining, "You fight same men who harm my people. They pay us pennies and kick us like dogs or worse." As Fong spoke, a painful memory seemed to wash across his normally impassive face. Sage hadn't probed the other man's wound. He and Mae accepted Fong's offer to help and had been grateful for it every day since.

That was the past. Today, keen interest shone in Fong's dark eyes as he asked, "Where is plywood factory?"

"Upriver, near that small town called Milwaukie. Not too far, maybe ten miles or less."

"I know of Milwaukie. Cousin own laundry there. What are names of missing men?" Fong's question wasn't an idle one.

"St. Alban wrote that the first organizer who went missing is a middle-aged fellow named Walter Amacker. The last one's name is Joseph Kincaid. He gave me the address of Kincaid's wife. I thought I'd start there—with the man's wife. Might as well figure out whether he deliberately scampered off or whether someone did something to him." As he spoke, Sage realized that it was not going to be an easy interview. Labor movement activists worked in constant danger. Too often their women and children end up alone in the world. His mother, Mae, was proof of that.

Fong sent Sage a sympathetic look as he said, "I will ask cousins if they hear anything about plywood workers named Walter Amacker and Joseph Kincaid."

The other man's use of the word "cousin" was not strictly correct. Sage doubted whether any of the men Fong called "cousin" were his blood relations. Rather, he'd told Sage that the term "cousin" referred to men who belonged to Fong's mutual aid organization; something Fong called his "tong." Over time it became clear that there was immense value in having access to Fong's fellow tong members. The cousins knew things about people, things those people thought securely hidden. And, often the cousins ferreted out what they didn't know. Sage gazed up the river. Again he mused over the strength of their team: Fong, his mother and himself. He was certain that their unbreakable unity was sufficient to overcome whatever challenges this search for the missing organizers delivered.

❀ ❀ ❀

An hour or so later, Sage was ready to make his exit from Mozart's as John Sagacity Adair. He'd need to arrive at the Kincaid's, however, as a man named John Miner. Miner was some-one else altogether different. As John Miner, Sage was an itinerant worker, just one more hungry fish in a sea of thousands.

At night, Sage used the secret tunnel extending from the restaurant's cellar into an alleyway one building over. It made his departure virtually undetectable. During the day, however, that exit was risky. There was too much foot traffic on the street outside the alley, making it more likely he'd be seen clambering up through the trap door. This dilemma called for a variety of stratagems. Today, as John Adair, he planned to stroll into the most elite parlor house in town just like any other gentleman cus-tomer. Once there, he'd change his clothes, traverse its basement and exit from a milliner shop one street over as John Miner.

His passage down the sidewalk was accompanied by fra-grant wafts of the extra bay rum face tonic he'd patted on just in case the establishment's proprietor, Lucinda Collins, was at home. He was looking forward to seeing her face brighten when he walked through her door. She always lifted his spirits, especially in these days following his recent brush with death. Although they hadn't discussed it, he believed that Lucinda now reserved all her affections for him. He found himself feeling sim-ilarly exclusive toward her.

❀ ❀ ❀

"Oh, Mr. Adair," said Lucinda's maid Elmira. Her cafe-au-lait-colored face twisted with distress when she saw him on the doorstep. "Miz Lucinda will be so upset that she missed you. It's been some days since you've stopped by. She took one of our girls to see the Sisters at the St. Vincent's hospital. Some kind of trouble in her internal workings, we're thinking."

"Which girl?" Sage asked, handing Elmira his hat. She hung it carefully on the hall tree, next to the two men's hats already adorning its carved branches.

"Carrie Lynn, her name is. She's down from Seattle, trying to escape from some persistent customer. Says he liked to hit her. We're afraid he broke something loose inside her."

Sage didn't have time to wait around for Lucinda's return. Kincaid had been missing for more than two weeks, Amacker for six months. It would take at least an hour to reach Milwaukie. Then he had to interview Kincaid's wife, talk to others and make the trip back.

"Please tell Miz Lucinda events prevented me from waiting for her return. If you don't mind, I'd like to take advantage of her special exit down the back stairs and through the basement after I pick up a few things I keep in her closet."

Elmira raised her eyebrows. A soul of discretion, she nevertheless didn't bother hiding that she knew he was frequently up to something. The twinkle in her eye told him that she was well aware of his odd duds in the madam's closet. She'd seen him in disguise sneaking out the back entrance like a dodgy politician. Lord knew what the woman thought. He'd always been afraid to broach the topic with her.

Once in Lucinda's room, Sage changed into what he thought of as his John-Miner-going-to-church suit. Minutes later, he was crossing the dim basement, grateful for its casement windows. He climbed the wooden steps onto the shop floor and strode to the alley door. As usual, the women treadling the sewing machines never glanced up from their work. They'd likely seen this bolt hole exit used by far more noteworthy townsmen than the nondescript John Miner wearing his Sunday best. Regardless, they'd never say anything—not if they wanted to keep their jobs. Poverty forged a strong chain, keeping them firmly beneath the milliner's heel. The milliner, in turn, kept quiet because of the extremely low rent Lucinda charged for the space.

The gray horse he hired had a smooth gait, so Sage enjoyed the hour-long ride through downtown, across the river and south along the river bank. He easily found Kincaid's house. It squatted down among other tiny clapboard houses in a weedy field just outside the plywood mill gates. Without a doubt, the houses were ones built, owned and never maintained by the factory owner. Sage could picture the inside layout. As a child he'd lived in a similar house. A typical mill town shack had a narrow hallway running down one side ending at a back door. On one side of the hallway, three doorways opened into parlor, kitchen and bedroom. A well-trod dirt path out the back door assuredly led straight as an arrow to a one-hole outhouse.

The Kincaids' weathered clapboard was distinguished from its neighbors by the sole personal touch customarily allowed mill town renters. An unpainted window box, holding a profusion of leggy red geranium blooms, hung beneath the single window next to the front door. The flowers gave the shack a defiant cheeriness. The sight of those flowers sent his thoughts back to that Appalachian shack. Springtime, geraniums had filled its window box, too, his mother having sheltered them inside throughout each bitter winter. Today, the sight filled him with pity and foreboding. His mother's optimistic flowers hadn't shielded her family from tragedy.

Sage stepped up and rapped his knuckles against a flimsy door that shook within its frame. A young woman, holding an infant, pulled it open. Murmuring something unintelligible, she stepped out onto the stoop.

An aurora of unruly light brown hair framed her pale, heart-shaped face. Her skin was satiny, like the rose petal his finger had stroked that morning. But her face was slack, without animation. This woman didn't care how unkempt she looked. Her faded pink cotton dress drooped off her shoulders as though she hadn't bothered fastening its buttons. When she turned to pull the door shut behind her, he saw that was the case. The infant against her shoulder gazed at Sage with wide, unfocused eyes that seemed to find the world bewildering.

"Mrs. Kincaid?" he asked.

"Yes, I'm Mrs. Joseph Kincaid." Her arms tightened

protectively around the child. "Are you here about my husband?" The muscles around her eyes tensed and her gaze sharpened. Hard to tell whether she was fearful or angry.

Sage doffed his hat. "Yes, ma'am, I am. My name is John Miner. The union asked me to find out what happened to him. I'm sorry, Mrs. Kincaid, there's no news of him yet. I stopped by hoping you will tell me about when you saw him last. Maybe, what he told you and what you knew about his plans."

His piece said, Sage waited, his hat pressed against the twill of his cheap blue serge suit, watching her closely for any sign of deception.

Her chin lifted and her lips tightened, her face taking on a mulish look as her blue eyes drilled into him. "The police stopped looking for him," she said bitterly. "They act like he deliberately abandoned us. He's not that kind of man. He loves us." She said the last three words emphatically, as if trying to convince herself. Her eyes filled with tears and she looked down, pressing her lips onto the silky down on the baby's head.

Sage shifted his feet and let the silence stretch out. It seemed she'd forgotten his presence, losing herself in some byway of memory or possibly in the dead end of despair. Grief seemed to drape across her bent shoulders like a soggy blanket. Sage cleared his throat to summon her back to the present.

She started. When she spoke her words sounded mumbled, as if clogged by unshed tears. "We fought. He stormed off to work mad. It was my fault. I'd been up with the baby all night and I . . . I hollered things I didn't mean. I said I was going to leave, take Faith with me." She sagged, as if her legs had suddenly lost their bones.

Sage grabbed her elbow. "Let's sit here on the stoop for a minute," he said gesturing with his bowler hat.

She nodded and he eased her down as she swung the baby forward to sit in her lap, wrapping both her arms around the child as if protecting her. The baby wiggled unsuccessfully against her mother's grip. Sage sat beside the woman, watching as his John Miner Sunday best boots collected the path's dust stirred up by a slight breeze. Tears once again coursed unchecked down her cheeks onto the baby's head. Guilt and grief. The most potent mix of pains.

Sage gazed about him. In one direction, down the dirt road, stood the mill yard with its clutter of heaped wood scraps and stacked plywood sheeting protected by rusted tin awnings. In the opposite direction, the dirt road intersected the main road leading to Portland. A ramshackle two-story building anchored one corner of the junction.

At last, she raised a sleeve to wipe her face dry. He cleared his throat. "Tell me how you and Joseph came to live here in Milwaukie, Oregon," he said quietly.

She sniffed, wiped her face with a grimy sleeve and began talking, almost to herself. Her words poured out. The story she told was one typical of the thousands of people flooding into the area, all looking to create a new life in the more sparsely settled West. Joseph, it seemed, was a strong union man so he had jumped at the chance to organize a union at the plywood mill. There'd been no extra pay for the work, so they'd been struggling from one paltry mill paycheck to the next. Men like Kincaid risked their jobs and their lives for no reward other than the hope that one day, they'd see economic and social justice for people like themselves.

Mrs. Kincaid looked at him with wide eyes, her face earnest as she explained, "I was hollering at him about the money, but that's not why I hate it here. Mostly, I've been sick to my stomach afraid. Every week, some man down there to the mill loses his finger or his hand. That's what I was worrying myself about. I didn't want to jinx Joey by talking about it. But every day when he left for work, I dropped to my knees and prayed that God would keep him safe from those saws. Every single day, up till the day he just up and disappeared." Her chin started to wobble.

Sage spoke quickly, "When's the last anyone saw him?"

"On July thirty-first, over two weeks ago, at that saloon right down there." She pointed toward the building at the junction. Her chin started wobbling again and she gulped before continuing, "It was after the union meeting. They all tell me that he only drank one beer before he left. He told everybody he was coming home to me and Faith." She laid her cheek on the silky hair of the drowsy baby and sighed.

"What does Joseph look like?"

Without a word she handed the baby to him and nipped into the house. He held the warm bundle, looked down into the sleeping little face and felt an unfamiliar stirring. Not a bad feeling—just unfamiliar.

She returned holding a photograph. Taking the child back, she gave Sage the picture.

It was their wedding picture. Though they were posed like stone statues, their wide eyes still shone with youthful optimism. His hair was curly like hers and his jaw was remarkably square and determined. The young man would be easy to recognize, if Sage ever laid eyes upon him. He handed the photograph back to her.

She didn't take it. "No, no. Take that away with you. Joey and I took a little silly. We asked the photographer to print a number of photographs. One for each child we wanted to have. We planned to raise four or five kids, some our own, some adopted. When he comes home . . ." she swallowed hard, "if he comes home, you can give it back."

As he stood to go, she struggled to her feet and clutched his forearm with small, tense fingers. "Mr. Miner, please find out what happened to my Joey. I need to know if he deserted Faith and me or if something bad happened to him." Her face crumpled and she fought for control. When she spoke again, her voice was calm. "If it turns out that Joey just up and left us, we got nobody who cares about us—nobody." Her voice trailed off, her staring eyes fixed on the dirt at the bottom of the steps as if fearful of the earth opening up and swallowing her whole.

The flat tone of that last word, 'nobody,' made Sage uneasy. He cleared his throat and drew on a confidence he didn't feel to say, "You need to keep up your hopes, Mrs. Kincaid. I'll do everything possible to learn what happened to your husband." He caught her eyes in a steady gaze and spoke from that center in his belly Fong always talked about. "I am absolutely certain he did not leave you of his own free will." As he spoke the words, he knew somehow, he was speaking the truth. "No matter what, I promise to return and tell you what really happened to him," he said.

Sage pulled out all the folding money in his pockets, pressed it into her hand and closed her unresisting fingers around the wad. "Right now, you must take care of yourself and take care of little Faith. You know that's what Joseph would want you to do."

When Sage reached the corner of the narrow dirt street, he glanced back at the shabby little house. Mrs. Kincaid still sat on the steps, her face hidden, her body hunched over the sleeping child on her lap. The sight made him ask a question of that nameless being he sometimes believed in: Why are such heavy burdens placed upon such frail shoulders?

FOUR

MILLMEN'S, THE SALOON where Kincaid was last seen, was the ramshackle, two-story, wood frame building visible from the Kincaids' front steps. When Sage stepped inside, he saw that the sunlight filtering through the clean front window provided the only daytime illumination. That light revealed a well-swept floor, and scrubbed wooden wire spools that served as tables surrounded by mismatched kitchen chairs. Overhead, unlit kerosene lanterns dangled from exposed beams. Colorful magazine pictures were pasted on the drab brown walls. A simple plank, extending the length of one wall until ending eight feet shy of the rear corner, served as the establishment's bar. Behind it, a wall shelf held glass mugs, shot glasses and a few half-full whiskey bottles. A large wooden keg, sporting a bunghole tap, anchored the plank end nearest the door. At the plank's far end, stood a cook stove, a huge battered tin wash pan on a table and stacks of plates filling rough wall shelves. This rude corner arrangement was the establishment's kitchen. An odor of pan-fried onions goaded Sage's stomach into rumbling.

All in all a welcoming place to men dropping by for a beer after work or when bringing their wives to socialize with neighbors. Drunken fisticuffs were the most likely danger in this establishment. Altogether, a decent watering hole. Not much like the North End's saloons except for the beer, whiskey and meager furnishings. Millmen's seemed an unlikely place for a Kansas farm boy to encounter danger.

The man behind the bar was drying beer mugs. He was a slight man, with pale skin, high forehead and watery blue eyes. Sharp intelligence lit the penetrating look he gave Sage. "Help you, sir?" he asked affably. Sage reached the bar and rested a boot on the wooden, floor-mounted foot rail that ran length of the plank. He nodded at the barkeep and said, "If you don't mind, a root beer will suit me fine. It's a little early in the day for the real stuff."

The man laughed and lifted a brown bottle from a box on the floor behind the bar. He pried off the cap, poured the deep brown liquid into a mug and handed it to Sage, saying, "Ain't too many of my customers with that idea. More's the pity for some of them."

Sage swallowed the heavy liquid, licking the foam off his droopy mustache. "I wanted to ask you about one of your customers," he began.

The barkeep's face stiffened. "And just which customer might that be?" His tone was chilly.

"A young man named Joseph Kincaid."

The barkeep's eyes narrowed, openingly suspicious now. "I guess what I might say depends on just who it is doing the asking. You with the police or the plywood company?"

With this man, Sage realized, truth would give a longer ride than a lie. "Neither. I'm helping the union and Mr. Kincaid's wife by trying to find the man," Sage responded.

"Just why the heck should I trust what you say, mister?" The bartender stepped back and crossed his arms across his chest, eyes still narrowed and face skeptical.

Sage pulled the couple's wedding photo from his pocket and slid it across the counter. "Mrs. Kincaid gave me this. Only person I could have gotten it from, don't you think?"

The barkeep stepped forward, took the photo and studied it longer than was necessary for him to identify those pictured. He laid it down on the plank and used a single finger to gently push it back toward Sage. When he looked up, the suspicion was gone, leaving only a worry crease wrinkling his forehead. "He's dead," he said, his voice flat.

Sage's mug clattered against the bar. Someone found Kincaid's body?

Sage's face apparently signaled his thoughts because the man rushed to say, "No, they ain't found his body. That don't matter. There's no question in my mind. He's dead."

"What makes you say that?"

The barkeep's finger tapped the photo. "Joey loved that pretty little lady and I don't believe he ran off from her. He left the saloon before anyone else that night because he wanted to be home with her. And that baby daughter of his—he was so excited about that little girl. Why, he babbled on and on about every little thing she did. It was like she was the first baby ever born. No, I'm certain he's dead or something worse. Nary a doubt in my mind 'bout that." He shook his head, his face sad, "Just two blocks to walk and poof, he's gone. Has to be somethin' bad happened."

Sage sighed. The man's confirmation of St. Alban's fear deepened Sage's own persistent foreboding without giving him anything to act on. Sage pressed for more information, "Can you think of anything Kincaid said, or anything unusual he did that night?"

"Nope, other than leaving early. Told us that the baby was colicky so he was going home to help his wife. Everybody else stayed. They were happy and celebrating because of the high meeting turnout. It meant they got the majority of the plant behind them and some bargaining power with the owner. Joey gets credit for that. He's hardworking and likable both." The man shook his head and made a half-hearted swipe at another beer mug before saying, "'Course now that Joey's disappeared and him being the second one and all, well, the men are afraid to support the union. I'd say the company's won this one."

"What's your opinion of the union?"

Fire flashed into the watery blue eyes. "I'll tell you what I think, and if you're working for the company and burn me out for saying it, well, so be it. I know these men, mister. They're fine, upright, hardworking men. That mill cuts expenses so close to the bone that the men and their families are near to starving. And those saw blades are chopping off fingers and hands every which way. And not because the men are careless. It's because they are being drove too hard and because the company don't take precautions to make it safe. Do those men need a union? Hell, yes, they need a union." He slammed the mug down onto the plank for emphasis. The handle snapped off. With a rueful tweak of his cheek, the barkeep tossed handle and mug into the bottle barrel against the wall. "Good thing this is my place," he said.

Sage laughed and then sobered, saying "I won't disagree with you about the need for a union. Too many places are like the plywood mill. That's why I support unions myself. That's why I'm trying to find Kincaid." He swallowed the last of his soda, thanked the man and was turning to depart when a thought stopped him. "Say, any strangers in here the night Kincaid disappeared?" he asked.

The barkeep crinkled his nose in concentration before his gaze sharpened with a memory. "Matter of fact," he said, "two strangers stopped in that night. Kept themselves to themselves. Didn't much like the looks of them. Never saw them before or since," he said.

"When did they leave from here that night?"

This time the barkeep's nose antics yielded no results. "Can't recall to mind when it was they left. It was busy in here, what with the union meeting and all. I just remember looking over to their table," here he gestured with his chin toward a corner table near the door, "and seeing they'd gone. Don't recall when it was that I noticed."

"Anything about their looks to help me pick them out if I go looking for them?"

The bartender smiled for the first time, revealing a wide gap between his top front teeth. "I right guess there is. Mighty rough-looking characters. The big one's face carried a nose mashed to one side and there were pits, too, like the pox got 'em when he was already grown. The other one sported a piss-poor mustache, not a full one like yours," he said, nodding toward the unwaxed sweep of hair across Sage's upper lip. "His was straight and narrow, like he drawed it on with a pencil. And he was so thin that if he closed one eye you'd think he was a needle. You spot them two together, you found the right ones."

Sage thanked the man again and headed out the door. He spent another hour of root-beering through every Milwaukie saloon. His effort yielded no additional sightings of Kincaid or of the big man with the pocked face and his pencil-mustached sidekick. Sloshing like a half-full keg of root beer, Sage called it quits and visited a convenient bush before reining his horse toward Portland and letting the animal set the pace. Whenever the horse took it into his mind to trot, the stiff cardboard of the Kincaids' wedding picture jostled in his shirt pocket so that its corners poked his chest. Those pokes kept triggering that sense of foreboding first stirred to life by St. Alban's letter. Nothing he'd learned on his Milwaukie trip lessened its potency. In fact, if anything, his sense of impending tragedy was stronger. He feared that Joseph Kincaid's baby daughter would grow up without ever knowing her father.

This was a pain Sage knew well. His own father chose to leave when Sage was only a year older than little Faith. Thought of that deliberate abandonment still weighed him down unexpectedly. That deliberateness was the hardest aspect to forget or forgive. If Kincaid was not going to return to his wife and daughter, it was important to discover why. "Never knowing is like forever pouring salt in a wound so that it never heals," Sage realized, "no matter how much time passes." Sage transferred the picture to his outside suit coat pocket and focused on the scenery.

Sage slipped in and out of Lucinda's without catching sight of her. He felt bad about that. "Still," he later told himself, "it's better she wasn't there." Given his low spirits, he wouldn't be good company.

Mozart's, however, didn't allow him to brood. The supper hour was underway when he opened the front door. As his mother disappeared behind the kitchen doors, she flung him a harried look and nodded toward the group of guests who'd preceded him in the door.

Two hours later, the distractions of his "charming host" role had lightened his mood. As he and his mother tidied the now-empty dining room, she explained that Fong had vanished without explanation, leaving Mozart's shorthanded.

Sage paused in his sweeping of the dining room floor. It was so unlike Fong to be irresponsible. "When did you last see him?" he asked.

"That's what's so strange," she said as she snapped a clean tablecloth down upon a table, her hands smoothing it flat with quick efficiency. "Mr. Fong scooted out of here right in the middle of the dinner hour, saying that he was going home for a minute. He told us he'd be right back. Except he didn't come back. We haven't seen hide or hair of him since."

"Well, maybe something happened at his shop and it was too late to return, so he just stayed home." Fong and his wife operated a small provisions store in Portland's Chinatown, just four blocks from Mozart's. Fong divided his nights between the store where he and his wife lived and staying in his third floor room above Mozart's. There was no particular pattern to his choices. "I'm sure he'll give us a simple explanation," Sage said.

Her raised chin and compressed lips signaled she wasn't buying that particular horse until she examined its teeth.

Her response compelled him to add, "You worry too much."

"Someone has to around here. If you'd worry a little more, I wouldn't worry as much." She said, pausing in her activity with the table linen to look at him, her smile tweaking the sting from her words.

"I worry," he protested.

"You do. Though not always about what's happening right under your nose."

"You're talking about Matthew now, I suppose?" he said.

She nodded grimly. The boy's sadness over the loss of his brother seemed to strike his spirits down on a frequent basis. When that happened, the boy disappeared into himself, leaving them to exchange worried glances. Still, only two months had passed since the boy's horrific trip riding the rails. No one expected that Matthew's awful memory of his brother's brutal murder would fade easily or soon.

"Did Matthew disappear today, too?" Sage asked. Generally, they could count on the cook's nephew to help out whenever the restaurant got busy because he tended to stay close to hand. Yet, the boy had also been missing during the supper hour.

"Yes, he left mid-afternoon and I haven't seen him since. I am hoping he's with that printer's boy." She idly picked up a napkin to sharpen its crease. "Don't tell me I shouldn't worry about him," she added, dropping the napkin onto the table.

He didn't. It wouldn't do any good. Until all the chicks were safely in the nest, his mother would worry.

As if summoned by their mention of his name, Matthew burst into the dining room from the kitchen, words tumbling out before him, "Excuse me, ma'am, Mr. Adair. My aunt just told me that Mr. Fong didn't come back. I'm sorry. I'd surely have stayed around if I'd known you needed help."

The reason for the boy's wide-eyed look of excitement came clear as he continued, "My friend Danny took me to that new Kinescope parlor. The machines have moving pictures inside 'em, pictures of horses running, people kissing," Matthew blushed, shot a glance at Mae Clemens and hurried on, "and even one man sneezing. It looked right funny–that man sneezing. Boy, oh boy, that Mr. Edison is smart. I wonder how hard it is to be an inventor." Matthew took the remaining tablecloth from Mae Clemens's hand, expertly snapping it across the last uncovered table. "Once we used up all our pennies, we just walked around," he said to finish his story.

Sage shot his most smug, see-I-told-you-so, look at his mother.

Her look in return was unabashed, even defiant. "Don't you worry about it, boy," she said to Matthew as she lowered herself into a chair and lifted her feet to rest them on a nearby chair rung. For the first time that night, the tired lines around her mouth showed deep. "We thought Mr. Fong planned to be here, too."

Now, Sage decided, was the time to spring his idea for perking up Matthew's spirits. "Say, Matthew, I'm glad you're here because I've been wanting to speak with you," Sage told him. The boy's posture stiffened and he turned toward them, a bristly bunch of cutlery clutched in his hand.

Why, the boy fears I'm going to tell him that he has to leave, Sage realized and rushed to say, "You've been helpful running errands for us around here. Your aunt tells me that you also pick up some loose change running errands for our neighbors."

The boy waited for Sage's next words with an anxious face, although a slight widening of his eyes meant curiosity was starting to take hold.

Sage continued, "I'm thinking you might be able to help us out more around here, and maybe make more money, if you owned one of those bicycles. So, I propose to purchase one for your use. F. T. Merrill's Bicycle Emporium sells good ones I hear," he concluded and leaned back in his chair to judge the boy's reaction.

Matthew's freckled countenance became instantly alert and his eyes sparked before gloominess caused his face to fall and he slowly shook his head. "I really thank you for that thought, Mr. Adair, but I must refuse. You've already done too much for me. You gave me a job, a place to stay and you've already paid my school tuition for this September. It just wouldn't be right for me to accept any more help from you. My folks wouldn't like it. Aunt Ida neither. I'm gonna make my own way. I can't be beholden to you for so much. Just wouldn't be right," he told Sage. His jaw set, the boy turned back to laying out the tableware.

Sage glanced at his mother. She arched an I-could-have-told-you-so eyebrow in his direction. He, however, did not relinquish the idea. "I thought that might be your position but the bicycle wouldn't be a gift. You will pay me back a little at a time, and while you're doing it, we'll ask you to perform more errands for the business."

Matthew didn't jump on that rationale as eagerly as Sage expected. Instead, the boy's face remained solemn as he said carefully, "Well, I certain sure like the idea but I'd need Aunt Ida's permission before I can take you up on your kind offer."

Despite this carefully measured response, Sage thought he detected a smidgen of that excitement he'd hoped to see. There'd been too many downhearted days for the boy, days when he tended to dog Sage's heels like a lost pup. No doubt about it. Matthew needed a distraction.

Sage nodded again. He was unconcerned about Ida's reaction to the idea. A few days prior, Sage diplomatically plowed that field. She was agreeable. All it had taken was Sage reminding her of Matthew's persistent preoccupation with the death of his younger brother. Agreeing to Sage's plans for the bicycle, Ida expressed the hope that "the contraption might take his mind off things," adding, "I'm at a point where I don't know how much longer I can keep wringing my hands over that boy before they fall off."

Sage wasn't being completely altruistic. Ida's inability to console her nephew weighed heavily on her mind and that, in turn, resulted in less than inspired cooking. Business could drop off if he didn't take action.

Sage studied Matthew more closely, noting a certain vigor taking hold of the boy. Matthew didn't seem to notice his scrutiny but he said, "Excuse me, ma'am, sir. I need to go talk to my aunt." He dropped the cutlery with a clatter and hastily exited through the double doors, nearly upending two chairs on his way. Although the gaslights were dimmed, Sage caught his mother rolling her eyes toward the tin ceiling.

"What?" he asked her with a touch of exasperation.

"A bicycle now? Sage, just remember that hero worship usually ends in disappointment, and not in a way that feels good to the hero."

"So what am I supposed to do? You just told me to worry about him. You agreed he needs something to pull him out of the doldrums. Besides, a bicycle will be a useful addition around here–like I told him."

"Yes, and the new clothes are good for him, daily pocket money is good for him, you taking him to that new public library all the time is good for him."

He smiled ruefully. "Well, when you list it like that, I may be overdoing it a bit."

"Humph. A bit?" She said, before shrugging her shoulders and giving in by saying, "Though I can't say I know of any better way to distract his thoughts."

He wasn't sure he could explain why getting the boy a bicycle was the right move, he just knew it was. "I guess I know how it feels when the whole world jumbles up and turns ugly overnight," he said at last, without accusation.

The silence that followed thickened with memories. Sage had been nine years old, working inside a Pennsylvania coal mine. A methane gas explosion had killed his uncle, his cousin, and the mine owner's only son. Stranded far below any hope of rescue, Sage saved himself and the mine owner's young grandson. The mine owner, imbued with a Protestant sense of moral obligation, insisted on taking Sage to foster. Assuredly, he'd provided Sage with every material advantage denied to him by birth. Years later, however, Sage finally understood the reason for the nasty undercurrent that ran beneath the mine owner's every generosity. The old man resented Sage surviving the mine explosion instead of his own son.

The scraping sound of his mother's chair being pushed back snapped Sage into the present. He thought of another argument, "Besides, I suspect he's taken to following me around. I don't want to lead him into trouble. A bicycle will send his mind somewhere else and away from my business," he said.

Mae stood and patted him on the shoulder, saying, "I am sure that's the case." Her tone said she didn't share his confidence. "In the meantime, I'm so tired that I can't wait any longer. I'm going to bed. Are you coming up?"

Sage was tired, too. It had been a grueling day and the grit of exhaustion stung his eyes. But Mrs. Kincaid's sobs seemed to echo inside his head and their pull was stronger. "Yes, but only to change clothes and head out again," he answered. "I need to start looking for Joseph Kincaid. I promised his wife that I would find him. Too much time has elapsed already." This news perked Mae up. She sat back down to listen as he related all he'd learned on his trip to Milwaukie.

"I don't like the sound of that. That poor young woman," his mother said, her voice softening. "She told you that there was no one around to help her?"

"Yes, my impression is that the couple was either shunned by their relatives or they are without any family. For certain, they've no people around here. She kept repeating that she and Faith were all alone. That there was 'nobody.'"

"Sounds like she feels hopeless on top of guilt and grief. Maybe I should take myself on out there to Milwaukie. See if there's something I can do to help. Lord knows, I can remember how she feels." Mae said that last sentence mostly to herself.

She didn't need to elaborate. Mae'd lost everything important the day the mine exploded–her brother and nephew. In the dire financial straits following those losses, she was forced to surrender her only child's upbringing to the very man responsible for the whole disaster. He'd promised to provide Sage with every material advantage, including a university education. Her life, on the other hand, could offer Sage only poverty and a miner's early death.

"You wouldn't mind going way out there on the train?" Sage asked. "You'd have to walk a good bit to get to the house from where the interurban drops off."

"No, I'd enjoy the fresh air. Anyways, I could do with looking at something besides this place."

Sage was relieved. She'd shifted some of the weight off his shoulders. "Thanks. I can't seem to loosen her from my thoughts. I'm afraid she's going to harm herself and that baby," he said.

She reached across the table to pat his hand before standing and heading toward their third-floor rooms. "Tomorrow, first thing," she threw over her shoulder.

Sage went into the kitchen to see if there was any coffee in the pot. The kitchen was clean and empty. Matthew and his aunt lay already abed in the second floor apartment where Ida, her husband, Knute, and now Matthew, resided. Lukewarm coffee remained in the pot. Sage poured a cup hoping it would liven him up. Leaning against the kitchen sink, he sipped, grateful for the dim gaslight filtering in through the window. It illuminated the various kitchen gadgets hanging on the wall. He hated the oppressive black of windowless rooms. His need for light was one reason he'd purchased a corner building to house Mozart's.

As he sipped, Sage made a mental list of the various saloons he'd visit that night under the guise of the itinerant worker, John Miner. As always, the biggest problem was how to ask his questions so that they would pass unremarked. Still, even as he planned his approach, the Milwaukie saloon keeper's emphatic belief that Kincaid was dead weighed heavily. That idea kept stabbing into his thoughts like a hungry woodpecker on a rotten stump.

FIVE

As HE TUGGED ON HIS John Miner canvas pants, faded flannel shirt and scuffed work boots, Sage considered how best to search for the missing union organizer. By the time he was dressed and heading down the hidden staircase, he'd formed his plan of approach. Asking after Kincaid by name would be a waste of time. According to his wife, Kincaid stayed close to home and seldom visited Portland. He hadn't liked leaving her and the baby alone. Besides, in Portland's North End, "Kincaid" was just one more unremarkable name among many. Throngs of destitute workers wandered through the City's beer joints, looking for cheap eats and the temporary release of alcohol. Their names were quickly forgotten–to the extent their names were ever known. All of which meant the best approach was to show the couple's picture to people and see if it stirred any recognition.

His search focused on the saloons north of the City's commercial center where poor men on a ramble always washed up, like so many pieces of bark trapped in a river's eddy. The North End was a hard walk. On every side, the darkened doorways of the closed stores supplied niches. From those manmade grottos, sprawled men called and dull-eyed women beckoned–begging for a few coins. Money needed neither for food nor shelter, but for the oblivion of booze or worse. The scene meant a dismal trek between watering holes. Overhead, signs creaked in a stiff night breeze, their faded letters touting ten-cent rooms. They offered a sagging mattress, a thin blanket and sufficient numbers of biting critters to keep a man fully clothed all night. Only gaslight torches flaring outside the dance halls provided intermittent light. The City's esteemed fathers hadn't seen fit to light the way for the North End's nightly revelers, even though the businesses here delivered more than their share of city taxes and bribes.

Hours passed as Sage dutifully trudged through the Happy Duck, Blazers, Jimmy Mick's, Slap Jack's and other saloons quick-ly forgotten. By the search's end, Sage ceased trying to match a saloon's name to its interior look. Their sameness and his own fatigue defeated him. Every saloon sported the same gouged wooden floor, scarred bar, and smelly miasma of beer and tobac-co smoke beneath dim lights. He'd been forced to down a signifi-cant volume of cheap beer before the din, produced by drunken patrons and ineptly played music, deadened to a bearable level. Once it did, he pretended the sound was babbling water.

In all the saloons Sage visited, not a single face matched the curly-haired square-jawed young man. Some faces were close—young rootless men being thick on the ground, so to speak. Worse, though, was the fact none of the barmen recalled ever seeing Kincaid's earnest face.

Finally, he reached Erickson's saloon, the last stop in his search and the one drinking establishment markedly different from the rest. Famous for having the longest bar in the world, Erickson's drew men from everywhere. Loggers rubbed shoul-ders with European sailors who, in turn, stood elbow to elbow with farmers from eastern Oregon wheat fields.

Overhead, an encircling balcony supported a stage. On the stage, girls in short skirts cavorted, while comedians traded rib-ald quips with an inebriated and loudly appreciative audience. The balcony was also where well-to-do townsmen soaked up the revelry while remaining aloof and above those they considered their social inferiors. They made a point of talking only to each other and the women Erickson's sold.

At each of the saloon's entrances stood hefty men wearing white shirts with arm garters. Their stance telegraphed that they were at the ready to oust any troublemaker.

The block-large saloon was too big for Sage to stand at the bar and observe the whole room. So he roamed, bleary-eyed from cheap beer, noise, a long day and the lack of sleep. His efforts yielded nothing. When at last he stepped out into the cool air of early morning, he was glad to be heading home. As he began walking toward Mozart's, he mulled over his lack of success. He hadn't found Kincaid. Not even the slightest hint of Kincaid. It was as if the young Kansan had dropped into a deep black hole. As he crossed Burnside Street, the demarcation between the City's commercial center and the rougher haunts of working men, Sage heard the tinny clatter of milk wagons rolling up the street in his direction. Dawn would soon begin to lighten the sky.

When he reached the south side, his ears picked up another sound. It came from a nearby alley. He stopped, listened, but heard nothing. He shrugged. Must be a leftover buzz in his ear from all those saloons. He started walking. There! It came again. This time, an unmistakable cry from deep inside the alley. It was a familiar sound. Just like his own cry that night when three men had jumped him and Fong's surprising intervention saved his life. He whirled toward the alley, shouting, "Hey! Somebody in there? What's going on?"

A weak voice responded, "Help! Please, help me!"

Sage squinted, staring down the black narrow space until his eyes adjusted. He saw that two dark figures were viciously swinging their boots into a third form on the ground.

"Hey, you there! Stop that!" Sage shouted as he leapt toward the men, skidding in the slimy garbage people had dumped from the windows above. The kicking men paused before bolting away toward the building's rear. They disappeared around the corner just as Sage reached the man on the ground.

Sage squatted. "Are you all right?" he asked.

A moan was the response.

Sage moved his hands over the canvas coat until he found the man's armpits. He rose from his squat, pulling the man upright. Wrapping an arm around the man's waist, Sage staggered back toward the sidewalk. The man tried to walk. Good, he was still conscious.

When they reached the street, Sage lowered his burden onto a shop step. The man leaned back against the door frame only to yip in pain.

"What hurts?" Sage asked.

"My ribs. I suspect at least two of them are broke." The man shifted, grimacing with the movement. In the faint light of a nearby street lamp, Sage could see that he'd rescued a middle-aged man. Alley muck smeared his sun-browned skin and head of light hair. A trickle of blood dripped down one side of the man's face.

"Were they after your money?" Sage asked as he pulled a handkerchief from his pocket and pressed it against a gaping cut on the man's forehead.

"Not hardly. No, the goal was to discourage my work. Money's involved, but not my money." Sage thought he placed the faint accent. Boston area or near about. More than one Bostonian had attended Princeton, so the odd pronunciation was familiar.

But what did this man mean by not his money, but money nonetheless? Sage gave a surreptitious sniff. No booze. So, why was this sober Bostonian in this area of town, at this time of the morning, dressed like a man living rough? Noting the man's increasing pallor, Sage said, "I think we'd better take you somewhere for a look at those ribs, just in case one's poking into something it shouldn't."

The man merely nodded, pressing his lips tightly together. Sage helped him to his feet, and they headed back into the North End. When the man realized their direction, his feet locked onto the sidewalk, "It is unsafe for me to be anywhere around here so soon after they jumped me. They might come back and they intend to murder me. They said so." For a second, Sage hadn't understood the man's words until his ear inserted a second "r" back into "murder." The man's accent made it sound like "murdah."

Sage tightened his grip around the man's waist. "I guarantee that those men won't think to look where we're heading. Come on now, it's just a few doors farther on."

When they staggered through the door of the New Elijah Hotel, the injured man summoned enough strength to weakly chuckle and say, "Oh, you are certain correct in your prediction, sir. They won't look heah for me, that's for sure."

The New Elijah was a traveling man's hotel. Rising three stories high and constructed of wood, it still projected the elegance that once made it Portland's preeminent hotel. Now, of course, it was obsolete, its prominence usurped long ago by the tall brick-and-mortar structures downtown. Regardless, Sage always felt a momentary appreciation for the front desk's looping swirls. Its wood face was carved years ago by Italian craftsmen. Imported to carve the woodwork and construct lead glass windows decorating many of the City's hilltop mansions, the artisans stayed in Portland to raise families, their skills in great demand by the humbler of pocket.

Sage raised his eyes to look into those of the man standing behind the desk. It was this man, Angus Solomon, along with the other sons of Africa filling the lobby, who had elicited his companion's wry chuckle. As one, their wary faces had turned to watch as the two white men staggered into their midst.

Solomon, for his part, didn't hesitate. He swiftly strode from behind the desk to pull Sage and his companion to one side, out of the sight of anyone passing by outside on the sidewalk. Taking his cue from Sage's attire, Solomon asked, "Mr. Miner, what has happened here?"

"Mr. Solomon, we'd appreciate your help. This man was attacked and needs treatment as soon as possible."

In answer, the tall black man snapped his fingers, summoning two younger men to his side. "Show these men to my quarters," he told one. "Fetch Miss Esther, clean cloths, and hot water," he instructed the other.

In ten steps, Sage and the injured man left the hotel's early morning checkout bustle behind them and entered a peaceful sanctum. The opulence of Solomon's private quarters was no surprise to Sage. He'd been there before. Not so his companion. Stretched out on a brocade divan, the man gazed about the room, taking in the elaborate walnut buffet, graceful silver candelabra, thick Persian carpet upon the floor and the long wall of leather-bound books. "I say, I didn't imagine a room like this existed among the colored folk heah in Portland," he said.

Sage bristled. "Why not? They're no different from you and me when it comes to appreciating beauty and fine objects."

The man raised his chin, looking offended. "Why, certainly I know that. Still, it takes a powerful lot of money to buy these kinds of furnishings and from what I've seen, black folks find it a bit hard going in this fair city. Too many restrictions on them. So, your friend must be quite successful with this hotel for him to afford the quality I'm seeing."

Sage didn't know this man or his business. If anything, he worried whether it was a mistake to bring this man to his friend. If the stranger worked for the other side, he'd endangered Solomon as well as their joint missions. So, Sage just nodded and said nothing about Solomon once being chief butler in a Carolina governor's mansion. Or, that he'd left that position for the chance to be in charge of the exclusive dining room of Portland's newest, whites-only hotel. Quietly dignified, he commanded respect from that hotel's most bigoted patrons. In sum, Solomon prospered because he was competent, prudent, hard-working and smart.

The door opened and their host entered, followed by a mahogany brown, gray-haired woman. Round scissor tops glittered in the pocket of her white bib apron. Her large hands carried a full water basin, strips of white cloth draped over her forearm. Her brown eyes softened when she saw the injured man. She briskly crossed the room to his side.

Solomon spoke to Sage. "May I introduce the formidable Miss Esther." Sage inclined his head in greeting as Solomon continued, "She has healing hands and will tend to your companion's injuries. While she is doing so, you and I shall retire to the dining room for some coffee. When she has completed her work, we will return." This last sentence was directed at the injured man. Miss Esther began gently removing his shirt, clicking her tongue sympathetically at what she saw.

In the hotel dining room, Sage and Solomon took a corner table and drank steaming coffee. All around them, men shoveled in hearty breakfasts and laughed easily with each other. Soon, they'd be setting out on their train runs where they'd have few opportunities to dine comfortably among their own kind. Sage noticed a few surreptitious glances but they were too polite to stare openly.

"I'm sorry we burst in on you like this, Angus. I didn't intend to. It's just that something the guy said made me curious about him. Also, he doesn't seem to be your run-of-the-mill itinerant laborer." Sage told Solomon that the stranger believed his attackers were intent on murdering him because of his "work." Sage shared the thought he'd had. "Probably, he's a temperance man who stepped crosswise of a saloon keeper. Still, I'm not so sure. His hands are rough from manual labor and he seems anchored to the earth, not the type to be carried away with some harebrained notion. That means he might be on our side, and if so, I want to help him."

Solomon's dark eyes held Sage in warm regard. "I'm proud you thought of coming to me, John. You know that I stand willing to assist your endeavors." Here his trademark smile split his face, triggering Sage's answering grin. Both of them paused to savor the success of their last joint effort. In addition to saving Matthew, Sage's train escapade also exposed a land fraud scheme that left a number of wealthy men, including a U.S. senator and the local U.S. district attorney, under prosecution by San Francisco's federal district attorney.

"I can't rightly claim that this man is one of us." Sage cautioned. He's a stranger and I think we need to be careful what we say around him. As for me, I was out tonight in an effort to find two union organizers. They just up and disappeared without a trace. The last of them left behind a wife and new baby."

As they ate breakfast and waited for Miss Esther to finish her ministrations, Sage told what he knew of Kincaid's disappearance. Solomon studied the young man's picture, his face taking on a sad cast as if he, too, felt the nameless dread that had been dogging Sage. Still, Solomon only said he would keep a lookout for the missing man.

Miss Esther appeared in the doorway and nodded in their direction. Grabbing a cup of coffee, Solomon led the way to his apartment. There they found the man leaning back against the divan, his bandaged face clean although scraped raw in places. A white cloth bandage was snugged around his naked chest. The skin around his eyes was dull red and turning black. He opened those eyes upon their entrance.

"Lady Estha' has the hands of an angel," he told them. Now that he wasn't gasping in pain, there was no mistaking that missing 'r' in the man's speech.

Solomon leaned his long frame against the buffet, folded his arms across his chest and sent an inquiring look toward Sage. He clearly thought it was not his place to ask the questions.

Sage moved a chair close to the divan and sat. "I don't want to mislead you," Sage began. "The fact is, you're here because of your comment about your work. You made me curious. What is your work that makes men try to kill you? You're not one of those temperance proselytizers, are you?"

The man laughed before grimacing and pushing a hand onto the bandage encircling his ribs. "Good Lord. Not me. I like a drink now and then, just like any other man. Sometimes more than any other man, given what I've seen happen."

Solomon's service experience sprang into action. Within seconds, the stranger held a glass. He gulped the whiskey and stretched out his other hand so they saw its trembling. "I thought for sure I was a dead man. And likely that's where I was headed except for yah fortuitous intervention—Mr. Minah, is it?"

Sage nodded, saying nothing, acutely aware that his original question remained unanswered. And it was odd that, despite his great pain, this man heard and remembered Sage's alias from Solomon's initial greeting. "And your name, sir?" Sage asked.

"Name's Stuart Franklin." Franklin swallowed the last of his drink, shaking his head at Solomon's wordless offer of more. "I've been helping out the Seaman's Friend Society. Last few weeks, I've been down to Astoria at the Columbia River's mouth. Been rowing out to interview ship captains anchored in the river as they wait for the tide to cross the river bar into deepwater ocean."

"Interviewing?" Sage repeated. Franklin's talking to ship captains made someone want to commit murder? If Franklin was weaving a lie, it was certainly an odd one.

"Yup. Interviewing them about the shanghaiing that goes on here in Portland." Franklin leaned forward, only to groan and sink back against the cushions. He made an obvious effort to battle the pain and when he spoke again, his voice was fainter, "You might not realize it, but this fair city here has a bad reputation for shanghaiing men aboard deepwater ships. Someone heah is making boatloads of dirty money out of it," he added.

"Shanghaiing?" Sage echoed. His eyes snapped to Solomon's, and the two exchanged a long look. Now, there was a possible explanation for Kincaid's disappearance—one not considered by either of them.

SIX

"You mean to tell me that you've nevah heard of shang-haiing?" Incredulity sent Franklin's pitch up a notch, grabbed the "er" off of "never" and for the first time, suspicion replaced friendliness in the man's eyes. Now, this man was as much on his guard as Sage was. Interesting.

To set Franklin at his ease, Sage gave him a dash of truth, saying, "No, of course I've heard of it. I worked around Frisco Bay a few years back and here in the North End there's always stories about men getting hijacked off the streets. Thankfully, I've no personal experience with the practice. It's just that your mention of it might connect with something I'm working on." Despite Franklin's face showing interest, Sage was done with his confiding. He wasn't going to talk about Kincaid with a stranger when he still didn't know exactly what the man was up to. "What I don't understand is why someone jumped you because you're interviewing ship captains," he prodded.

Franklin sighed, winced and pressed a hand against his ribs again. "It's because of how we plan to use those interviews," he told them. "A group of us, the Seaman's Friend Society and a few of the foreign consuls in town, have been raising a fuss and calling for a state law to protect seamen from the crimps. Some of them are nothing more than circling sharks." Although the word came out "shacks," the man's bitter contempt still evoked the vivid image of huge jaws and razor teeth.

"Protect seamen how?" Sage asked, not recollecting reading about any such "fuss' in the newspapers. And, wasn't the boarding house crimp game pretty much on the up-and-up? Didn't the crimps give seamen a landside berth in exchange for signing them onto ships when their money ran out? Exploitive, sure. But what wasn't these days? Maybe Franklin means those back alley cutthroats. The ones who pour knock out drops into a fellow's beer or thump him senseless before dumping him aboard a departing ship. Men in the saloons muttered about so-and-so disappearing and sometimes wondered aloud whether the missing man was on his way to China. There was no way of knowing. Hard living and the transient life meant men routinely disappeared without warning. Shanghaiing was yet another danger in an already hard, perilous, world.

Still, the practice might explain what happened to Kincaid. The young man had a job, family and success in his efforts at organizing the plywood mill. That kind of stability considerably reduced the field of likely possibilities. Shanghaiing, therefore, was an avenue requiring investigation. Still, was a shanghaiing likely to happen in Milwaukie? The Millmen's saloon was relatively far away, at least eight miles upriver from the North End. Sage found the possibility unlikely.

Franklin picked up the whiskey glass only to set it down when he realized that it was empty. Solomon stepped forward and poured a few more ounces of the amber liquid. Franklin acknowledged the courtesy with a rueful smile and a careful nod before continuing, "We want to stop men from being sold to ship captains like indentured slaves." His eyes flicked sideways toward Solomon. "No disrespect meant to your own people's horrifying history, suh," he said. He struggled to sit upright, his face grimacing at the movement, before explaining, "Not all crimps are bad. Tobias Pratt, he's okay. But there's other crimps, bad ones like Kaspar Mordaunt. He's nothing but a bloodthirsty land shark preying on defenseless men. Crimps like him must be stopped. Mordaunt's one of the last of the really bad crimps. He's scared off most of the others. He controls the port's dirty land shark business and he's undercutting the more decent crimps so that they're giving up the business. Tobias Pratt's one of the few of those remaining."

Seeing he still held their interest, Franklin launched into an explanation of the crimping business. "Not all crimping is illegal but most of it is immoral. Your ship usually docks with a full crew. The boardinghouse crimps pull a bunch of shenanigans to entice its sailors to desert ship. That way the captain has to pay blood money to the crimps for a new crew because the ship can't sail without a full crew. The blood money works like a finder's fee. That is not all. The captain is also forced to advance the crimp the sailor's first two months of wages. Supposedly, he's paying off the sailor's board and room.

So, here the sailor is leaving the port, already having to work for at least three months without any pay. Usually, it's longer. Crimps dump the men on board without clothes or tobacco or any necessities. So, the sailor also owes for what's issued to him out of the ship's stores. That's your legal, so-called 'willing' sailor. Paying off a crimp debt is how a willing man ships out, no matter how bad the bargain. Some crimps are at least somewhat legitimate, even if they gouge the sailor past all that's godly. The sailor accepts the deal with his eyes open.

"Not every man delivered on board arrives willingly. Land sharks like Mordaunt shanghai some of them."

Sage crossed to the sideboard and poured himself a drink from a water pitcher. There was no way Joseph Kincaid volunteered to ship out. He'd never willingly leave his wife and new baby. Besides, he disappeared so suddenly and completely. Franklin's description of crimping didn't fit the facts of either Kincaid's or Amacker's disappearances. Yet, both men were gone.

So, what about the land shark crimps? Would land shark crimps travel as far afield as Milwaukie when there were such easy pickings here in the North End? It didn't seem likely. And then, there was the opportunity for escape in that hundred-mile trip downriver to the ocean. Turning to the man on the couch, Sage asked, "Why don't the sailors avoid the crimps or jump overboard while the ship's still in the river?"

"Answer to the first question is that you'd think they hit port flush with months of unspent wages. There, you'd be wrong. Most ship captains won't pay their sailors but a fraction of their owed wages when the berth is a U.S. port. Otherwise, too many men would take off and leave the ship stranded in port for lack of a crew. A sailing ship needs a minimum number of sailors to work the rigging. Without them, it can't sail. That's why sailors are prey for anyone who plies them with drink, knockout drops or maybe the chop of a sap behind their ear. Same thing happens to landlubbers who wander the streets penniless and hungry. They accept a friendly drink and wake up on their way to China."

Franklin cautiously shifted position, sipped his whiskey and continued, "Mostly they don't jump ship in mid-river because they're below deck knocked out, tied up or locked in. And even if they reach the railing, that water's mighty damn cold. A man can't last long in it, especially close to the river's mouth where the current's treacherous. That's how come my arms look like a gorilla's. It's all that rowing to and from the ships anchored in the river, waiting for the tide to turn." Franklin extended heavily muscled arms that looked as if he made his living swinging an ax. More proof the man was telling the truth.

"So, tell us more about men being drugged or beaten and delivered aboard ships against their will," Sage asked.

Franklin's eyes took on a melancholy cast, as if he felt a pain more profound than his broken ribs. But he merely sighed before saying, "Sometimes they're tricked aboard too. Maybe promised a job on a riverboat only to find themselves delivered to an oceangoing ship. That's shanghaiing too. Sometimes I row out to a ship, and as I'm leaving a man dives into the river hoping I'll fish him out and carry him back to shore. I've done so more than once."

"Can't make the captains too happy with you," Sage observed. A small row boat, an immense river and an unscrupulous ship captain sounded like a deadly combination.

Franklin smiled grimly. "Been a few of them shot at me, even hit the rowboat. Ain't been sunk yet but I've done some snappy bailing. Some ships, I don't bother talking to the captain; I know he won't cooperate. I just circle the ship in case someone wants off. 'Course, if a man's below deck tied or drugged up, he never gets the chance." For a moment, Franklin gazed into somewhere else with unfocused eyes, a sadness washing over his face. Then he seemed to give himself a mental shake because he shrugged and sipped his whiskey, before saying, "Drugs, beatings, imprisonment, and trickery. That's the evil, shanghaiing side of the crimping trade. That's a different story." Franklin gave a disgusted snort, "and not all of the bodies they sell are even living. There's the sea captains, desperate short of men, willing to take any body delivered on board–just so they can raise sail. One crimp, Bunco Kelly, dumped twenty-six unconscious men onto a ship stranded in port. The captain paid top dollar for them, too.

"Anyway, the ship crosses the Columbia River bar, the captain goes to rouse them and finds his forecastle full of dying men. Turns out, they'd gotten their snoots full of the wrong stuff. They found an unlocked cellar full of barrels they thought held drink so they tapped into them and partied. Wouldn't you know, it wasn't drinking alcohol but embalming fluid, a mix of wood alcohol and formaldehyde. Bunco ambled by, heard them groaning and took advantage. 'Course, nothing at all happened to Bunco. The captain was forced to berth in Astoria and report the deaths. Not because he was a good citizen but because he lacked sufficient crew members to attempt the open ocean.

"That captain kept his mouth clamped shut about who'd dumped the dying men onto his ship. Told authorities that it was dark and he didn't know. No choice about that. Not if he wants to berth in Portland again. That kind of crimp has a very long memory. Make one of them mad and the next time that captain's in port the crimp will strand him by stealing away all his men. A crimp does that, the shipping company loses too much money. And that usually means the captain loses his command."

Mrs. Kincaid's grief-stricken face seemed to shimmer before Sage's inner eye. "Do shanghaied men ever find their way home again?" he asked.

Franklin shrugged, grimaced and said, "Depends. It's called 'shanghaied' because, most times, the ships ride the current across the Pacific to Shanghai, China. Ships don't usually beat back from that direction against the trade winds and they make more on cargo if they head east toward Europe. So, if a man wants to return heah, he must survive long enough to circumnavigate the globe. Takes about two years. If misfortune is his lot, he doesn't make it."

"Misfortune? What kind of misfortune?" Sage prodded, thinking of storm-tossed waves and evil-faced pirates. Sage didn't particularly like sailing the ocean. Too much water. The last time he'd landed in the wet stuff, his boots acted like rocks tied to his feet, pulling him down toward the mucky river bottom. Maybe he wasn't sailor material because he'd spent the first nine years of his life far from the ocean. Or, maybe, he drowned in a prior life. Some folks believed in such things. Whatever the explanation, Sage liked the water only so long as land lay within swimming distance.

"Well, there's always the weather or a stray ice berg or two," Franklin said. "But often, the greatest danger is your fellow shipmates. They'll gut you for something you own or just for sport. Worst of all are the captains who help a crimp by disposing of a man the crimp doesn't want seen again. Tidy, lasting way for the landlubbers to rid themselves of a troublemaker. Anyway, those captains work the man down to the nubbin before dumping him overboard. Voila! He disappears from the face of the earth, after swallowing too much deep blue sea."

Sage and Solomon exchanged a long, serious, look. It fit. The idea of Joseph Kincaid being tossed overboard in the middle of the Pacific while still alive was horrific. Sage instantly decided that was one possible explanation he'd keep from Kincaid's wife, no matter what. He'd make up a lie before he'd put that image into her mind. Still, how the heck was he ever going to find out whether shanghaiing was behind the young Kansan's disappearance?

Franklin, oblivious to Sage's dilemma, was continuing his explanation, "Then, of course, there's the whaling ships. That North Pacific is a death trap. Even willing sailors gamble when they ship out on a whaler. Since kerosene's invention, whaling isn't nearly as profitable. So most whalers are leaky buckets and that Bering Sea is the roughest ocean in the world, except for the hellish Cape Horn around the tip of South America."

Sage sent a questioning look toward Solomon. Was this man trustworthy? Solomon's small slow nod indicated cautious assent.

Sage took a deep breath. It was a gamble, telling this stranger their business. Yet, he had to know. "Mr. Franklin, I've spent all night searching for a young man named Joseph Kincaid. He disappeared from outside a saloon upriver in Milwaukie over two weeks ago. He's left a wife and baby behind. Is there a way to find out if Mordaunt or some other land shark shanghaied him?"

Franklin didn't speak for a minute, just stared into the whiskey he was swirling around in the glass. Slowly he began, "There might be. Tell you what, I owe you for saving my life and bringing me here. I'll ask around. What's he look like?"

Sage pulled out the photograph, its edges bent from repeated handling, and passed it to Franklin. He took the picture, holding it up to the gaslight. "Nice looking boy. This here woman the wife?"

"Yes. That's their wedding picture. Since they posed for it, a baby daughter named 'Faith' was born."

Franklin shook his head slowly. "Well, it's sure hard to believe he'd desert a looker like this gal of his own free will. So maybe he was shanghaied. About how long ago, you say?"

"The night of July thirty-first, over two weeks ago."

Franklin swung his legs down to the floor, pain creasing his face as he struggled into a sitting position. "I am catching a steamboat back to Astoria in the morning. Tell you what. I'll have a friend of mine ask about Kincaid here in Portland, and when I reach Astoria, I'll ask around there. You know the Seaman's Friend chapel building situated at the corner of Third and Davis? It's whitewashed brick."

Sage took a moment to picture the street corner. That intersection was where noisy religious proselytizers frequently gathered. He tried to avoid it. "Yes, I know the place," he said.

"Well, I'll meet you Wednesday night in the chapel there. Entrance is off Davis Street. That's when the Floating Society of Christian Endeavor holds a prayer session that's open to everyone. I'll sit on a rear bench. Take the seat next to me." Franklin paused, his brow knitted. "Best that you act like you don't know me. Something's not right. I've been pondering on how those bushwhackers knew I was heah in town. This was supposed to be a quick trip upriver to meet with Reverend Quackenbush, the president of the Society. I possessed information I couldn't entrust to writing. That's because a ship captain told me that copies of my reports are ending up in the crimps' hands. Tonight, Quackenbush and I made sure we met out of sight of any crimp. After we parted, though, this creepy, crawly feeling came over me. Like somebody was behind me, breathing down my neck. I told myself I was being overly anxious. Hah! Seems I wasn't anxious enough." Franklin's rueful chuckle cut off abruptly. He pressed a palm to his ribs and sweat broke out across his forehead. After a few moments, he continued, "I can't let loose of the idea that those two killers knew right where to find me."

Sage knew the feeling. You sense danger until reason pushes it aside as fancy rather than fact. "Anymore, my rule of thumb is 'trust your instincts.' We've been given them for a reason," he told Franklin and stood up. "Wednesday night at the Friend's Chapel. I'll be there. What time?" he asked.

"The second evening meeting starts about 9:00 o'clock. All the singing, preaching and amening ought to cover up our talk if we sit in the back. Say, if I need to send you a message, where do I send it?" Franklin asked.

Sage looked toward Solomon, who stirred to say, "You can send a message to Mr. Miner care of this hotel, Mr. Franklin. I'll make certain that he gets it."

Minutes later, as dawn began graying the eastern horizon, Franklin hobbled out the hotel's rear door and headed deeper into the North End. Seconds later, Sage stepped from a nearby doorway and began following the injured man. He wanted to ensure that Franklin arrived safely at his destination. Sage also wanted to see where he went. Company spies riddled the labor movement.

Ten blocks later, he watched as Franklin climbed a flight of wooden steps and let himself into a nondescript boarding house on the west side of the North End. Sage noted its address. That done he headed south toward his bed–discourgaged. He was probably not a whit closer to finding Joseph Kincaid than when he'd begun.

❀ ❀ ❀

The sounds of Fong setting the small table in the bay window penetrated Sage's sleep. "Hello, Mr. Fong," Sage rasped, as he struggled into a sitting position out of the nest his body had made in his horsehair mattress.

Fong started, dropping cutlery that shattered the china plate. Sage froze, astonished. During the nearly two years he'd known Fong, the man never displayed anything other than absolute physical control. He seemed incapable of clumsiness. And ordinarily, Fong sensed when Sage was awake before Sage raised his eyelids.

"Are you all right, Mr. Fong?"

"Sorry," Fong mumbled, picking up the broken pieces. "Thinking of something else." It was a mindlessly spoken response. Sage squinted at his friend. Fong's lips formed a grim line and dark smudges surrounded his eyes. The sight brought Sage thoroughly awake. Before he could say anything, Fong departed abruptly, leaving a dumbfounded Sage staring at the closed door.

What the heck was wrong with Fong? Sage swiftly surveyed his own recent activities and found no clue to the answer. Try as he might, he couldn't imagine anything he'd done to offend Fong. And even if Fong felt offense, he wouldn't show it or act this way. Something else. It must be something else.

"Whatever has gotten into him, I'd better find out what it is," Sage muttered, flipping aside the bedclothes and snatching up his trousers.

Fong slid back into the room carrying a new plate. He finished setting the table in absolute silence.

Uncertain what to say, Sage took a chair and reached for the coffee pot, his head feeling sodden from lack of sleep. "We missed you yesterday evening, Mr. Fong," he began.

"Very sorry," Fong interrupted. "Something came up. Not possible for me to return." He didn't sound sorry, he sounded irritated at being prodded.

Sage waited for more explanation. Instead, Fong snatched the John Miner clothes from the floor and disappeared once again.

Hearing a step in the hallway, Sage looked up from his food, fully expecting Fong to return. This time Sage wanted Fong's explanation for leaving them in a lurch. Fong owed them at least that.

It was his mother, not Fong who entered. "Oh, I thought you were Mr. Fong," Sage said.

"Good morning to you, too," she responded. The quirk at the corner of her lips said she wasn't offended.

"Did he tell you where he disappeared to last night?" he asked.

Before answering, she sat, filled a cup with coffee, and leaned back in her chair. Flour dusted the shine of her hair. Evidently she'd been baking up a storm. "No," she said, "he hasn't said a single word to me about where he was. He told me he was sorry, but I can't say for certain that he felt sorry." She drummed her fingers on the table. "I'm getting worried. It's not like Mr. Fong to disappear without a word. I can't think what's got ahold of him. He's not acting like himself."

"No kidding," Sage said as he forked into his eggs. They were cold. Another mark against the man. What was the explanation for these changes? It might take a little prodding, but Sage was sure Fong would give him one. After all, they'd been friends for some while. "Oh, well, it's probably nothing, Mother," he assured her. "We'll find out eventually."

Sage gave up on breakfast and pushed the half-eaten eggs around his plate. "Besides, we've bigger problems right now to worry about. Were you able to visit with Mrs. Kincaid?"

For a brief instant she studied him before apparently accepting his change of topic. "Indeed I did, while you slept half the day away. I took the interurban train out and back. And I must say that having talked to her, I see why you're worried. I feel unsettled about her state of mind. I suppose she told you about her upbringing and all?"

"No, we never talked about that." Sage laid down his fork. Damn, she was right. He should have asked Mrs. Kincaid more about their background. Maybe it held a clue to her husband's whereabouts.

"Well, she started out being orphaned somewhere back East," Mae reported. "Her mother died when she was born and after hauling her from pillar to post for a few years, her father dumped her in an orphanage, and that was the last she saw of him. When she was twelve or so, the orphanage shipped trainloads of adolescent girls to the Midwest. She landed in Kansas to work as kitchen help for Joseph's family. The Kincaids needed the help. They have a big farm with a lot of farmhands to feed. One thing led to another, the two young folks fell in love and they eloped. Probably had to, truth be known. It made his folks furious. Their social aspirations for their only son were higher than an orphan girl. Their anger hurt her terrible. After having lived six years with them she thought of them as family. Anyways, she and Joseph headed out here to start a new life."

Sage pushed aside the lace curtain to study the sky that showed above the building across the way. Two gulls wheeled silently in its summer blue. A sailor once told him gulls mated for life. "So," he said thoughtfully, "she really is all alone, like she told me." The young woman's plight felt like a blow to the heart.

His mother nodded. "That's how it looks," she agreed. "But it's hard to believe her in-laws are so unforgiving that they wouldn't want to see their only grandchild. Such a precious little baby, Faith is," she said, her tone wishful.

Sage spoke quickly. A discussion about future grandchildren was definitely someplace he had no desire to go. "Maybe we might try to contact Kincaid's parents; let them know what's happened."

She nodded, pulled a scrap of paper from her apron pocket and passed it across the table. "The same idea came to me, too. So, I talked her into giving me their name and the town where they live. Thought I'd send them a telegram to let them know what's happened. Once that's done, it's up to them.

"I'm worried, Sage. That girl's itching to act something foolish. Somehow, she has taken it in her head that her husband has abandoned her just like her father did. I blame those ignorant policemen for that idea. Too darn lazy to go looking so they harped on with that explanation. Given her background, it likely rang true in her mind. I tried talking sense to the gal." Mae shook her head. "There's no saying she took it in. I tell you, my boy, and this is going to sound hard, but I think it's better she knows he can't return to her. It will be a sight better than if she keeps on thinking that maybe he just headed off to start a new life. Besides, I don't think he left her on purpose. That idea just doesn't have teeth. Everything she told me about the boy says differently."

Mae's fingers chased stray breadcrumbs across the tablecloth with the intensity of a hungry dog turned loose on a dirty kitchen. She was a tough woman, used to tough times. If she was that worried about Mrs. Kincaid and her baby there was no time to waste. Sage shifted uncomfortably. What else was there for him to do? He'd searched all last night and found nothing.

He cleared his throat and she looked up from her crumb herding, "I can't shake the awful feeling that Joseph Kincaid is dead," he told her. "It weighs down my thoughts. Makes it hard to keep looking for him."

She wasn't in a sympathetic mood. "Well, I think you better be finding out what happened to him sooner rather than later. At least find his body. That young woman is hanging on to hope by a fingernail. I hate to imagine what will happen when that fingernail gives out. She needs to know what really happened to that man of hers."

"The search has gotten more complicated," Sage began and heard the defensiveness in his voice. The sound of heavy boots clumping up the stairs saved him. "Matthew," he mouthed.

Sure enough, the young man appeared in the doorway, "Miz Clemens, my aunt says to tell you the butcher man is downstairs and is there any particular cuts you want her to buy?"

"Yes, I told Mr. Fong. Ask him to talk to the butcher for me, please."

Matthew shuffled awkwardly in his large boots. "Ah . . .well . . . ah . . . Mr. Fong isn't here anymore."

Sage broke in. "Go look in the attic, Matthew. He's probably preparing for our exercise. It's time."

Consternation reddened the boy's face and he again shuffled uneasily on his big feet. "Well, sir. He's not in the attic, either, because I saw him leave my own self. And when Aunt Ida asked when he was coming back, he didn't say nothing, just scooted out the door. She says he's been acting peculiar all morning."

Sage and his mother exchanged a look. It was one thing for Fong to spurn his partners' questions, but Ida's? Fong was usually quite courtly in his relations with Mozart's cook.

Mae started piling the dirty dishes onto a tray. "You go tell the butcher that I'll be right down," she instructed the boy. Neither of them spoke until his boots began clumping back down the stairs.

"Something's not right with Mr. Fong," she informed Sage, her tone emphatic.

"I expect whatever it is will work itself out in a few days," Sage responded with more confidence than he felt.

"I surely hope so. What with this Kincaid matter, we need things to operate smoothly around here. It won't do to for everybody to be in an uproar because Mr. Fong has decided to turn mysterious on us." She strode toward the door, halting on the threshold. "By the way, you haven't forgotten your promise to Matthew, have you? Remember, you promised him one of those newfangled safety bicycles. I just heard him down in the alley telling his friend, the printer's devil, all about it. Don't want the boy disappointed–even if I don't cotton to all you're doing for him." Her declaration made, she swept from the room.

SEVEN

EVERY PLACE HE'D MISSED searching the previous night, Sage covered during the late afternoon on Tuesday and most of Wednesday. He visited every money-grubbing job shark. Even though the coins Sage offered had them near drooling, not a one admitted to sending the square-jawed Kansan out on a job

Sage also canvassed the waterfront, thudding down the docks, boarding ships, questioning stevedores and wandering through the warehouses stilted out over the river. He visited every building site and interviewed every day laborer he encountered. Nothing. Absolutely nothing.

So, it was not until Wednesday, late afternoon, that he and Matthew finally strode into F. T. Merrill's bicycle emporium. A few tall wheel cycles hung from wall hooks, their purpose already that of historical oddity and adornment. Brightly colored two-wheeled safety bicycles crowded the showroom floor, their nickel-plated sprockets spotless. The pungent rubber smell of the single-tube tires snared Sage's nose and made him sneeze.

Boxes of accessories filled shelves attached to a side wall. Sage ambled over to read their labels. He learned they contained all the bits and pieces a fellow needed to be a successful wheelman. Things like engraved handlebar bells, foot pumps, locks and chains, trouser guards and toe clips. Bicycling apparently was a complicated endeavor and, no doubt, one that was making F. T. Merrill wealthy.

Turning, when he heard a salesman greet Matthew by name, Sage raised an inquiring brow at the boy. Matthew flushed and stammered an explanation, "I . . . I . . . ah . . . stopped by and I . . . ah told them that maybe I'd be getting me one of these . . . ah . . . bicycles."

Sage grinned. "That was good thinking," he said.

The boy relaxed with a shy smile.

"So, you know the particular model you want?" Sage asked.

The salesman laughed. He looked to be only a few years older than Matthew. The spare stubble of blond whiskers, on his otherwise baby smooth face, signified his wish to distinguish himself from the ranks of boyhood. Sage glanced at the new-fangled bicycles. Why is it that youth are so quick to grab the reins of the technological bandwagons?

"He's been studying hard on it the last couple days, let me assure you of that!" the salesman said, clapping Matthew on the shoulder.

Matthew's flush deepened as he responded to Sage's question, "No, I really couldn't pick one because I didn't, you know, whether . . . ah. . . ." His voice trailed off into awkward silence.

"Oh. Right," Sage said. Matthew hadn't known whether Sage would follow through on his promise or how much he'd be willing to spend if he did.

The salesman interceded, "Let me show you some of the models this young gentleman and I discussed. As I am sure you know, today's bicyclist is interested only in those bicycles having tires of equal size. We call them safety bicycles because the rider is far less likely to tip over, and," he pointed toward the hanging high-wheeler, "if he does hit the ground, he won't tumble nearly as far." The salesman escorted them down an aisle between two rows of bicycles angled side by side, their rubber tires lined up exactly so. For some minutes, they discussed the inventory of brightly painted frames and leather perches, squeezing hard rubber tires as the salesman nattered on about structural soundness and durability. After a certain point, Sage's eyes crossed because, to him, every bicycle looked identical except for its color. At last, they reached what appeared to be the salesman's final offering.

"Now, this one here," he said, resting reverent fingers on the handlebars of one sporting the name of Blue Beauty scripted in gold along its cross-frame, "is our top-of-the-line model. 'Course, being top of the line, you pay for it. I'll tell you, upon my word though, you won't find a sturdier machine than this one. It's just the thing for all the jostling a fellow gets riding over the cobblestones, wood pavers, potholes, and such here in the city. 'Course, it's just the ticket for the country rider as well," the salesman hurried to assure them.

Yearning suffused Matthew's freckled face as his bright blue eyes gazed upon the shiny contraption. This was the bicycle, then. "We'll take this one. It's just the thing," Sage announced.

Matthew immediately began shaking his head. "Oh, no, Mr. Adair, You can't buy this one. It's way too expensive. My aunt will skin me alive if I came back with the most expensive bicycle in the shop. You've already done way too much for me as it is."

Sage squeezed the boy's shoulder to stop the rushing words. "First of all, like I told you, Matthew, I'm buying it for you to use in going to school and to help Mozart's. If you want it to be yours alone, you can pay me for it, as you earn the money from running errands and such for our neighbors. And it's up to you to maintain it in sound condition since it's going to be getting a tough workout."

In that instant, a powerful twinge of foreboding compelled Sage to add, "And don't use it to get yourself into any trouble, either."

Matthew shook his head vehemently, "Oh, no sir!"

Sage studied him. Earnest, honest, hardworking, smart. He was the kind of kid likely to go far in the world, provided he lived long and well enough. "I want you to keep around the restaurant and go where we send you. And stay out of the North End. It isn't safe for young fellows. You hear me?"

"Yes, sir," Matthew promised quickly. The boy was at a point where he'd likely agree to anything in his eagerness to obtain the coveted bicycle. Sage ignored the faint warning bell in the back of his head and nodded to the salesman. That decision made, the salesman directed Matthew's attention to the various accessories. Sage listened with one ear as the salesman began a new series of spiels.

It is hard to distinguish between a fear and a premonition, Sage thought. Still, just two nights ago he'd advised Stuart Franklin to trust his instincts. Now, those instincts landed him on the horns of the same dilemma. With a mental shake, Sage let go his niggling worry. Probably just the protectiveness he felt toward the likable boy who'd become part of the family. Besides, he was tired and edgy from looking for Kincaid.

Thirty minutes later, the Blue Beauty wheeled into Mozart's kitchen, its chrome-plated carrier basket filled with a variety of wheelman necessities. Attached to the bottom of the perch was a small tin license plate. "A legal requirement," the salesman informed them. "The City uses the proceeds to construct various bicycle paths."

The bicycle's arrival created a minor ruckus. Ida Knutson immediately proclaimed that the "dirty contraption" was not welcome in her kitchen. Sage made a beeline for the stairs, leaving Mae Clemens to sort things out.

When Sage returned downstairs an hour later to take up his duties–seating the clientele and making small talk–Mae managed to pinch him on the arm. "You owe me, son. It seems I gave birth to a coward," she said, clearly referencing his hasty exit from the kitchen.

He rubbed his pinched arm as he paraphrased Shakespeare, "Retreat is the sometimes the better part of valor." Flashing his best smug smile and sidestepping her attempt to pinch him a second time, he advanced past her to greet new arrivals.

The supper hour moved smoothly along until it the time arrived for him to again become John Miner and exit through the cellar tunnel. As usual, he moved swiftly down its length to reach the opening into the alley. Even that short trip made his chest tighten. The tunnel's brick walls seemed to squeeze inward as he passed, giving off the same musty earth stench that always pervaded his recurring nightmare. Sage plunged ahead, holding his breath against that smell and against the dust his boots kicked up.

❀ ❀ ❀

Tooting clarinets and the rousing vocalizations of a Salvation Army band heralded the presence of the Seaman's Chapel before it came into sight. The Sallie's god-fearing soldiers proved to be up to their old tricks–trying to entice potential converts into attending the Salvation Army's religious services instead. The chaplain of the Seaman's Society, a white clerical collar squeezing his neck until it bulged, stood in the chapel doorway, his doughy face mottled red, his small chin quivering as he shouted, "Go away. Take yourselves off to your own church. Stop bothering our congregants." His efforts seemed only to increase the volume of brass horn, tambourine jangle and human caterwauling.

Sage slid past the Sallie's proselytizing soldiers to mount the concrete steps at the building's corner. Seeing him, the chaplain stopped his haranguing, hurried down the steps and grabbed Sage's elbow–almost as if he thought the opposition was going to snatch Sage themselves. The chaplain's voice transformed into a melodious purr, "Come in, my son, come in. So glad that you've decided to worship with us tonight. The Lord has guided your steps, I am sure. Welcome, welcome." He paused to shoot a glare at the momentarily quiet band. Its members interpreted his look as a goad to strike up another raucous tune. "Pay those fools no mind," the chaplain said, his voice still a purr even though his teeth were clenched.

The chaplain guided Sage up the steps, through a vestibule and into a large room where he let go of Sage's elbow. With a pat on Sage's shoulder, the chaplain returned to his post on the steps. Moments later the preacher again raised his voice to drown out his competition. Sage gazed about the sparse room. Except for the cross mounted on the wall, it looked like a union hall. Unpainted benches stood in ranks before a low dais that supported both a small organ and a lectern. A big, potbellied stove filled one corner, no fire behind its mica window, doubtless because of the day's lingering warmth. There was enough bench space for a hundred. Only about twenty shabbily dressed men were present, however, talking quietly or staring vacantly. Not a lively crowd by any standard. On a table, up near the dais, a canning jar held a bedraggled fistful of daisies. Next to it stood a battered tin coffee pot, a collection of mismatched cups, and a dish piled high with cookies. It looked like most of the attendees had already helped themselves. It's probably a tossup over which is the biggest draw, Sage thought: free coffee and cookies or eternal salvation. Sage grabbed a cup of coffee and took a seat on the rearmost bench.

Franklin wasn't there. Sage sighed in frustration. Franklin was the only lead that might explain what happened to Joseph Kincaid. If Franklin didn't show, the search was at a dead end. Not only that, he'd be stuck here for who knows how long, listening to rants about a vengeful god whom he found particularly objectionable. He refused to believe in a god who wasn't a kinder spirit than he, himself, tried to be.

Feeling like he had little choice, given that warring Christians blocked his exit, Sage slumped on the bench and resigned himself to enduring a long hour. He felt conspicuous. Everyone else sat clustered together on the benches up at the front. A few more men straggled into the room, filled their coffee cups, grabbed a few cookies and took their seats, some nearer the back of the room. Finally, the chaplain entered, paused to take in the attendees and mounted the dais. Franklin trailed the chaplain , stepping carefully. His bruised face was somber as he slid onto Sage's bench. He made no comment. Just kept his eyes fixed on the chaplain, who made a theatrical show of clearing his throat to bring the men to attention.

When the chaplain's first words rang out, they sounded both sonorous and distant, as if he were preaching to strangers filling a soaring cathedral. "Brothers, this day is for rejoicing. Why? You ask, 'why'? Why, when your life has been nothing more than endless pain and loss? How can I stand here speaking to you of rejoicing? I'll tell you why. It is because I know, as you shall know before this night has ended, my brothers, that God's good grace drew you to this humble place to hear news of your glorious salvation! Don't turn your back on His message! Salvation is yours, provided you don't spurn his love nor incur his wrath!"

"Miner, I'm glad you made it." Franklin shifted on the bench and leaned closer. "I'm thinking the news is bad." His low voice was barely audible beneath the chaplain's fervent exhortations.

Sage half-turned his face toward Franklin, who looked away and said quietly, "No, best that you not look at me when we're talking. I don't know all these men heah, and I still don't know whether those crimps are on my behind."

Sage faced the front. "What bad news?" he asked out of the corner of his mouth.

"A Chinese fisherman found a body floating just outside the Columbia River bar. It is almost certain that the man came off a ship. Maybe it's that boy you've been looking for–they described the fellow as having light hair and being about the right age. Can't be sure, though."

"When was the body found?" Sage asked.

Franklin's shoulders slumped. This new death had clearly dealt a blow to the shanghai-fighter's spirit. Another man Franklin failed to save. Sage wondered how many times in the past Franklin carried similar sad tales of loved ones vanishing into the ocean's wide, wild expanse.

A heavy sigh, audible to Sage even over the preacher's loud haranguing, preceded Franklin's next words. "The fisherman pulled it out a few days or so ago. Hadn't been in the water too long. By the time I reached Astoria, they'd already buried him. The police told me that the poor fellow's face was mostly gone, what with the crabs. And his body was kept on the deck of the fisherman's boat for a bit." Franklin paused, as if to force his thoughts away from the image. "Police said it was too late for a photo to help identify the man so they didn't take one. If you want to make sure, you'll need to show the kid's wedding photo to that Chinese fisherman who pulled the body from the water. His name is Hong Ah Kay—maybe he got a good look at the face before it swelled up too bad," he said.

Sage started calculating the days. The timing was off. Kincaid had been missing for longer than that. "Was there a gunshot or knife wound or anything like that?" Sage asked, cringing away from the thought of that handsome young face reduced to corrupted flesh.

"They tell me it looked like he drowned. If he jumped ship in the middle of the Columbia, down by Astoria, he'd surely drown. Only a fool or someone ignorant about the tides and current jumps into the water right there. Happens more times than you'd think, though. Shanghaied farm boys don't know anything about the river or the ocean either, for that matter. If it is any comfort, the cold likely put him to sleep first."

Poor Kincaid. Can't be more "farm boy" than someone from Kansas. Sage cleared his throat. "Astoria is where I'll find this Hong Ah Kay?" he asked.

Franklin shifted on the bench and pretended to tie his boot laces. "Yup, he has a small boat with a single sail. Sells to his people and to one of the canneries–the one on the wharf right next to where the sternwheeler, *Hassalo,* ties up. Can't say if he'd be ashore when you land there but maybe some other Chinese fellow saw the body. You show them the picture and they might say whether it's your fellow. Just ask around Astoria's Chinatown. I expect you'll find someone there willing to talk to you."

Sage was silent. The chaplain's exhortations and threats of eternal damnation continued to wash over him but Sage was deaf to the words. Astoria. Maybe Fong and his tong connections could convince the Chinese in Astoria to talk to him. Fong. Now, there was a little jab to the gut. He used to be able to count on Fong's help. Evidently, not anymore, considering how things had gone the last few days. Would he even be able to find Fong to ask for help?

"If it turns out that it is Joseph Kincaid's body, I am going to find out if he was shanghaied and who is responsible," he told Franklin.

Sage's peripheral vision caught Franklin shaking his head slowly from side to side as the man said, "Shanghaiing is a mighty nasty business, Miner. There's more involved in it than you realize. People are making money–important people and big money. Not just the crimps. Why else do you suppose we haven't been able to stop the practice? Shoot, you can't trust anybody. Not the police, not the judges, not even the harbormaster who's supposed to enforce what little law we got. I can't even trust the people in my own organization. No, you best stay away from the whole mess. I'm sorry about Kincaid. But if it's him and you poke your nose into it, you're liable to find yourself following him."

"To hell with whoever sees us talking," Sage thought and twisted to face the other man. "Franklin, I hear what you are saying and I plan on being careful. I'm telling you though, if that body is Joseph Kincaid's, I promise that somebody is damn sure going to pay." That statement gave each man pause before Sage continued, his mind already roving over possible actions. "What foreign consuls in Portland are trying to change the law? Might one of them talk to me? Give me some idea of how, who, and what is involved?"

"Well, if you're determined to push ahead, then you best talk to James Laidlaw, the British consul. He has better details about the business-end than me. He's leading the charge and doing a damn fine job of it too. Makes me wish I was a Brit."

Sage started. He'd seen James Laidlaw more than once. The man's office occupied a storefront about a block from Mozart's. Moreover, the sardonic Scotsman was a regular customer.

Better pick Franklin's brain while he still could. "Tell me, Franklin, if a man wants to work for one of these crimps, how does he go about it?"

"Well, first of all, he darn sure wouldn't want to be seen in my company." Franklin went silent, wriggling on the bench as if trying on the question. "I guess if I was to go about getting next to the crimps, I'd start by working for Tobias Pratt, just to familiarize myself with the trade. Pratt's always looking to fill a runner opening. He says that's because the men he hires are lazy but that's not the reason."

"Why can't he keep men? He drive them too hard or something?"

"More like 'or something.' Still, overall, he's fairly decent for a crimp. Has a heart and a small measure of principle. You work for him, you'll find out for yourself why his workers run themselves off after a few days or so. Can't hurt you none. Listen to 'ole Tobias–not that there's a choice in the matter."

Franklin softly cleared his throat, as if words were trapped there, before hesitantly continuing, "After that, you might be ready to get taken on by Kaspar Mordaunt. But before you take any steps in that direction, you'd best talk to Laidlaw. Survey the lay of the land, so you don't act like some greenhorn. Otherwise, Mordaunt will spot you as a ringer for the real thing. If he does, I wouldn't give a plug nickel for your chances of staying alive."

This last sentence extended beyond the end of the chaplain's sermon and seemed to roll across the silent hall. Sage sneaked a look toward the other men, checking whether anyone had heard it. No one gave an indication that he had, except for the chaplain. He paused to glower at them before moving to sit before the organ and slam his stubby fingers down on the first chord of the old standby, "Amazing Grace." Sage and Franklin clambered to their feet with the others, both opening their mouths wide to sing with a gusto neither of them felt.

When Sage returned to his room above Mozart's, no one was there. He'd expected to see Fong, waiting to pack up the Miner disguise while he listened to Sage's report. Instead, the room was empty. There'd be none of Fong's penetrating questions to help Sage sort the information into a coherent picture. It was irritating to ponder, alone, the question of what to do about the body found down at Astoria. And, he missed talking to Fong about the particulars associated with the shanghaiing business. In the past, their two minds working together, somehow added up to three minds.

After stuffing his John Miner duds into the trunk and shoving it under the four-poster, Sage climbed into bed only to lie staring up at the ceiling while he tried to mull over the Kincaid situation. He wasn't successful. Like the babble of a small stream, a growing disquiet over Fong's seeming abandonment of their mission overpowered all other thoughts. "I'm getting worried about Fong," he finally confessed out loud before dropping off to sleep.

EIGHT

No breakfast waited on the table when a "yee-hawing" teamster in the street below woke Sage late the next morning. Fong was still absent.

Donning a day suit, waistcoat, white shirt and long tie, Sage descended to the restaurant kitchen. His mother was wielding a wickedly sharp knife and attacking a pile of scraped carrots, her lips blanched from being pressed tightly together. She glanced at him while her knife continued dicing. She seemed to address the carrots, "No, before you ask, I do not know where Mr. Fong is. He sent a message by one of his cousins that he was delayed. That's all I know. If you're hungry, fend for yourself or wait until dinner's ready." Her tone of voice telling him that she was a snapping turtle best avoided.

He looked around for something to eat. Golden biscuits overflowed a basket on the counter. So, he grabbed the basket, jam pot and coffee cup before retreating into the empty dining room without saying a word. At tables situated farthest from the kitchen, two waiters laid out place settings. Obviously, he wasn't the only one choosing to keep out of Mae Clemens's way. Sinking his teeth into the biscuit, he started cataloging all the incidents signaling Fong's change in behavior. There was no getting around it, his mother was right. Fong certainly was acting strange.

Sage tried to recall the last time he'd spoken to the "normal" Mr. Fong. Last Sunday, when they'd sat on the roof talking about the mission, the Chinese man was his customary, teasing self. Later that day, Fong mysteriously disappeared during the dinner hour. When he returned to Mozart's on Monday, he was acting differently. So, Fong changed between the time they'd talked on the roof and before Monday morning. That meant Sunday supper hour was the most likely time something happened.

His mother swept through the swinging doors from the kitchen, her arms straining beneath a high stack of clean plates. He jumped up to take them from her, setting them on the buffet. She thanked him with a weary smile.

Good. The snapping turtle was gone. "Mrs. Clemens," he began, feeling slightly foolish as he always did whenever he used the pretense of having a more distant relationship with her. Just in case the two waiters were listening, though, he put on the show. He lowered his voice. "Do you recall whether anything unusual happened here in the restaurant last Sunday afternnoon? Anything that upset Mr. Fong? Or was there a message from one of his tong 'cousins?' Sunday was the night he disappeared during the dinner hour," he reminded her.

She was on her way back to the kitchen. At his question, she paused and turned, her forehead wrinkling with thought. "I'm certain no message came for him. As for something happening . . . we were very busy and ran short on dishes and all. Mr. Fong noticed and volunteered to clear the tables to free up an extra hand for washing. He did that for a while. Suddenly, he came into the kitchen, whipped off his apron and announced he was leaving. In two seconds, he'd bolted out the back door without even a never-you-mind."

Sage looked around the empty room, envisioning Fong serenely moving among the patrons, clearing the dishes, moving back and forth to the kitchen. "Tell me, Mrs. Clemens, were any strangers in the dining room just before Mr. Fong vanished that afternoon?" He was thinking that it had to be a man who triggered the problem. Surely no woman would upset Fong. Fact was, Mozart's female patrons, whenever they noticed him, seemed to like Fong. Besides, could mere words make Fong abandon St. Alban's mission with no explanation? It just didn't make sense. Given the years of brutal racism Fong had already endured, it was inconceivable that words, no matter how vile or ignorant, could work such a dramatic change in the man. Sage couldn't buy it.

Mae pulled a chair out, sat and sighed wearily. She reached out and began mechanically folding the clean napkin lying there, even as her eyes stared out over the tables, her brow furrowed. "Let's see, the Kearneys were here, the Saltzmans, and a large group from Baker's Theater. Most everyone, customers we know. People that Mr. Fong has seen here before." Her strong fingers began idly sharpening the napkin's edges only to stop as her eyes widened slightly. "Wait a minute. I do recall two strange men. Kind of rough." She nodded toward a table in the far corner of the restaurant, near the front windows. "They sat over there."

"Can you remember whether Mr. Fong worked anywhere near them?"

Once again, she considered before saying, "Yes, he must have, because that big Baker theater party sat at tables next to them. The theater group finished dining before the two men did. So the two men hadn't left when Mr. Fong began clearing the theater folks' table."

"What do you mean, 'kind of rough'? Were they dressed like working men?" Such patrons were unusual because Mozart's was too pricey for them. That fact, and his disguises, were the reason why he could play Mozart's debonair restaurant host without worrying that he'd be recognized as "John Miner, itinerant working man" from the North End.

"No, they wore fine enough clothes. It was more that they had the look of field mules wearing parade saddles, if you know what I mean. They'd look more natural-like in work pants, suspenders, and long johns."

Shouts from inside the kitchen sent Mae hurrying away. When she returned to the dining room, she carried two pitchers of water and her earlier irritation was back. Some kind of kitchen brouhaha–probably another dispute with the butcher. The two of them squabbled every time they saw each other. She didn't bother explaining, instead, saying sharply, "Mr. Adair, if this restaurant is to open in time for dinner, you best shake a leg and clear off that table. Customers are going to come through that front door any minute and this place is not fit to open."

Sage jumped to his feet, snatching up the jam pot, biscuit basket, dirty knife, coffee cup, and used napkin. His prompt obedience drew snickers from the two waiters, both of whom immediately sobered when she sent a sharp look in their direction. "What are you two gawping at? You think there's time to fool around? Half these tables aren't ready," she snapped before steaming back through the kitchen doors. The two waiters returned to laying out the tables at twice their previous speed.

Sage waited until they looked in his direction to throw a smirk at them. A man didn't risk stepping to Mrs. Clemens' bad side when she was in her no-nonsense mood. No smart man. Her tongue could lash hide off cattle.

Near the dinner hour's end, James Laidlaw entered Mozart's ready to eat. The British consul usually took his noontime meal at Mozart's. A vocal admirer of Ida's cooking, he often threatened to hire her away. Although Laidlaw's threat had a jovial tone, Sage was never quite sure that the other man was joking.

Sage greeted Laidlaw, scrutinizing his clean-shaven face. His thinning brown hair started far back on his forehead while the bland regularity of his features rendered the man unremarkable except for the penetrating intensity of his eyes. In retrospect, Franklin's identifying Laidlaw as a champion in the fight against shanghaiing was less a surprise than it was a confirmation. Sage had already taken Laidlaw's measure, deciding he was an easy man to underestimate if you overlooked that keen intelligence in those pale gray eyes.

"And a good afternoon to you, Mr. Adair," Laidlaw's cultured Scot's voice replied in response to Sage's greeting. "And am I not thinking correctly, but what the excellent Mrs. Ida might be saving me a piece of her chicken pot pie? Is that not the special for this day of the week?"

"It certainly is and she always does, Mr. Laidlaw. She'd never disappoint such a faithful devotee of her noontime specialties." And indeed, Ida had set aside the last piece of chicken pot pie for the British consul. Laidlaw tucked into the dish with the intensity of a hungry logger.

Sage bided his time, waiting until Laidlaw was nearly finished. He approached the consul and asked whether he might sit and join him for coffee. After momentary confusion, Laidlaw inclined his head graciously, saying, "Why, certainly, Mr. Adair. I'd appreciate the pleasure of your company with my coffee. A most enjoyable meal. Please convey my compliments to Mrs. Ida."

"I shall," Sage said, taking the seat that put his back to the rest of the patrons. That way, they wouldn't overhear him. Once seated, he cast about for how to begin, picking up an unused dinner knife idly pressing its rounded tip into the tablecloth. There was much he must not say. The other man stirred, his curiosity piqued. Sage drew a deep breath and began, "Actually, Mr. Laidlaw, I need to make a rather unusual request of you. And I must begin by asking that you keep our conversation strictly confidential."

Laidlaw laid down his fork and scooted his chair closer to the table, his pale eyes now piercing. "Why, certainly, I will honor your confidences, Mr. Adair," he said. "How is it that I can be of help to you?"

"I need to learn about the business of crimping and shanghaiing," Sage answered.

Laidlaw's face closed as if hit by cold water. "Now, what, I wonder, has gotten the owner of an elite restaurant like Mozart's Table interested in the despicable business of crimping?" He leaned forward. "Don't tell me that you are thinking of branching out? Need to invest surplus cash or something of that nature?" His tone was light but his smile was rigid and his eyes chilly.

Sage spoke quickly, leaning closer so that people dining at adjacent tables would not overhear, "Quite the contrary. I think it possible that a young man I'm trying to find was shanghaied. If so, I am at a loss as to how to find him. I know so little about the practice." Not the truth, of course. His experiences in San Francisco and Portland's North End, together with Franklin's recent revelations, meant he knew quite a bit. Still, he couldn't tip his hand just yet. Not until he could gauge both Laidlaw's willingness to share information and his ability to keep secrets.

Laidlaw's skepticism twisted his lips. "Just how is it that you know someone who'd get themselves shanghaied? I would think," here he cast a sardonic look around the elegant dining room, "that your associates' social status would be more than adequate to shield them from such dangers."

Sage's anger flared at the man's judgmental tone of voice. What a pompous ass. He stifled a retort, though. In situations like this, it is better to be underestimated. Might as well satisfy Laidlaw's expectations. Sage faked what he hoped appeared to be awkward embarrassment. "Actually, you are correct, he said. "The problem does lie far outside my ken. It seems that one of Ida's nephews has gone missing and, well, she's not an attentive cook when she's worried. We can't afford to have her distracted, you see. Bad for business."

Laidlaw's eyes narrowed momentarily and he stared at Sage for so long that Sage felt the urge to fidget. He willed himself to remain still. The British consul abruptly withdrew his searching gaze, seeming to accept Sage's explanation. Laidlaw leaned back in his chair and drank from his coffee cup. "Fair enough, Mr. Adair. It just so happens I am the ideal man to enlighten you on the dastardly business whereby sailors are bought and sold. I condemn it under all circumstances. It is my intention to eradicate it from this seaport, whatever the cost. Of course," he paused to peer into his almost empty cup, "right now it will cost you an additional coffee because it's not a short lesson."

Sage gestured and they waited silently while a waiter re-filled their cups and moved on to the next table. Once the waiter was out of earshot, Laidlaw began, "If Ida's nephew has vanished then he could have been shanghaied. There is always a market for cabin boys. Still, as I just indicated, shanghaiing is usually a danger only to certain types of men. Rarely to the locals, mind you. No, the danger is to those sailors on shore leave or to homeless loggers and farm hands–able bodied men lacking roots in our community or without nearby families who are likely to raise a ruckus if they disappear. Like I stated, not the sort of men you'd know, old chap."

That last jab seemed calculated because Laidlaw's eyes turned measuring and watchful. Sage decided it was time to work a slight adjustment in Laidlaw's mistaken view of Mozart's owner. "Actually, I bought Mozart's with gold I prospected in the Yukon. And I wasn't a provisions trader, either. I froze my rear end melting permafrost, nearly lost my toes more than once and wintered over at 40 below in a dirt-floored hut. And this blaze of white at my hairline is thanks to a wild sled ride down the backside of Chillakoot Pass that came near to killing me."

Speculation once more narrowed the consul's eyes. Still, Laidlaw only laughed. "Well, I have heard tell that looks can be deceiving. I beg your pardon. Seems like there may be more to you than I originally surmised."

Again, it wasn't the man's words. Instead, it was Laidlaw's superior tone of voice that rankled Sage. He, however, only smiled though he wanted to say, "More than you'll ever begin to guess, you smug so-and-so." You'd think that a diplomat whose national dish was a sheep stomach stuffed with rutabagas might think twice about taking that high and mighty tone with others. Sage gave himself a mental shake and forgave the man. People filled with righteous indignation often developed an annoying sense of superiority. Heck, even he had, on occasion. Sometimes that sense of superiority was a man's only reward for fighting on the moral side of things.

Oblivious to Sage's thoughts, Laidlaw shrugged and began, "For most men, being shanghaied starts with a glad hand and a friendly drink and ends with kidnapping or even worse. For the financiers, many of them Mozart's patrons, shanghaiing is a matter of cold cash economics. Otherwise, it doesn't touch their lives at all." He nodded in the direction of the other diners. "That is why the ones leading the fight against the practice are the foreign consuls and a few Christian souls who carry their religion home on Sunday rather than leaving it behind in the church pew."

"Don't the police try to stop it?" Sage asked despite already knowing the answer. Nefarious activities like crimping and shanghaiing drew demands for bribes like rotten meat drew flies.

Even without the bribes, the police tended to ignore back alley villainy when it didn't affect regular folks. Not that Sage blamed the officers entirely. A Portland street patrolman earned far less than most bartenders, thanks to the rich reducing their tax rates even as the population exploded.

"Hah!" Laidlaw responded. "The police receive their slice of the proverbial pie as kickbacks. Not just them. Many others gobble from that particular trough, if you'll forgive my clumsy metaphor. First, there are the semi-legitimate boardinghouse masters or 'crimps,' as most call them. Their gain is obvious. They tend to use trickery and indebtedness to crew the ships.

"After that are the building owners. They provide both the lures of entrapment above ground and those underground locations where the land shark crimps imprison shanghaied men before transferring them onto a departing ship. So, that means the North End building owner gets a cut—twice.

"To my mind, the most disgusting of all are the 'investors.' They are the ones who finance the crimps and land sharks, underwrite the buildings and get payoffs in exchange for providing political protection. No matter what happens, they make sure their profit from the shanghaiing business exceeds the interest rate obtainable from a bank or other legitimate investment."

As he'd told Franklin, the kidnapping aspect was something Sage knew about. He'd received plenty of warnings about the dangers of drinking with strangers during those months of hard Frisco living. Later on, while snugging close to lumber camp stoves or sitting in North End swill joints, there'd be tales of loggers and others who'd disappeared from the streets. Speculations usually focused on shanghaiing as the culprit. But, investors? Somehow, he'd never considered the economic underpinnings of the trade. "But surely the crimps who shanghai are arrested sometimes? I've read about such arrests in the paper," Sage said, leaning forward.

Laidlaw's laugh was a humorless bark. "Yes, they might arrest a crimp or his runner," he said. "Nothing comes of it. The court either dismisses the charges or reduces them to a finable offense. Think back. You never read about the aftermath of a crimp's arrest, do you?"

"Are you saying the judges are in on it, too?"

"Near as we can learn, all but one of them are beholden to the crimps. You see, on election day, the crimps haul drunks by the wagonload from one polling place to another to cast their votes, over and over. It doesn't matter that most of them aren't even American citizens, or that not a one of them is sober. Because of this welcome political 'support,' few local politicians challenge the crimps–including those judges who swear upon on a Bible to uphold the law." Laidlaw sipped from his cup, his face scrunching as if he'd swallowed bitter coffee.

"What about the captains? Don't they object? It sounds like the crimps are extorting them."

"Some of them do. Most captains hate the crimps as much as I do. That doesn't mean they can stand up to them. When a crimp is mad at a captain, that captain loses his crew and cannot find replacements." Laidlaw's brow tightened and the corners of his mouth sagged slightly. "Then, of course, there are the other captains. Brits among them, I'm ashamed to say, who embrace the situation. They see the shanghaiing game as an opportunity to line their own pockets."

Laidlaw fumbled in his waistcoat until he found and extracted a small silver toothpick. He didn't use it, only turned it end over end as he continued the story. "Under British seafaring law, sailors on British vessels cannot be paid more than a paltry shore leave allowance until they return to British soil. Other nations also generally require sailors to sign round-trip contracts that fully payoff only if they return to their home port.

"The thought behind the delayed pay off is that if they receive all their wages while they're in a foreign port, they'll jump ship and be gone for good. During the gold rush that happened every time a ship docked in San Francisco. Got so you couldn't find a ship willing to berth there. Abandoned ships crowded the Bay. The rotting hulks of some of them are still there.

"But like many reasonable ideas, the purpose for withholding pay was quickly corrupted. It now serves the bloody bastards' self interest. Some captains deliberately exploit the situation by working hand-in-glove with the crimps. They pay the crimps to keep the sailors from returning to their ship. That way, the captain and the owner split those unpaid wages."

Sage pondered Laidlaw's explanation. He'd never taken the time to reason the economics out. Shanghaiing was clearly a commercial venture with a full complement of exploiters, foot soldiers and victims. He asked, "But I thought there was a harbormaster to stop that sort of thing? I also heard that the law limits what captains can legally pay a crimp for a sailor."

Laidlaw's face tightened as he said bitterly, "In a single month, Portland's harbormaster takes more in bribes than he receives as his annual salary. And yes, the law sets a maximum limit on how much blood money the crimps can charge captains. But that limit is insufficient to render the trade in sailors economically unfeasible. Right now, it's fifty-five dollars per head in blood money and sixty dollars to pay the crimp for what the sailor supposedly owes for two months of board and lodging. Of course, the crimps lay claim to that sixty-dollar advance even if the sailor has been in port less than a week. That sixty dollars is an advance on the sailor's wages, by the way. It means he ends up working two months at sea for no wages at all."

"Isn't there a way to stop shanghaiing?" Sage asked, thinking that sailors were treated even worse than timber workers. And at least a logger could walk off the job and out of the woods.

"Ah, might it be that the practices I relate offend your sensibilities?" Laidlaw asked, his tone again sneering before his face sagged and weariness seemed to wash over him. He looked down and away. With a rueful twist of his lips, his gaze returned to Sage. "I am sorry, my man," he said, his voice apologetic. "You've done nothing to deserve such unwarranted sarcasm. It's just that I've told this story so many times to people like you. Each one expresses outrage but afterward they do absolutely nothing. When I try to again raise the issue with them, they brush me off. It is as though someone warns them to keep out of it 'or else'." He huffed an abbreviated chuckle. "Who am I kidding? I know bloody well that someone's warned them to keep out of it."

He straightened in his chair to say with slightly more vigor, "To answer your question, a growing number of us are asking that the state legislature prohibit all trade in sailors. We've introduced a bill. The crimps and their powerful friends are fighting that bill tooth and nail. One factor in our favor is that your legislators hail from all over Oregon. Many rural legislators answer to constituents whose sons are in danger of being snatched off Portland's streets or Astoria's and all the points in-between. Plus, their farmer constituents complain that crimping raises their costs. That's because the crimps' surcharge gets passed on, forcing the farmers'shipping costs up and their profits down. Money again, always the money."

Sage swallowed the last of his coffee and looked around for a waiter. "Sounds like you're making progress, changing people's minds," he observed.

Laidlaw's smile was crooked. "Excuse my cynicism, but the fact is, the legislators from the interior can afford to be outraged. They don't receive any of the financial or political benefits of the crimping trade. So, my powers of persuasion deserve little credit. And we have yet to succeed. Thus far, the Portland legislators wield sufficient political power to resist the tide of change, so to speak."

The man's too modest, Sage thought. He suspected Laidlaw was due much of the credit. Franklin seemed to think so anyway. "How's it looking?" Sage asked. "Will the bill pass?"

This time Laidlaw's smile was straightforward, hopeful. "It's looking more likely. There's a man whose been rowing out to meet with the ship captains before they cross the Columbia River bar into the ocean. His reports are compelling because they prove how dastardly and widespread the practice is. This new information might make the difference."

"Stuart Franklin," Sage said.

For the first time, Laidlaw looked taken aback. "Our group does not bandy his name about. It's dangerous work. How is it that you came to learn of him and his work?"

"He told me about it himself. He's the one who suggested that I talk to you, as a matter of fact."

Laidlaw relaxed in his chair. "Well," he commented, "if Franklin vouches for you, there must be much more to you than I thought. He's a careful man."

"There's reason to believe they're on to him," Sage said. He related his rescue of Franklin without discussing its aftermath at the New Elijah. In the ensuing silence, Sage thought about how the pain had creased Franklin's face, and about his muscled shoulders and his sun burnt face and asked Laidlaw, "Why's Franklin willing to do this? To risk his life like this? Was he shanghaied? Or is he one of those practicing Christians you talked about?"

The British consul shook his head. "Neither one, actually," he replied. "I take it that he didn't tell you about his younger brother. Here, maybe you should read this." Laidlaw pulled two folded sheets of paper from his inside coat pocket and handed them to Sage. "That's a copy of a letter Franklin's youngest brother wrote to their grandfather. Franklin gave me permission to pull it out whenever I talk to folks about shanghaiing."

Sage carefully unfolded the fragile papers, spread them flat on the table and leaned forward to read the letter's faded script.

NINE

LAIDLAW'S VOICE WAS SUBDUED as he watched Sage smooth the folds from the sheets, "Franklin's grandfather copied the original letter and forwarded it to me. He hoped that I would encounter or find the boy. The old man is three years dead now."

Sage studied the sheets of paper. Cramped script covered all sides from edge to edge. The spidery copperplate handwriting was proof, indeed, that an elderly, failing hand wrote the words. A momentary aching pang transfixed Sage. He sensed the fear, hope and yearning the old man must have felt as he copied his grandson's words.

Dearest Grandfather, It will surprise you to hear that I am in destitute circumstances, but if you knew how it came about you would sympathize with me. As you know, I started out from home with a good deal of money, but as I was thoughtless I spent and wasted more than necessary. I found myself in Portland, Oregon, without money or employment. After trying hard to get work and starving five solid days, I chanced to meet a man who said he would give me employment on board a steamboat that ran up and down the

Columbia River between Portland and Astoria, at forty dollars per month and board. I thought that was a good chance and took it of course. This man treated me very well and bought me anything I wanted. He paid my board bills and then took me with him to Astoria.

When we got there, he left me in a boardinghouse until he sent me out on a small boat with a lot of sailors (all drunk). I thought it was heading to the river boat I was going to work on but instead it took us to a ship called the *Cody Bell*. I was what they call shanghaied. I had not the least idea where we were going but I made up my mind to do the best I could to please the officers. I was seasick but that made no difference with them so I had to work just as hard as though I was well. Then I was thinking of home so that I got homesick. The other sailors, seeing that I was no seaman, got down on me and treated me like a dog. I had to take the fat meat that they left or have none at all. They would make me tobacco their pipes and wash their clothes. I was working day and night, very seldom ever getting three hours sleep in one night. If there was anything to do I had to do it and if I forgot any little thing they would treat me very rough. I resisted their cruelty once and got put in chains all one day and all one night without a thing to eat or drink. When I got out, the hard chaff bread tasted good.

Worst of all they stole my clothes and divided them amongst themselves and were clothed warm around Cape Horn while I was shivering with cold, wet through in a shift with no dry clothes to change into. The carpenter gave me an old pair of drawers and an old shirt. I looked forward to the time when I should see land again hoping and expecting to get (30) thirty dollars per month but just when we were within one day, the captain said that I was getting nothing and he was selling me to another ship for the money I owed for what he paid the crimp. I am now working from daylight til dark for nothing but three ladles of soup a day on a ship named the *Lucifera*, a devil ship. I am not telling you lies for all I have said is as true as I live. I don't think I can last much longer and this ship's timbers are rotten through.

How is grandmother? I hope she is well. I send my love to Stuart, and Mary and Laura. I hope to see you soon. We stopped in a port on the South African shore and I am sending this letter care of a sailor from another ship. I hope it reaches you. From your loving grandson,

Donald B. Franklin

As Sage read, he found himself picturing Matthew's innocent face. He could see a young boy like Matthew, totally overwhelmed by his dire circumstances, penning just such a letter. And, Sage realized this was precisely the kind of trouble naive young men, like Kincaid or Matthew, could easily stumble into Sage carefully refolded the worn paper. "What happened to him?" he asked, already sure of Laidlaw's answer. Stuart Franklin was here in Portland after all.

"The *Lucifera* sank to the bottom, off the coast of Argentina, shortly after young Franklin wrote that letter. All hands were lost."

"So Stuart Franklin is here to find the man who shanghaied his brother onto that ship?" Sage asked. Franklin's willingness to repeatedly risk his life in a small rowboat at the Columbia River mouth now made perfect sense.

"That is what brought him here. The outcome of that particular search is unknown. I am careful not to ask. These days, his mission is to stop shanghaiing. He worries me, though. He is unrelenting in his efforts to expose and stop the shanghai crimps—the land sharks. It leads him into taking too many risks. Like rowing out to the ships. One of these days, a captain is not going to let him leave. He says he's careful, knows what ships to approach. Still, if the crimps want Franklin stopped badly enough, they will find a captain disposed to take care of him for a price."

Sage looked down at the folded letter and said, "Don't know that I blame Franklin. I'd feel the same in his place. His brother sounded like a nice boy. A bit like Ida's nephew, Matthew." Sage handed the letter back to Laidlaw, asking as he did so, "Why aren't the town merchants yammering for this practice to stop? Doesn't it drive off their customers? I mean, why visit a city where you might be snatched off the street and shipped out to China?"

Laidlaw's bark of bitter laughter turned faces in their direction. The consul didn't notice. "That just shows how little you understand the world of commerce as it relates to ocean shipping, my friend. If the sailors jump a ship here in port, then that ship is stranded until it obtains a full crew. That hurts the City's commercial men. They want to receive and ship goods in a timely fashion. More important, a port can get a reputation for allowing desertion to strand ships. If that happens, it becomes a port where the merchants are forced to pay markedly higher shipping costs. That's what started happening in San Francisco during the gold rush. It remains a problem today because many sailors want to become Americans living on the West Coast."

Laidlaw studied him, his fingers idly tugging at an earlobe. Then he straightened and pulled a watch from his vest pocket to check the time. "Tell you what Mr. Adair, if you've an hour or so to spare, you can hear for yourself what our esteemed city leaders really think about the reprehensible business of shanghaiing. Come be my guest at the Cabot Club. It's been some while since I stopped in there to give them a poke."

Sage accepted Laidlaw's offer with alacrity. The two of them exited Mozart's and strolled toward West Park and Salmon Streets, a location conveniently near Lucinda's establishment. As they passed the fourteen steps leading upward to her lacquered door, guilt stabbed at him. In the midst of all that had been happening, Sage thought of her only fleetingly. She deserved better treatment. He glanced toward her parlor windows, hoping she wasn't at the window watching him walk right past. It seemed that a curtain edge twitched. Or, probably, his guilt had him imagining that furtive movement.

They mounted the three steps and entered deep shade. Considered one of the City's architectural attractions, the Cabot was a four-story gentlemen's club constructed of yellow Japanese brick trimmed in white. Its entrance lay behind a broad tiled veranda held up by Ionic columns and enhanced by two large bay windows. Inside was a small reception room, where Sage and Laidlaw relinquished their hats and the consul's briefcase. Beyond stretched the polished wood floor of the main hall, exposed beams arching overhead and a large open fireplace anchoring the far end of its expanse. Mingled scents of expensive cigars layered the air, while the clack of billiard balls sounded from a room on the right.

A nattily dressed old man approached and gestured toward a gilt-edged journal that lay open on a small table nearby. "Sir, please also sign your guest in." Laidlaw nodded and as he signed he told Sage in a low voice, "The old boys are strict about guests in the club. Inviting too many of the wrong kind brings approbation down on your head. And certainly, no women enter, ever. Well, they've been allowed twice, once when the club opened in its original location and once when it opened here. That's it." He returned the pen to the attendant. "Gerald, be kind enough to bring us brandies in the library."

Inside the library, a pristine Wilton carpeted the floor, its thick blue pile contrasting with red drapes swagged to either side of the tall windows. Crystal chandeliers sparkled overhead. It being summer, a huge flower arrangement of scarlet bee balm spikes screened the opening of the yellow Sienna marble fireplace.

The commonality between the Cabot Club and North End saloons lay in the density of tobacco smoke and the opportunity for excessive alcohol consumption. There were, however, no rickety chairs, spool top tables, rowdy musicians, or dingy lighting. Instead, the Cabot's members lounged in deep leather chairs, reading or conversing in quiet tones, their brandy snifters resting on polished tables at their elbows, the bright windows and chandelier light being supplemented by glittering crystal wall sconces.

Laidlaw headed toward a pair of chairs sitting off to one side though still within voice range of a few groupings of men, many of whom Sage recognized as frequent Mozart's customers. Gerald appeared with the brandies and the two men sank into the soft padded leather.

Sage sipped the smooth, sweet fire and spoke softly, so that his voice wouldn't carry, "If these men support shanghaiing, it's surprising they permit you in their midst."

Laidlaw snorted. "They have no choice in the matter," he said. "By virtue of my consul position, I'm automatically a member and, more significantly, I am shipping master of all the British ships entering this port. If my fellow Club members desire to sell their products in merry old England, they need make nice to me." He leaned forward, a mischievous quirk to his lips, and said confidentially, "And I must say, I rather enjoy giving them a poke now and again."

By way of demonstrating, Laidlaw raised his voice so that it carried to three men sitting nearby. Sage knew them from their frequent patronage of Mozart's. "Mr. Knapp, there's concern that the *Birmingham Bell* will be stranded in port for lack of men. You have a rather large shipment aboard her, do you not?" Laidlaw asked.

All three heads swiveled toward Laidlaw. The whippet-faced man Sage knew as Melbourne Knapp, concern tightening his features, quavered, "Not sail, you say? Oh, surely not. She's supposed to set sail this evening." Even protected by the sturdy bricks of this exclusive club, Knapp acted like he was scared of his own shadow. Not for the first time, Sage wondered whether Knapp had married into, or inherited, his money. He seemed altogether too timid to have grabbed it on his own in this era of the robber barons. The new century's ruthless moguls would stampede over Knapp like thirsty cattle sensing water.

Another one of the three men, his figure as stout as Knapp's was meager, made a show of guffawing, before saying reassuringly, "Don't you worry, Melbourne. James is pulling your leg. The crimps won't miss an opportunity to make money from the *Bell's* predicament. She'll go out as scheduled, mark my words."

"You seem remarkably confident about that, Gordon," Laidlaw's voice was deceptively mild since Sage observed a slight whitening at the corners of his companion's tight smile.

Gordon waved his smoking cigar dismissively, saying, "Yes, well, I'm a businessman who ships goods. And as you well know, not a few of my properties are situated there in the North End. So, I keep myself fairly well apprised as to what is occurring with the oceangoing labor force."

Sage was familiar with Gordon's habit of making confident assertions. When dining at Mozart's, Gordon proved himself to be the exact opposite of the timid Knapp–loud and boastful with the patrons and bullying to the staff. Today, the man's bragging revealed something interesting–that he might be one of those Portland businessmen profiting from the crimping trade.

Laidlaw sent Sage a surreptitious wink. To Gordon, however, he said, "So, you're betting the crimps will successfully snatch enough innocent men off the street to crew the *Bell*?" Laidlaw's voice remained dead calm although his eyes narrowed to mere slits above the rim of his brandy glass.

"Oh, oh. James is about to mount his soapbox," said the third man, also a Mozart's customer, whose name Sage did not recall. "Clear the way and plan to stay." The chortling his rhyme elicited from the other two, far exceeded its comedic merit.

Gordon made a show of suppressing his laughter before directing a comment toward Sage. "I say, Adair. Has our Mr. Laidlaw gnawed your ear bloody over his pet interest yet? Revealed our fair city's shameful reputation for allowing poor innocent men to be shanghaied off its streets?"

Sage sipped brandy before answering. Better not to tip his hand to these men. "Actually, Mr. Laidlaw was indeed informing me of the practice. I am learning that I am quite ignorant in that regard," he said, striving for a noncommittal middle ground between the two men. He needed to remain free of suspicion–a disinterested bystander in this dispute. Laidlaw would have to fight this battle unaided. Otherwise, Sage wouldn't be free to delve more deeply into the crimping business. His top priorities had to be Kincaid and the other missing man, Amacker.

Gordon nodded. "Well, before he has you weeping into your brandy like some fainthearted miss, let me inform you that most of us Americans don't agree with James on the issue of crewing deepwater vessels." The other two nodded when Gordon looked toward them. He continued, "These sailors and lumberjacks blow into town and hang about the streets, disgustingly drunk and accosting decent women. They are their own worst enemies–shiftless, lazy, and weak-willed. Sending them to sea is doing them a favor. At least out on the ocean, they aren't drinking themselves stupid and offending decent people." The moral force of Gordon's statement was blunted by the faint slurring that accompanied his words. The man was already drunk at midday.

That fact, and the fate of Stuart Franklin's brother, forced Sage to struggle at keeping his face blank. Laidlaw, however, exercised no such restraint. His sharp retort echoed throughout the room, bringing every other conversation to a standstill, "Surely, Gordon, you cannot be claiming that every shanghaied man falls into that category. Some of them are decent Christian men and others are mere children."

"Damn few of them. Otherwise, they wouldn't be down in that part of town. Besides, it's a good way for a young man to toughen up. We have far too many these days who don't know the value of work or a dollar."

"When you say, 'that part of town', do you mean the part of town where you own a number of the buildings–buildings you rent to the poor and to the crimps at exorbitant prices? Or so they tell me." Laidlaw's volume remained raised. Avid faces began staring openly in their direction, not a few of them appearing gleeful at the promise of a tussle in their midst. In that respect, there was little difference between these men and the denizens of the lowliest waterfront saloon.

Deep red flushed Gordon's round face and Sage suppressed an urge to chuckle at the sight. "You listen here, Laidlaw. I won't tolerate your damnable insinuations right here in my own club! If you think . . . ," He was sputtering, his fleshy lips flicking spittle.

The third man hastily intervened. "Now, gentlemen," he said, his voice urgent and low as he pointedly glanced around the room toward eager faces staring intently in their direction, "Let's keep things civil. This is, after all, a gentlemen's club."

Sage felt the urge to jump in. What was "gentlemanly" about cudgeling, drugging and kidnapping people? Sage clamped his lips tight, swallowing his observations. Don't show your cards to a potential opponent, he cautioned himself.

The peacemaker raised his voice to reach the attentive listeners seated around them. "I say, Laidlaw, when are you going to let me beat you at bowling again? Gerald tells me that the lanes downstairs have been sanded and lacquered until they are smooth as a whore's backside." Gerald, entering the room with a tray of brandy glasses, halted, his prim mouth agape at hearing the simile being attributed to him. Laughter exploded across the room. There was no telling what triggered the merriment: Gerald's reaction to the statement being attributed to him, the unlikelihood of such a bawdy phrase ever crossing Gerald's lips, or the need of those present to release tension.

Laidlaw's fingers relaxed around the stem of his brandy glass. Apparently he was ready to back down from an obviously familiar fight. "Kimble, your last win was a lucky fluke. It is the only time you'll win against me, no matter how smooth Gerald claims the lanes are." His humorous response evoked more laughter and the room's other occupants ceased their scrutiny. The Cabot Club's subdued ambience was restored.

Sage and Laidlaw soon finished their brandies and departed. Stepping onto the sidewalk, Laidlaw said, "If there's still time remaining, I'll show you how we British sign men onto ships. Britain alone requires them to come to the consul's office to sign their shipping articles."

"What are shipping articles?"

"Some years back, the United States enacted a law that requires every sailor to signify he is shipping voluntarily. Those papers are called the 'shipping articles.' Usually the articles are meaningless. Men make their mark thinking they are signing one thing only to discover that they placed their mark on shipping articles. Some of their marks are forged. We Brits make it a little more difficult. A sailor signing aboard a British ship has to sign the articles in the consular's office before a consular witness. Unfortunately, there are ways to defeat that safety precaution. Anyway, if you come along to my office, I'll show you what I'm talking about."

Sage agreed, and within minutes, Laidlaw's shipping office was in sight. The office occupied the entire ground floor of a narrow brick building situated a few blocks west of the river and one block north of Mozart's. Its one dusty window displayed an arch of large black and gold lettering proclaiming "Laidlaw, Shipping Master" with smaller gold letters underneath stating "British Consular Office."

"Ah, good." Laidlaw's voice close to Sage's ear startled him. "It seems that one of the crimp's victims is inside signing the articles."

"How can you tell?"

"See that scruffy-looking character lurking near the entrance?" Laidlaw nodded toward a man leaning against the wooden post that held up the sidewalk awning. The man's suit and waistcoat hung loosely on his string-bean frame. His overlong face, with its narrow slash of a mouth, was a pasty contrast to the cords of greasy black hair hanging from beneath the brim of a tattered panama hat.

"Another one like him will be standing guard at the side door. I know them. They're runners for one of the boarding house crimps. Their job is to make sure the sailor steps onto the ship. I refuse to allow the crimp's runners into our office to intimidate men into signing. Out here on the street, though, I cannot control what awaits them if they don't sign."

Laidlaw gave another of his mirthless snorts. "Truth is, my restriction is largely ceremonial. If a sailor refuses to sign, the crimps obtain a warrant against him for theft, and the police hold him until he pays whatever the crimp says the sailor owes. A few days in the City's dank jail and he's ready to sign. I try to intercede whenever the sailor's a British national, but most men end up shipping out whether they want to or not."

A man came shuffling out the office door, and within seconds the runner was at his elbow nudging him along, talking in his ear. Sage watched as the two men rounded the corner. What future lay ahead of that sailor-to-be when his ship reached the ocean? Which danger would he find the most threatening? That of man or that of nature? Sage mentally shook himself back to the present but not before sending a heartfelt thought of "Go well and safely" after the departing man.

Inside, the office consisted of just two rooms. The front and largest room was sparsely furnished with a wooden desk, a swivel chair and a few wooden file cabinets. Except for the break of a single hatch gate, a tall wooden counter stretched across the entire space, creating a customer lobby separated from the desk area. It reminded Sage of the job shark storefronts. Inside this office, however, the atmosphere was clean, calm and genteel, the whole being watched over by a portrait of the bewhiskered King Edward and the ticking of a large, pendulum wall clock.

A mild-faced clerk stood at the front counter. He was helping an old man whose canvas duffle sat beside his scuffed boots. Without opening his jaws, the old man stuck a pale tongue through the gap in his teeth to wet a pencil before making his mark on a sheet of paper. When he looked up to see Laidlaw, his toothless grin split a bronzed and wrinkled face. "Hey there, Consul Laidlaw. It's right good to see you before I goes. I landed me a right fine berth on a British ship this time, the *Birmingham Bell*. They tell me the grub don't hold too many weevils and that the captain is slow to use the whip. Likes his grog in moderation, too, if you catch my drift. Even better, I'm berthing as an able-bodied seaman so the boarding house crimp, he'll just be getting my first month's pay and the blood money, too, of course," he added. The man's tone carried no resentment.

Laidlaw clapped the man on his back. "Mr. Puckett, you've a way of landing feet down in this port. Who is the crimp shipping you out this time?"

"I took your advice, Mr. Laidlaw, and went with ol' Pratt. He charged me pretty fair for board and vittles and the other amenities. And ole Flappy Lips didn't cheat my duffle," the man said, using his foot to nudge a half-full canvas duffle bag near his foot. "So, I won't be freezing my arse off 'round the Horn like some do." After folding his papers away, he snatched the duffle up and with a carefree wave, he departed taking with him Laidlaw's hearty best wishes.

"He doesn't seem a victim," Sage observed.

"Some men aren't victims. Old Puckett is a sailor through and through. It's the only life he knows or wants. There are men like that. They land in port and spend what little money they've got before shipping out again without complaint. As consul and shipping master I'm here to protect those men and try to better their lot. Unfortunately, when the crimps control the show, like they do in this port, even old salts like Puckett undertake grave risk whenever they come ashore. There is always that dark underside to the business." Laidlaw patted the faded letter in his breast pocket. The gesture set Sage to envisioning a younger version of Stuart Franklin, ocean waves sloshing across his upturned face.

Reaching the rear office, they settled into comfortable armchairs. Laidlaw leveled an unblinking gaze at Sage. "Now, Mr. Adair," he said, "suppose you tell me why you are really interested in the crimping business. Don't think for a minute I swallowed that story about Ida's nephew. I know your cook has only one nephew here in town–that being the boy, Matthew. And I saw him as I walked to Mozart's Table. He was happily jumping curbs, trying to break his foolhardy neck on that shiny new bicycle of his."

TEN

SAGE DID NOT TELL LAIDLAW everything. He did reveal that Kincaid was a union organizer, someone Sage was trying to find for a friend. But, he said nothing about Amacker's similar disappearance. Despite Sage's vague explanation and a decidedly skeptical glint in Laidlaw's eyes, the British consul remained willing to help.

Laidlaw touched a match to the bowl of a well-polished pipe and huffed the tobacco to life before saying, "Ordinarily, I oppose unions. Ruling class prejudice and all that. Lately, I've come to be of a mind that we need the help of the Sailor's Union to bring shanghaiing onto its knees for good. I heard the union's leader, Andrew Furuseth, speak, and he made excellent points. I found myself agreeing with him on every one." Furuseth's speech had evidently worked a revelation of sorts because a certain wonderment tinged the British consul's words.

Who knew? Maybe sometime down the road this stuffy Brit might extend his open-mindedness to the plight of those people laboring ashore under equally hellish conditions. Although rare, some notable elites did cross the class barrier and throw their lot in with the common people. Still, Sage only nodded and resisted the urge to confide his own role in the union movement. That might come later. For now, all Laidlaw needed to know was that Sage was performing a favor for a friend. Sage took a chance and told Laidlaw the plan he'd hatched while they were strolling back from the Cabot Club. "I'm going to get a job with the crimps. Working on the inside, maybe I'll find a lead on the missing organizer."

Laidlaw studied him intently for a few moments before saying, "I'm thinking I way underestimated you, Mr. Adair. Such action is fraught with great danger. Somehow, though, I suspect my warnings won't change your mind. So, I'll give you the best advice I can in the hope you'll have the good sense to follow it."

Sage worked through the supper hour with a preoccupied mind. Rarely did he meet a man like the crusty Laidlaw, someone who inspired the conflicting emotions of irritation and admiration. Complicated fellow. Strong mixture of arrogance and compassion. Oh well, as his mother liked to say, "The day you think you've found a perfect man is the day your mirror reflects a fool." He'd never asked her why she'd come to that conclusion. Though, from the bitterness coating her words, he gathered that it had been a hard learned lesson.

After musing on the idea for a while, he thought of Fong which, in turn, led to that new worry over his friend's strange behavior. At this point, Sage purposefully turned off all thoughts except those calculated to coax smiles from Mozart's customers. Time enough later to mull everything over, he told himself.

Hosting duties at long last finished, Sage climbed to the third floor to pack for his early morning steamboat trip to Astoria. He might be gone overnight. Fong also needed to make the trip so he could translate for the Chinese fisherman who'd found the body. While folding clothes into a valise Sage realized for the first time, that the changed Fong might not agree with his plans, might not even appear. As if summoned by those thoughts, the Chinese man slipped into the room. He entered so quietly that, if the door hadn't been in Sage's peripheral vision, Fong's entry would have taken Sage by surprise.

"Mr. Fong?" Sage's voice sounded tentative to his own ears, as if he were addressing a stranger instead of a friend whose loyalty had been tested and proven many times over.

"Yes, Mr. Sage, I came to tell you that I will not be at Mozart's tonight or tomorrow." Fong's tone was formal, without its customary teasing warmth.

A hollow, sinking feeling filled the pit of Sage's stomach. It seemed that the time for discussion had arrived. No more beating around the bush. Sage closed the valise before saying quietly, "Mr. Fong, I don't understand. What's going on that we can't find you when we need you? Did we offend you in some way?" Sage's throat felt constricted by the familiar ache of abandonment that had dogged him periodically since childhood.

The remoteness that had been wrapped around the other man like a repelling mist, momentarily dissolved, allowing a spark of warmth to kindle in Fong's dark eyes. "I cannot tell you, Mr. Sage, why I must be gone. It has nothing to do with you or your lady mother. You both are kind and friendly. I am most sorry for trouble."

Fong's words brought relief of a sort. Still, the mystery had endured long enough. Once again, Sage saw in his mind's eye, Kindcaid's desperate wife and little baby. Their lives depended on whether the three of them could find answers quickly enough. Not to mention Kincaid, himself. Sage spoke firmly, hoping to compel Fong's assistance, even if he wouldn't explain the reason for his changed behavior. "Nevertheless, I need you to go to Astoria with me. I've heard that a Chinese fisherman may have pulled Kincaid's body from the ocean. He speaks no English. You must go with me. Help me talk to the man."

"It not possible for me to go away now. I am sorry." Fong was emphatic, cutting off any argument. His eyes hardened to black obsidian in a face rigidly set against further entreaty.

A hot flush of anger traveled up Sage's neck and he snapped, "Your 'sorry' is cold comfort to that poor mother and her innocent baby. She is alone, with no means of support and full of unanswered questions about what happened to her husband." Sage turned away to jerk open a dresser drawer. He was afraid to look at the other man's face, afraid of what he'd see.

"The sternwheeler's leaving the Couch Street wharf at five in the morning. I hope you'll try to make it," he said, staring blindly into the drawer.

The silence that greeted this declaration was so thick and heavy that it forced Sage to turn back around. A muscle twitched in Fong's jaw, though he responded matter-of-factly, as if Sage hadn't spoken, "I must go now. I ask permission to use room in attic."

Room in the attic? Sage mentally flailed at the odd request before saying with some exasperation, "Oh, of course, the room's yours to use. You built it, after all. Why even ask?"

Fong dipped his head and was gone, leaving Sage staring at the empty doorway. "Shit," Sage said and slammed the drawer shut so hard that it bounced the silver brushes atop the dresser.

Far into the night, Sage lay awake, listening to the slap of bare feet above him. Fong was exercising like a demon–a behavior contrary to the moderation he'd always preached to Sage. Until a few days ago, he considered Fong the nearest thing to a perfect man that he'd ever encountered. Given Fong's strange behavior these last few days, Sage ruefully admitted that, if he looked into a mirror, he'd see the fool his mother warned him about. He jammed a pillow over his ears and drifted off into a few hours of restless sleep.

Thick fog crawled across the predawn river, muffling the swish and mechanical thumps of the sternwheeler's departure. Its moist weight was as dampening on the day as Sage's spirits. Fong hadn't shown up. Sage waited near the gangway, staring up the street until the boat pulled out into the river. Moving forward toward the bow, Sage leaned over the railing to stare into the sullen water mounding away from the hull. He pictured the impassive face of the man who'd been his daily companion. He admitted to himself that it hurt to feel cut off from that friendship, to see Fong transform into an unreliable and secretive stranger.

Sage straightened, mentally casting his gloom into the river. His mother was right. He was certain of it. She believed Fong was in trouble and too proud to ask for help. Well, when he returned to Portland, he intended to reach the bottom of it, even if he had to tie the man down and sit on him. The vision triggered a laugh. He had a better chance of flipping a Brahma bull than of overpowering Fong.

Hours later, the faint stench of rotting fish guts rolled upriver from Astoria's canneries to meet the boat. The cannery where Stuart Franklin instructed him to start looking for the Chinese fisherman, Hong Ah Kay, stood on a wharf next to the sternwheeler's docking pier. Within minutes after the paddlewheel stopped revolving, Sage was standing just outside the wide-open doorway of the cannery building.

The dim light inside came from the door where he stood, a few filthy window panes and the chinks in the cedar shingles overhead. A calliope of clanking leather drive belts, engine chugs, whistle toots, and valve releases blasted around the space. Wiry Chinese men, each wearing a black rubber apron, stood in the slime of discarded fish bits. Standing at butchering tables, they grabbed fish from a conveyor belt, cutting off their heads and gutting them, their knives silver blurs in the gloom. Not a single man glanced in his direction. Sage hesitated. Should he approach one? And if so, which? Not a one would meet his eyes.

"You done worked up a liking for the stink of fish?" came a raspy American voice at his shoulder.

Sage twisted around. A big man stood there. A few days beard growth stubbled his pale face. His heavy forearms were crossed atop a rounded belly encased in a slick black rubber apron. His grin was gap-toothed and engaging.

"Guess I gave you a bit of a start." The man's laughter was a gasping wheeze.

"That's all right. My name's John Miner," Sage said as he held out a hand to shake.

The other man didn't reciprocate. "Nice to meet you, Mr. Miner. Unless you want to stink of fish the rest of the day, we best not shake mitts. That what you're looking for—a nice fish for your dinner table?"

"No. Actually, I'm trying to find a fisherman called Hong Ah Kay. I heard he might work out of this cannery." Sage shrugged.

"'Course, I can't speak Chinese so I wasn't sure how to go about asking."

The other man grinned again, acknowledging the difficulty. He nodded in the general direction of the Chinese. "Wouldn't make no difference. Ain't a one of them Hong. He sells to us, all right. Right now, he's out on his fishing boat. Don't know what day he'll be back. The fish are running pretty good and he's a hard worker. Won't come back in until his catch threatens to swamp him. Meanwhile, those men ain't going to tell you a thing."

Sage's heart sank. He'd been hoping that Hong was a day fisherman or that he was ashore. Evidently neither was the case. That meant the body probably lay for days on the fishing boat's deck. No wonder the face was unrecognizable. And just how many days had elapsed before the fellow returned to land with his grisly find?

"Do you think some of the men here might know Hong Ah Kay?" Sage asked, nodding his head toward the dark interior. Maybe Hong told someone something about the dead man, something that would indicate whether the body was Kincaid's or not.

"It's for certain they all do. China folks are thick as thieves here in Astoria. Ain't that many of them."

"Would you mind if I tried to find one of them who'll talk to me about Hong Ah Kay?" Sage was going to make the effort since there was no knowing when Hong would return to shore. All he needed to know was whether or not Astoria was a dead end. Time was passing. Mrs. Kincaid's anxiety was undoubtedly growing by leaps and bounds. He couldn't hang around on the off chance Hong would return in the next day or so.

The man set meaty hands on his hips, irritation suffusing his face, his words clipped as he said, "Well, mister, like I said, they're not going to talk to you. The China crew don't speak to white men. They only speak to the China boss and through the China boss, and he ain't here right now." The man began turning to go, all affability gone.

Damn. If Fong were here, there wouldn't be this problem. Fong would walk right up to that line of closed-mouth fish gutters and receive answers in no time. And, Sage wouldn't need to cajole this gatekeeper into cooperating. "Quit whining, Sage," he told himself. "Deal with reality. Fong isn't here." He tried again, saying to the man, "Well, maybe if I let them know who I'm looking for, offered to pay . . . if you'd help me, I will pay . . ."

The man interrupted, waving his large scarred hand, "Oh, I'm not stopping you, just warning you what's gonna happen. Go ahead on, try to talk to them. More power to you. I can't help because they won't talk to me neither unless it's strictly necessary. See that you watch where you step, though. Them wood floorboards are slick as snot." That said, the man waved a hand at Sage before lumbering away down the wharf toward dry land.

Sage peered inside the cannery. The straightforward, friendly approach would be best. It usually was—honey rather than vinegar. He stepped across the threshold into the gloom. To one side, a line of men gutted and sliced fish. On the other side, a big boiler oven hissed steam out the small valves dotting its metal dome. Next to that stood a towering stack of large wooden boxes, the word "Salmon" on their sides in heavy black lettering.

The rumble of steel wheels across the uneven floorboards caused him to turn. A Chinese man was pushing a wheeled tray loaded with tin cans in the direction of the boiler, his back bent at a nearly 90-degree angle by the effort. Sage stepped forward, close to the man's path, a tentative smile on his face.

"Excuse me, I was wondering . . ." The man neither paused nor acknowledged Sage's presence, just rolled right past him. Reaching the boiler, the man swung open a metal door. He used his heavy gloves to extract a tray, slide it onto the cart and insert a new tray in its place. Slamming the door shut, the man began trundling the cart back toward Sage. Again, Sage stepped forward and again the man acted blind and deaf to Sage's presence.

Great. So much for his Black Irish charm. It might turn the trick at Mozart's but this fellow was definitely impervious to its effect. Unwilling to accept defeat, Sage swiveled, looking around for somebody else to approach. His eye settled on an old man tucked away in the far corner of the work area. He was perched on an upturned wooden box, a stack of labels and a paste pot at his side. With repetitive precision, he was affixing labels onto the soldered cans that surrounded him in shiny stacks. Maybe it was better to approach someone stationary.

"Excuse me, sir. I'm looking for someone who knows the fisherman Hong Ah Kay."

The old man's yellowed eyes cut to him before snapping back to his work without ever pausing in his rhythm: brush into paste pot, paste onto label, label onto can, and can onto finished stack.

Maybe the combined din of steam hiss, knife whack and conveyor belt rattle had deafened everyone working in the cannery. Sage had seen that happen to men in the rolling mill attached to the mine and that mill was only a bit noisier than this place. Or, maybe, these men were simply an unfriendly wall erected against "sharp noses" like himself. Sage studied the others, searching for a single friendly face.

Behind him, the old man began hollering at the men working on the fish line. Sage thought he heard Hong Ah Kay's name somewhere in the stream of sounds. His gaze returned to the labeler, uncertain whether to try again. Despite that steady gaze, the old man remained stolidly unwilling to acknowledge Sage's presence.

A stringy white man in bib overalls and cap entered the scene from out of an adjacent room and began attending to the hissing boiler. Sage headed over to him. The man saw him approach, but he checked the boiler's gauges and made notations on a pad in his hand before turning to Sage.

"Sorry," he said, "have to keep close track of the heat in this here retort, otherwise the fish'll cook too fast. Makes them dry and mealy." He tucked the pad into an overall pocket. "Anyway, somethin' I can do for you, mister?"

"Well, maybe. I'm having a little bit of trouble getting even one of these men to talk to me. I wonder if you will kindly direct me to one of them who speaks English."

The man glanced at the Chinese workers before saying, "You'll be wanting their China boss and I don't see him."

"The big man on the wharf told me the China boss wasn't here right now."

"Well, mister, then I'm afraid you're out of luck."

"Surely, one of these men speaks a little English?"

"Aye, some of them speak it pretty well outside the cannery. Here, in the cannery though, these men won't speak to a white man. You'll just have to wait for the China boss, I'm afraid." He gave Sage a friendly nod before disappearing through an archway into a room where the conveyor belt's steam engine roared at full throttle.

Sage huffed in exasperation. He wandered over to watch the lines of men standing on either side of the moving belt, their knives flashing as they gutted, scaled, and sliced the silver fish in quick, economic strokes. From the light pink of the meat, Sage realized this was the beginning of the Chinook salmon's fall run. Life as a restaurateur delivered its own little lessons—like how to distinguish one salmon species from another. At the end of the line, other men packed salmon into tin cans, their fingers nimble as those of a seamstress. Sage clenched his jaw, frustration lengthening his stride as he moved closer to the line's end. Dammit, one of them is going to talk, China boss or no! That frustration was his downfall. Literally.

Suddenly, his feet were skidding across the plank floor as his arms flailed for balance. He landed with a resounding thud on his backside, pain his first sensation, chilly wet his second. Both in the same location. He'd stepped onto a section of the floor slick with entrails and water. He quickly tried to regain his footing, only to have his hand slip in the slime and send him down onto his shoulder. Deciding that dignity must give way, Sage gingerly raised onto his hands and knees so he could slowly lever himself onto his feet. Fully erect, he caught more than one pair of amused dark eyes looking in his direction before they immediately flicked away. He was about to become invisible again.

Churlishness took hold as Sage studied the slime on his hands, coat and pants. How entertaining for them, seeing a white man land on his butt in a mess of fish guts. Probably these men wouldn't come to my aid if I broke my leg falling down right in front of them.

As if rebuking these unspoken thoughts, a man with one wandering eye stepped away from the line and silently handed him a dingy rag. Sage took it, smiling ruefully. "Thank you," he said. He wiped muck from his hands, knees, shoulder and tail end before returning the rag and quickly asking, "Do you know Hong Ah Kay?"

The man's wide smile showed sparse teeth black at their roots. He shook his head. "No speak English me. Talk to China boss. He come back sometime soon."

ELEVEN

SAGE WAITED, SITTING WITH HIS boots dangling over the edge of the wharf. Eventually, he found himself watching the sun sink into the ocean beyond the river bar. He tried to ignore the fishy stench wafting to his nose from his damp trousers. The water slapping the timbers beneath him hit with no discernable rhythm, serving to underscore the disjointed and glum train of thought that had ahold of him.

What if the China boss never came back? What if he proved as uncooperative as the rest of them? After traveling all this way, wasting all this time, was Sage going to discover nothing to tell Joseph Kincaid's wife? Was it a waste of time to wait for the China boss? Sage clenched his jaw. If so, the fault lay at Fong's door. In Fong's presence, the strange cadence of the Chinese words would have flowed. Already, Sage would be aboard the *Hassalo* as it chugged upriver with the evening tide. And, he'd know for sure whether or not the drowned man was Kincaid.

Fong's absence pressed down on Sage so heavily that he felt as if the sinking sun were tugging his spirit down with it. Just as the bottom of that glowing disk touched the horizon and sent a pathway of light flowing toward him up the river, Sage saw a Chinese man approaching. This man wore a dark suit, a natty brocade vest, a high-collared shirt and a somewhat battered top hat. While all the men in the cannery wore their black hair in ropey queues, this man was westernized. His coarse black hair was evenly short, as if someone had upended a porridge bowl on his head and traced around it with scissors.

Sage scrambled to his feet. "Hello, sir. Are you the China boss here at the cannery?"

"I am." The man said nothing more, just looked at Sage, his face an expressionless mask.

"I wanted to talk to the men here about Hong Ah Kay."

"Why you police are still after poor Hong Ah Kay?" The man's voice rose an octave.

"No, I'm not the police. They want to talk to Hong Ah Kay?"

"Police ask Hong Ah Kay many, many questions about body he found outside river mouth. Police think he kept body too many days or something. They not understand fisherman can not go all the way out on ocean and come right back. Hong Ah Kay did nothing wrong with white man's body. No belongings with body, not even shoes."

This outburst made Sage pause. Apparently, the dead man had caused problems between the Chinese and Astoria's police. No wonder he'd met stiff resistance from the cannery workers. "No, no. I have no reason to think that Hong Ah Kay did anything wrong. I'm just trying to see if the body is that of a man I'm trying to find."

"He your friend, this man?" The China boss was still wary, though Sage thought he detected a slight relaxing of the man's stance.

"If the body is that of the man I seek, his wife is my friend."

"I not see the body. Hong Ah Kay is now out on boat. Body brought to shore late at night. Most everybody sleeping."

"If Hong Ah Kay is still out on his boat, did anyone else at the cannery see the body?"

"Maybe Loke Tung. He help Hong Ah Kay unload body and talk to police."

Sage felt hope rising. This might be it.

"May I please speak to Loke Tung?" Sage asked.

"Not now. Wait until after eight o'clock tonight when work over. Come back at that time to China house, over there." He pointed toward a weathered building that looked similar to the bunkhouses Sage lived in when he worked in the woods. Except this building had a tidy vegetable garden and a chicken coop in its side yard.

"After eight, you say? Loke Tung will be there?"

"Yes. You come back after eight o'clock." With that, the man strode into the gloom of the cannery without a backward glance.

The silence was the first thing Sage noticed when he returned to the wharf at 8:00 o'clock. The only sounds were the faint swish of water as a solitary Chinese man washed down the cannery floor and the distant cry of the gulls wheeling above discarded fish bits scumming the river.

Sage stepped onto the porch of the worker's bunkhouse and knocked on the door. The China boss answered and gestured for Sage to enter. Inside, the ordinary hubbub of men at the end of their workday ceased the moment he crossed the threshold. Garlic, ginger and other exotic smells wafted through the air of the ramshackle building–the mixture familiar, strange and poignant. Fong's provision shop smells like this, Sage thought. Another stab of loss hit him. He valued the fact that he'd been accepted into that strange other world. Was that connection lost as well?

"Please, take seat." The China boss directed him toward a straight-backed wooden chair next to a plank table that was situated in the cooking area of the large whitewashed room. Another man, an apron tied around his waist, placed a tin teapot and small white porcelain cup at Sage's elbow. The man turned away to stir a simmering slant-sided pan on the wood cook stove. The pan rested in the hole left by the removal of a stove top lid. Sage found that the tea was mildly sweet and needed no sugar. Just like the tea Mrs. Fong served. That stab again. Fong was supposed to be here.

Conversation around him resumed, although much more subdued than before. Sage examined his surroundings, curious about the difference between the bunkhouses where he'd lived and this one. The first thing that struck him was that there were no mattresses on the iron cots. Instead, a pile of folded blankets covered their rope webbing. Here and there a man lay stretched out on the blankets. One of them appeared to be in distress. Two men hovered over him, one with a sharp knife in his hand.

Sage watched as the knife holder slit the man's rubber boots apart and gently pulled them off making the man's face scrunch in pain. Sage was close enough to see the angry red swelling and sores covering the man's feet and ankles. A painful rush of blood must have hit the injuries because the man moaned softly. The second man, after darting a glance at Sage, touched a match to the bowl of a water pipe. He handed the hose tip to the man on the cot who sucked hungrily until his head fell back onto his pillow, smoke streaming upward from his nostrils. Opium's cloying scent drifted across the room. Sage looked away, careful to keep his face expressionless. With feet like that, oblivion was the logical choice. Besides, opium was sold legally to whites in the form of patent medicines, despite increased efforts to ban its use.

"Here he is." The China boss appeared at Sage's elbow. Beside him stood a heavy squat man whose narrowed eyes and jutting chin telegraphed his unwillingness to be there. "This is Loke Tung," the China boss told Sage before turning to bark something in Chinese at Loke.

Sage stood, realized he was towering over Loke, and quickly sat down again. He pulled Kincaid's wedding photo from his pocket and held it out toward the man.

Loke barely glanced at the photo. Sullenness lacing his halting words, he said, "Don't know if this is man who die. Man without face. Too many days in ocean and in boat. Right age."

Aggravation washed through Sage. He spoke rapidly to control it. "Please, the man in the photo has a wife and a baby . . ." Loke's lower lip jutted forward before he shook his head and backed away.

Sage watched Loke cross the room to lie down on a cot. In the silence that followed, Sage became aware that all eyes were again fixed on him, more than one pair surrounded by wrinkles of amusement. Embarrassed, he waited a beat or two before rising from the table. Absolute silence accompanied his steps from table to door.

Outside, Sage punched the porch railing hard with his fist. He would not wait around for Hong Ah Kay. There was no way to tell when the fisherman might return to shore. Besides, there was no guarantee that Hong would be any more helpful than the rest of the Chinese. A wasted trip. He was no closer to finding out whether the body was Kincaid's than when he'd boarded the sternwheeler in Portland. All this time and all this way and all he knew was that the body was that of a man about Kincaid's age. And that's what Franklin had already told him. The face of Kincaid's grieving wife was as sharp in his mind as when he'd sat on her stoop, waiting for her sobs to stop. He hated the idea that he'd learned nothing to tell her, not a single thing to ease her mind.

A hissing sound came from the building's corner. When Sage looked in that direction, he saw the scrawny Chinese man with the wandering eye who'd handed him the rag in the cannery. The man was leaning around the outside corner of the China house, his hand beckoning. When Sage moved closer, he saw the man's hand was cracked and scarred by work. After a moment, Sage realized the man wanted to see the Kincaids' wedding photo, so he handed it over.

The man stepped forward and tilted the photo until the twilight illuminated its surface. "Your friend wife?" he asked softly, his accent much less noticeable than when they'd talked in the cannery.

"Yes, his wife. Now, they have a baby."

The man's face saddened. "I have wife and two sons in China," he told Sage.

"Two sons? That is most lucky. How old are they?"

Sage's question brought a smile to the man's face. "They are seven and nine. Soon I have enough money to return to them." The man's face sobered once again as his thumb gently stroked the surface of the photo. "Best you come back. Talk to Hong Ah Kay. He will help you. He unhappy about finding man in water. He worry nameless man's spirit is wandering because he kept body too long on boat. And because man buried without name. You come back few days."

"Maybe he'll be like Loke Tung and not want to help."

The man shook his head. "No, Loke Tung always cranky. He not like anyone, not like to help anyone–not even China man. Hong Ah Kay different. He write poetry. A learned man. My wife's brother. I promise, he will help."

Sage thanked him and tried to give him some coins only to be rebuffed by the man raising his palms in refusal, bowing his head and disappearing back around the corner.

The next day, as light rimmed far off jagged mountains and brightened the forested hills along the river, the little sternwheeler paddled eastward atop the tidal surge. Sage had spent a sleepless night above a saloon, his pillow pancaking flatter with each passing minute even as the sprung bed coils poked into him. Not an experience to improve his mood. In the deserted area below the wheelhouse, on the flat roof of the passenger promenade, Sage lowered himself down onto metal beginning to warm in the morning sun. With the warmth came the faint aroma of fish that spot washing by the saloon keeper's wife hadn't eliminated from his clothes. Ahead of the blunt bow, tendrils of mist curled and skittered across the water. Its wispy essence seemed akin to the illusive "chi" substance that Fong's snake and crane exercise allowed him to sometimes feel. When it flowed unimpeded, it had substance. Try to grasp it in any way and it vanished.

What the hell was wrong with Fong? A growing complicated knot of exasperation and anxiety was taking up residence in Sage's gut. In Fong's presence, the surly Loke Tung might have cooperated. As it was, Mrs. Kincaid still would not know whether she was wife or widow. Swirling thoughts, the warm breeze on his face, and the steady vibration of the boat, at last combined to tip him into a doze made restless by visions of musty subterranean passages, where the only light was an evasive pinprick bobbing in the distance.

❁ ❁ ❁

Sage stomped from the wharf to Mozart's with long, angry strides. He'd lost a day, learned nothing of value and was damn sure out of patience with Fong. His surly mood evidently showed because his mother's eyebrows shot up as soon as he entered his third floor room and threw himself into the chair across from where she sat filling out a provision list. Supper in the restaurant below wouldn't start for a couple of hours.

"No luck?" she asked.

"They wouldn't talk to me. Dammit! Apparently, cannery people talk to white men only through their Chinese foreman and he wasn't eager to expend much effort to help."

"Did you learn enough to eliminate the possibility it was Kincaid?"

"No, instead I learned just enough to strengthen my suspicion that it was his body that the Chinese fisherman pulled from the water. But I don't know enough to tell Mrs. Kincaid that. Do you know how she's doing?"

His mother laid her pencil on the table, took a swallow of coffee and carefully replaced the cup in the saucer before saying, "Sage, she just doesn't seem to be doing well. She's wearing the same dress. I'm certain she hasn't taken it off since last we saw her a few days ago."

"When did you find time to visit her again?"

"Yesterday, between the dinner and supper hours. It was a quick trip. I didn't sleep the night before for all my worrying about her. Figured I might as well go see how she was doing."

Sage told her the details of his visit to Astoria and at first she commiserated. Her sympathy was short-lived, overcome by Sage's description of his pratfall onto the fish guts. Her laughter rang out and Sage joined her, saying, "Oh, you go ahead and laugh. It wasn't you lying there in stinking slime in front of an audience trying not to show their delight!"

Then his faced sobered abruptly. "So, where is our Mr. Fong? Eluding his responsibilities once again?"

"Now, Sage . . ."

"Don't 'now Sage' me. It's time Mr. Fong and I straightened

out whatever has him acting this way. I am out of patience. Either we settle this right now, or we'd better start planning how we're going to continue St. Alban's work without him."

She surprised him by simply nodding and saying carefully, "I think his burden, whatever it is, may be breaking him. If you're his friend, you will figure out how to help him carry it." She stood up. "He's up in the attic, I think."

The attic space was empty. A hatchet, one Sage had never seen before, lay on the grass mat in the center of the room. Its steel blade shimmered in the light streaming downward from the skylight. The trap door to the roof stood open.

TWELVE

FONG SAT ON THE BENCH, his profile toward Sage. Any residual anger Sage felt drained away the instant he saw his friend. Fong's face was long and thin with prominent cheekbones. He claimed his angular facial features were inherited from his northern Chinese ancestors. Now, those cheekbones jutted sharply beneath sunken eye sockets, making him look ill and years older. Sage could hardly believe this was the man who'd stood on this roof just a week ago, mischievous humor lighting his eyes, while he instructed his Occidental friend on the inner workings of the universe. Today, those eyes were flat pebbles lying deep inside black shadows. Sage wanted to leap to his friend's side and touch him reassuringly.

Instead, he joined Fong on the bench and kept silent, just like when he'd sat next to Kincaid's inconsolable wife. It somehow felt the same here on this rooftop in the middle of the city. For long minutes, both men sat while birds swooped overhead and Fong's carrier pigeons burbled in their coop. The smells of river, wharf and horse dung hitched rides on the breezes that stirred the rosebush leaves and mingled with the flowers' sweet scent.

Fong finally spoke, his voice wistful, his eyes fixed on the far distance. "It is China music I miss the most, the bamboo harp, the semisen, the moon fiddle." He raised the smooth bamboo tube he'd been holding loosely in his hand. "And flute, played by monks who make much better music than me."

Sage, lacking positive thoughts about Chinese music, remained silent. He found Fong's efforts on the flute painful despite knowing that the local Chinese considered Fong a most accomplished musician.

Fong continued. "I am from good family in China. I trained with temple priests and brought much honor to my father. Very sudden father die and my only uncle and his sons came here to 'Gold Mountain' as we Chinese called America. Later my uncle ask me to join him. I think, why not? America door closed to Chinese men, so I travel to Mexico and sneak across border. It was hard journey. Many people died.

"I find my uncle in San Francisco where Chinatown is controlled by tongs. Like I told you before, tong is like white man's club, a China man's 'Knights of Columbus.' So, I join a tong and my fighting skills make me esteemed soldier, valuable boo how doy. Many times the boo how doy of different tongs meet in battle. I show that I am good fighter. My tong pays me well, people respect me on street, and sing-song girls fight to be seen with me in noodle houses." His tone carried no pleasure at the memory.

"My uncle is different. He ashamed of what his brother's son has become in America. Other China men are also angry at the power of tongs. My uncle try to talk to me. I don't listen. Instead, I make fun of him. I tell him I am successful. I say that he and my cousins are jealous of my success." Fong leaned toward Sage to make a point. "My blood cousins, not my tong cousins."

Fong looked down, staring into an internal abyss. He swallowed audibly as if forcing a lump back down his throat. "My uncle just shake head and pat arm." Fong rubbed his forearm as if recreating the touch.

"One day, my uncle, cousins and other neighbor men from my district in Canton decide to go to river of the Snake in Oregon. They say government mineral department permit Chinese men to sift river sand for gold. White miner's always let tiny gold flakes escape down sluices into river. It is so little gold they won't do hard work to take from sand. My uncle ask me to come to Snake River with them, for protection and to find the gold. I tell him 'No.' I want to stay in city."

Fong closed his eyes and said nothing. Sage saw a tear glint and fall. Fong continued, uncaring of Sage's scrutiny, "My uncle begged me many times to go with him. He pleaded, saying I was falling from priest's way. He warned me that way of the boo how doy, killing other tong's men for money and prestige, was bringing death to my soul and grave misfortune to my life. When I not listen, he become angry. He tell me that my life dishonored and shamed my father's memory. I told him to go away. To strike me off the list of family names. That I was American now." Fong's sigh issued from deep in his lungs, as if he were venting an excessive pressure.

"Thirty-two Chinese men travel with my uncle, in one party, for protection. Among them is no trained fighter. When they reached the Snake River, the party split in two. One group of twenty-five men made camp at base of cliff, by wide sandbar. Other six haul two rowboats farther up Snake. They go explore for other places along river where gold maybe trapped. They plan to float back down to first group. My uncle and all cousins, but one, stay with first group on sandbar. There was little gold, but we Chinese are patient. Work very hard."

Here Sage nodded, thinking back to the old man of the day before, endlessly labeling the fish cans with exacting precision.

Fong continued. "Many hours spent crouched over gravel in pan yield some little gold. Not enough gold for white men. Still, it is enough for men like us.

"I hear nothing from my uncle. I continue to advance as boo how doy, even become tong's boo how doy leader. One day, a messenger comes to take me to Chinese General Consul of San Francisco. I cannot think why esteemed man want to see me. I dress in best suit and go to him."

Another deep sigh made Sage's hand twitch with the desire to cover Fong's hand with his own. He restrained himself. Sage somehow knew that this story was revealing a sorrow that lay at the core of his friend's essential being. He feared doing anything to interrupt the telling. Besides, his friend's obviously deep and abiding sorrow was beyond a touch's power to comfort at this point. Better to let him get it out, uninterrupted.

Fong's voice was near a whisper now. "General Consul tells me that word has come from Lewiston, Idaho. My uncle and every man with him, every single one, was murdered for gold."

Sage felt no surprise at hearing these words. Somehow he'd known this was the inevitable outcome of Fong's story.

"So, I travel to Lewiston to kill the men who'd done this terrible thing to my uncle and my cousins, all of whom followed the Way, never giving injury to another man, except to defend self or others.

"I stood on that cliff with sheriff and look down on sandbar. The sheriff told me six white men rode up from a small ranch where they'd been camping. They tie horses back from edge of cliff. They crawl forward and lay in bunch grass along its edge. Very quiet they load rifles. Next they shoot every Chinese man below on sandbar. No place for Chinese men to run away. Once everyone dead, they ride down to rob bodies. After that, they take axes and hack bodies into bits. They throw bits into river. Why, I don't know. Maybe blood thirst take them or maybe they think to make victims disappear.

"Two rowboats came around river bend when killers chopping at bodies. White men shoot Chinese men in rowboats. That when last surviving cousin also die. I know this because I find uncle's journal saying cousin go with second group to explore.

"No one knew this happen until parts of bodies wash on riverbank near Lewiston, Idaho. Sheriff rode upriver to investigate. When he visit small ranch house, rancher tell him everything that happen. Rancher not help murderers. He sorry they kill my uncle and others. He was good man."

Sage stirred to ask, "The sheriff knew the names of the murderers?"

"Yes, he knew their names, and even before I arrive five of them in jail: younger one of five confess. So, all of them in jail except one. Man named Homer LaRue. They all say he was leader. Killing of China men LaRue's idea." Fong raised his black blouse and extracted a photograph from a long pouch around his waist. He held it so that Sage saw the image of a big man with a heavily bearded face, leering into the camera, his arm draped across the bare shoulders of what was certainly a prostitute.

"This is LaRue?" Sage asked.

Fong nodded.

"What happened? Was LaRue caught?"

"No, he gone from Snake River place. He took stolen gold. Left other killers behind."

Sage waited.

"I hunt for him. I travel everywhere. I go someplace, take any work and begin looking for him. If he not there, I travel on to new place. Finally, I hear he is in Arizona."

Sage envisioned Fong, an endlessly searching stranger, drifting through the parched towns of the southwestern desert. What a lonely quest it must have been through that barren landscape of prickly plants, azure sky and a blazing sun that silently wicked water from a man's body.

"I go there to Arizona. I ask many places. Finally, they say LaRue in Mexico. I try to think how to cross border and come back when word comes he is dead. Killed by Mexican bandits." Fong rolled his shoulders slightly, like a pugilist remembering the end of a successful fight. "I surprised because I feel relief at news. Not angry like a boo how doy. I sit on rock in desert for long time. I think about my uncle and his last angry words to me. All around me is his spirit. I promise him that I am no longer a boo how doy. I promise to find the Way again and to follow it, in honor of my father and my uncle and my cousins.

"I take money I save from San Francisco and during my search and I come here, to Portland. I stay member of tong but I tell them I am retired. No boo how doy ever returns to the work from retirement. They believe me, and over time I become counselor to tong leaders. I become a peacemaker between tongs."

Here Fong paused, clearly weighing his next words. "I also buy beautiful sing-song slave girl, free her and make her wife when she accept me."

That revelation hit Sage with a wallop. Fong was talking about his wife, the dignified, self-possessed and demure Kum Ho, or "golden peach" as Fong translated her name and as Sage ever after called her whenever she strayed into his thoughts. She had been a prostitute? With a snap, Sage realized this explained Fong's subtle tenderness toward Lucinda Collins, Sage's own "sing-song girl."

The end of Fong's story was easy to deduce. Sage spared his friend by taking it up. "Then a week ago, as you cleared dishes from a table near two strangers, you realized that one of them was LaRue."

Fong gave a single slow nod.

"What are you going to do?" Sage asked, thinking that it was no wonder Fong was so upset. My God, how the hate must burn in him.

Fong turned to look at Sage, his eyes dark within their hollows. "I follow him, I know how to find him. Where he sleeps. He not know I am watching. He make no plans to leave. Room paid up for few days more." Fong again stared into the distance as he said softly, "I still trying to decide what to do."

"Let me help. Maybe the police . . ."

"Of course, I think of police. Idea make me laugh. I am Chinaman, he is white man with money. Stolen money." Bitterness laced his words.

"What if we try to find out whether the police will take action against LaRue? Ask Sergeant Hanke to contact Lewiston and ask about LaRue without anyone here knowing of our interest?"

"Do you think Sergeant Hanke will do that? For me?" Hope sounded in Fong's words for the first time.

"Are you making a joke?" Sage felt certain of the big policeman's willingness to help Fong. Hanke, after all, owed his recent sergeant's promotion to Sage and Fong. That was because they'd insisted Hanke take credit for solving the three murders that had sent Portland into a tizzy. Their work for St. Alban left them no choice but to swear Hanke to secrecy and to make him take all the credit. During this adventure, the brawny German policeman and the diminutive Chinese man had developed a friendship of sorts.

"Hanke is happy to do anything for you, for both of us," Sage assured his friend.

Fong's eyes rested on the mountain sentinel guarding the

eastern horizon, its pure white cap washed pale orange in the setting sun. His voice was low as he said, "It be better that way."

Sage took this as Fong's assent to the plan, even if it was not wholehearted. He jumped to his feet. "I think Hanke is down in the kitchen relieving Ida of some of her 'extras,' as he calls them. Please, Mr. Fong, let's go talk to him."

At this, Fong stood up.

One more question came to Sage. "How does that phrase, 'boo how doy,' translate?"

Fong didn't respond. Instead, he stepped to the trapdoor and began descending the ladder. Sage hesitated, puzzling over Fong's lack of response, before following his friend. At the attic door, Fong paused, his hand on the door knob. Without turning around, he spoke. The words bounced off the door and hit Sage like a pail of icy water.

"'Boo how doy' mean 'hatchet man,'" Fong said.

THIRTEEN

When they entered Mozart's kitchen, the big police officer was sitting at the worn table methodically consuming a heaping plate of Mozart's pricey vittles. At Sage's silent head jerk toward the kitchen door, Sergeant Hanke surged to his feet, picked up his overflowing plate and shuffled out onto the back porch. Fong and Sage followed, closing the kitchen door behind themselves.

The nearby street was empty of foot traffic. Hanke held the plate with one hand and continued forking in the food as he listened to Sage's shortened version of the Snake River massacre and Fong's connection to it. Not for the first time, Sage considered the policeman's stolid expression. That wide genial face was misleading in that some might consider the fellow dull-witted. A false perception, as he proved by summarizing their request neatly: "You're asking if I'd be willing to find out, without letting on why I'm doing it, whether the law on the east side of the Cascades wants LaRue. And if he's not wanted, you want me to forget you asked, just in case something unpleasant happens to him. That about it?"

Sage and Fong both nodded and stayed silent, awaiting the big policeman's decision.

Hanke forked in another bite, chewing slowly and thoughtfully before saying, "My mother used to say that a person can't lie to himself no more than he can lie to God. So, I'm not fooling myself about what it is you're asking me to do. And I don't believe in a wink-and-nod approach to truth like some policemen."

After setting his empty plate down on the narrow porch rail, Hanke faced Fong. "I'm pretty certain I know what you might do, Mr. Fong, if it looks like this LaRue fellow will escape justice."

Fong returned Hanke's gaze without saying anything, his bland expression unaltered, although Sage saw a muscle twitch in his jaw.

"Still, can't say I blame you. I'd feel the same if he'd murdered my kinfolk," Hanke continued. Keeping his gaze on Fong, he flicked crumbs off his uniformed chest with one hand and picked up the empty plate with the other, "I'm going to do what you ask for two reasons; because I owe you and because it's right. What you do with the information is between you and your God, or gods, or whatever it is you folks believe. I won't take steps to protect you, I can't do that. What I will promise is to forget that you ever mentioned the man's name to me."

In the silence that followed, Sage looked at Fong who merely nodded. Hanke turned toward Sage and the two exchanged a sober gaze that was their tacit acceptance of Fong's right to retribution. That look seemed to forge a bond between them although neither one spoke. Hanke reached for the doorknob and, opening the door, said over his shoulder in an overly hearty voice, "Mr. Adair, you suppose Miz Ida's squirreled away any berry pie?"

Sage was telling Fong, and retelling Mae, about his trip to the Astoria cannery when the sound of heavy boots mounting the stair drew their attention in that direction. Mae craned her head toward the third floor hallway before saying, "Mr. Fong, might that boy galumph a smidgen softer if I bought him a pair of those cloth slippers you wear?"

Fong shook his head. "No, Mrs. Clemens. I think of that. Problem is, his feet way too big. No slippers to fit him. Maybe teach Matthew snake and crane so he learn to move like bird instead of like big tree with feet."

Matthew's red head appeared around the half-open door.

"Excuse me, Mr. Adair. Ah, you told me I was to come on up when I got back from Mr. Laidlaw's house."

"That's right, Matthew, I said that. How's the bicycle running?"

The boy grinned. This was an expression Matthew seldom displayed in the days before he acquired his two-wheeled treasure. "Oh, crikey, Mr. Adair, she's a real sweet goer. I pedaled up to Mr. Laidlaw's house in twenty minutes instead of having to walk for near an hour. He gave me this, too! For being so quick and all, he said." Matthew held up a coin that glinted silver in the room's gaslight.

"And did Mr. Laidlaw give you anything for me?" Sage prompted.

A flush spread across the boy's face as he shoved the coin back in his pocket and reached inside his shirt. "Yes, sir. He told me to be careful with it and not let anyone see it, so I stuffed it inside my shirt. I hope that's okay?"

"That was exactly the way to handle it. Thank you." Sage took the proffered envelope and laid it on the table. The adults continued to look at the boy. He shifted uncomfortably before saying, "Ah, looks like you are having one of those restaurant meetings of yours, huh?"

"Afraid so, Matthew, otherwise I'd ask you to join us."

"Oh, that's okay. I told Aunt Ida I'd help with the cleanup, seeing how she's a bit shorthanded." He began to leave, then stopped.

"Anything else you need me to do, just ask, Mr. Adair. Anything at all."

"Thanks, Matthew, I won't hesitate. I appreciate your offer."

With grave dignity the boy bowed slightly and exited the room, closing the door softly behind himself.

The three shared a smile before getting back to the problem of the missing Kincaid and the other union organizer.

"From the description, it sounds like the man pulled from the ocean is Joseph Kincaid. Anyone else looking like him gone missing around here?" Mae asked thoughtfully.

"Hanke says no one's come forward looking for a missing man," Sage responded before falling silent as he momentarily re-lived his Astoria frustration and his anger over Fong's absence. This moment was pushed aside by the worse reality of Fong's situation. A few days of inconvenience didn't begin to match it. He looked at his friend.

Fong lifted a hand, saying quickly, "That cannery is not my tong people. I am Hop Sing man. They all Gee Kung. Most likely they not tell me anything either."

"Not your tong so they won't talk to you?"

Fong shrugged, saying with a rueful smile, "Well, maybe they talk to me. Our tongs not at war, they might talk to me. Still, much better someone from their own tong ask questions about white man. We Chinese always careful not to tangle in white man's business."

"What? No Chinese are involved in shanghaiing?"

Here Fong tilted his head in slight assent, "Most Chinese not involved. Sometimes bad Chinese shanghai China man to be cook on ship. Not happen very often. But this is about dead white man. Dead white man is white man's business. Period."

"Guess it doesn't matter now whether they would have talk-ed to you. There's no time to send you downriver to Astoria."

Fong smiled ruefully and said, "I already possess solution if you give me picture of Kincaid. I will send friend who is Gee Kung man to Astoria. He take photo and carrier pigeon from roof. He find Hong Ah Kay and send pigeon home with message. Time come for pigeon to earn his seed. A few hours after Gee Kung man speaks to Mr. Hong, pigeon message arrive."

Sage considered Fong's simple elegant solution to the problem that had kept Sage chasing his mental hind end like a dog after a burr in his tail. Fong evidently mistook the pause because he quickly said, "I will pay for friend to make trip. Least I can do after trouble I make this week."

Sage's peripheral vision caught his mother's slight twitch of surprise at Fong's oblique acknowledgment of the concern he'd been raising. She shot Sage a questioning look but asked Fong, "How long does it take a pigeon to fly in from Astoria? And where does a pigeon carry a note?"

Sage didn't listen to Fong's answers. Instead, his mind snagged on the fact that Homer LaRue, murderer of Fong's relatives, remained on the streets. He might, at any minute, reappear in Mozart's. If that happened and he, Sage, was there, he wasn't certain he'd forego the opportunity to make LaRue pay for his crime.

From the questioning glances she kept tossing toward Sage, it was clear that his mother wondered what had transpired to bring the three of them back together again. Fong hadn't asked Sage to stay silent about LaRue, so Sage mouthed the word "later" in her direction and saw her shoulders relax. Since he'd be embarking on a new career as a crimp, he'd be absent in the days ahead. There was no way he'd let Fong carry such a burden alone. Fong needed someone to call on. Nor, did he want his mother unknowingly depending on a man whose thoughts were decidedly elsewhere.

Sage's eyes focused on the unopened envelope from Laidlaw. He'd been absently turning it 'round about in his fingers. As he began to tear it open, the other two fell silent, waiting while he scanned the heavy parchment.

"When I told Laidlaw I was thinking about investigating the crimps, in order to find out what happened to Kincaid, he promised he'd look into some matters for me." He looked up at them, then back down at the letter. "What he says is more evidence that the body in Astoria is Joseph Kincaid's. Listen to this: 'As you asked, I made discreet inquiries of the seamen coming into the office over the past few days. More than one told me that there is indeed an unsavory pair, newly down from Gray's Harbor. I am told they fit your description of the two men seen in that Milwaukie saloon and who also waylaid Franklin in the alley.'"

Sage looked up from the paper. "He goes on to say that he couldn't find out their names or which crimp they work for. He thinks they're free agents, runners for hire by anyone needing their services."

His mother sighed. "I think, Sage, we must assume, unless Fong's friend learns differently, that Mrs. Kincaid's husband is dead. She needs to know it as soon as possible. Not knowing is tearing her apart."

Sage compressed his lips into a thin line, hating the fact that she had reached the same conclusion as he had about Kincaid's and Amacker's probable fates. "It all fits," he said. He looked at his mother. "What are you thinking? Should we go talk to her tomorrow? It's Sunday, so Mozart's won't be open during the supper hour. Let's head out as soon as the noontime dinner hour is over. You'll go with me to see her? I think maybe we need to talk to her before I start my new job tomorrow night."

"I'll go, of course." Her brow furrowed. "Just what do you mean by 'job'? What exactly are you going to be doing tomorrow? And don't you roll your eyes at me, young man!" The rebuke came sharp as a mother dog's bark. Not the time to treat Mae Clemens lightly. The last time he'd made that mistake she'd shown an alarming propensity for inserting herself right into the dangerous heart of things.

Sage held up a hand pretending to ward off a blow and saying in an exaggerated aside to Fong, "Have I not repeatedly indicated my intent to join the ranks of the land sharks to learn their methods of preying upon our seagoing brethren?"

Much to Sage's relief, the Chinese man caught the whimsy and chimed in, "Ah yes, Mr. Sage you speak very clear about intention. Maybe mother crane's head too deep in the water to hear cheeps of baby chick."

"Hey, now," Sage began in mock indignation.

"You hush, the both of you! I heard your intention, too. It's just that I recollect that you and Lucinda Collins made some plans. Can't see how you're going to follow through with them looking like some hard-luck seaman."

Sage flushed with embarrassment and exasperation. He'd forgotten Lucinda and their plans to attend a play at the new theater tomorrow night. Lord, was she going to be disappointed. Still, some things couldn't be helped. And right now, Mrs. Kincaid's tragedy exerted the strongest pull. He'd have to somehow make it up to Lucinda later.

"There's no choice but to cancel those plans. I must discover what happened to Kincaid, who is responsible, and take that criminal out of the picture. That's more important," he said. The air of finality in his words was intended to stop further comment.

It didn't work. Mae's face turned disapproving. "Sage, she's been looking forward to this, and it's not the first time that you've . . ."

"Mother!"

She raised both hands in surrender to show she was through with talking on the subject.

The next words came from Fong and concerned an entirely different topic. It was a topic equally disturbing to Sage.

"Shanghai mostly take place in tunnels. In dark. Smells like dirt. You afraid of dark places that smell like dirt."

"I will handle it."

"Sage . . ." his mother started to say.

"I can handle it!" Irritation rapped in his voice.

"Mr. Sage . . ." Fong tried to continue.

Sage raised an eyebrow at Fong. He regretted that he'd told Fong about his fear of underground cave-ins. His mother, he didn't need to tell. She'd been there, reaching down from the air vent's opening, as nine-year-old Sage clawed his way into the sunlight, the mine owner's grandson strapped to his scrawny chest. Besides, there were the nightmares. No way to hide those from her once they'd started living together a few years back.

"I can handle it," he said. But he could hear the subdued hesitancy that lay beneath his words. Fong and his mother didn't bother hiding the skeptical looks they exchanged.

Sage sighed. "Well, maybe the time has come for me to learn how to handle it. I'm tired of being afraid of the dark like some kid who thinks there's a monster hiding under his bed."

His mother reached over to pat his hand.

Late that night, three candles illuminated the two men who danced a silent duet of attack and retreat in the otherwise dark attic. Fong intruded again and again into Sage's space, forcing him back. The student was sweating and breathing heavily while the small Chinese man moved effortlessly, his face expressionless, his drooping eyelids the only evidence of his intense concentration. Finally, Sage could continue no longer. He stepped away and raised both palms in surrender.

"Enough, Master Fong." The words came from a throat aching for air, "I've reached the point where my entire concentration is now on how to avoid collapsing."

Fong brought his palms together and bowed.

As he struggled to breathe normally, Sage voiced a question even though he feared the answer, "Are you going to be all right, when I'm gone?"

"I will be fine. I wait for Sergeant Hanke to get information from other side of mountains. After that, I know what to do."

"Mr. Fong . . ." Sage didn't know what plea to make so he voiced his fear. "I don't know how we could continue without you. Not just the missions, but you, your presence in our lives. And you and Mrs. Fong risk losing so much if you kill LaRue."

At first, Fong made no response, instead looking into the blackness that pressed against the edges of the fir flooring. When he spoke, his voice was heavy, "Life is sometimes like river. Crane standing in shallows cannot know what flowing water bring next. He must stand ready to act quickly. Life current has pushed LaRue against my legs. Now, I must act quickly." Here he paused, looking at Sage, his eyes sad in the candlelight. "If I have to."

Sage's huff of exasperation lifted the hair off his sweaty forehead.

Fong smiled, his eyes now soft with affection. "Mr. Sage, as the lady mother always like to say, 'You have no room to talk.' Days ahead also hold danger for you. You are crane, about to wade in strange water full of sharks. You also must be ready for what current brings."

Sage saw only impenetrable black. His heart pounded in his chest as he fought to breathe through the dust clogging his throat. Dust so thick that his lungs wheezed. His legs strained to escape the rubble that had him pinned to the dirt.

There was a gentle tug on his shoulder and a faint glow began to fill the tunnel.

"Sage. Sage." The pulling on his shoulder became forceful as he struggled to lift his dust-caked eyelids. His mother stood there, a sleeping wrapper clutched around her body, a lit taper on the bedside table. Relief slowed the pounding in his chest and sweet-smelling air flowed across his sweat-drenched body.

"You awake now, son?" she asked softly.

"Yes, thank you. Sorry I woke you."

"Don't worry about it, son." Tenderly she brushed a hank of hair off his forehead, squeezed his shoulder and went back to bed, leaving the candle burning on his bedside table.

After she'd gone, he focused on the flickering candle's warm light until his eyes closed and he slept.

FOURTEEN

THE RENTED BUGGY ROLLED along the river road at a spanking pace. Sage's mother rode without complaint although she bounced atop its tufted seat like a corn kernel in hot grease. Her sparkling eyes meant she was enjoying the mad afternoon dash to Milwaukie. Generally her activities were limited to working at Mozart's or shopping about town. For a woman who'd been raised in the wooded crumples of Appalachia's landscape, a trip into the countryside was a rare treat. As the buggy rolled toward Milwaukie, Mae voiced her observations: "Grass over there is the kind that makes good baskets; tried once, I was all thumbs; farmers around here like a tidy field, bet they go to bed with the cows; my Lordy, look at all the filberts on the trees. They call them hazelnuts back East, you know"; and, "there's some sturdy bones, beneath that haystack over there," she said, pointing toward a tidy hayrick.

Her obvious pleasure in the surrounding countryside sent Sage's thoughts rambling down a dirt lane to an imaginary farmhouse where she wove baskets on the front porch, baskets he filled with green velvet balls of newly dropped filberts. "We need to get you out more," he teased, earning a swat on the arm.

Her face sobered quickly. "I don't understand why it is you think you should start working in the shanghaiing business tonight." Her words came in spurts, as ruts in the road jostled the buggy and made her clutch the side rail.

"James Laidlaw advised me to start out with a crimp named Tobias Pratt. As crimps go, he's a fairly honest man. I won't be in danger working for him. Thing is, Laidlaw wrote that Pratt just lost his runner and is looking for a new man. It's an opportunity I can't afford to pass up. I'll go down to the North End soon as I return today, figure out how to find Pratt, convince him to hire me and maybe room in his boardinghouse," Sage explained. Catching her frown, he quickly said, "If I wait too long, Pratt's going to find himself another runner. That forces me into approaching a less honest crimp. First, I need to hook up with a decent one. Otherwise, I won't know enough to achieve the acceptance of the crimping crowd. It's not a familiar world to me."

He'd thought the situation through and Pratt really was the best approach. It beat the other obvious option—using himself as shanghai bait. Just imagine Mae Clemens's response to that idea. He'd get more than a swat on the arm from her.

She stayed silent over another mile of jostling road, apparently mulling over his plan. She slowly nodded, "I guess your plan makes sense." But there was one more objection up her gingham sleeve. "But Lucinda's expecting . . ."

"Darn it, Mother, Lucinda is my business. I already told Matthew to take her my note. She'll understand."

"She's supposed to understand a note from a delivery boy? After you haven't seen or visited her in days?" Incredulity laced her words. "I tell you, Sage, you do this one too many times and you're going to lose that gal."

"We'll be fine. Lucinda understands my work." He spoke firmly to cut off any objection or further discussion.

As the buggy wheeled around the corner onto the Kincaids' dirt street, they saw the young woman sitting on her stoop holding her baby, watchful, as if expecting someone. She wasn't sitting there waiting for them.

"Oh, dear," Mae Clemens muttered, "she doesn't seem to be doing any better."

Sage reined the horse in, noting that the window box

flowers hung wilted, like the young woman already turned gaunt and colorless. She pulled herself to her feet and stepped toward them, a flicker of hope in her eyes when she recognized Sage.

"Mr. Miner, is there news of Joseph?"

Sage nodded, took her arm and guided her back down onto the stoop.

His mother evidently concluded that it was better for the woman to receive bad news without an audience, because she quickly said, "Let me see to the tea and child." She took the baby from the arms of the unresisting mother and disappeared into the house.

Sage remained standing, turning his hat brim around in his hands. "How have you been doing?" he finally asked.

She looked at him, her forehead wrinkled, as if puzzled why he'd driven such a far distance to ask the question.

Sage said, "The baby is looking very well. That's good."

Again silence. He breathed in and out. "I'm not positively sure yet," his words came slowly, painfully, "I think your husband was shanghaied, taken aboard an ocean ship against his will."

Mrs. Kincaid's spine straightened and her gaze sharpened. "Shanghaied?"

"Kidnapped, taken against his will and dumped aboard a seagoing ship. For money."

"Then Joey could come back to me and Faith? Once he reaches a port?" Hope suffused her face so completely that Sage dreaded speaking the next words, "Mrs. Kincaid, I don't know how to say this, . . . I think, . . . I'm afraid, that Joseph died trying to return home to you and Faith."

Blood drained from her face as if a plug had been pulled, "No, please no" she whimpered, burying her face in her hands.

To her bent head, he quickly recounted his fruitless search and told her about the strange men in the Millmen's saloon on the night her husband disappeared. And, worst of all, he told her about the body found at the river's mouth, a body that fit her husband's description. At last there was nothing more to say. Her shoulders shook with sobs, as she murmured, over and over, "He's dead, he's dead. I knew he was dead. I felt it these last few days. I didn't feel it at first but, lately, I just knew."

Sage took a seat beside her, waiting as her body heaved with sobs. He didn't know whether to pat her back or murmur words of comfort. Relief from the dilemma came with the call of Mae Clemens from inside the house. The sobbing slowed. Kincaid's wife raised her head, dashed tears from her face with shaking fingers and stood. When Sage started to enter the little house, his mother rested a gentle hand on his chest to keep him outside on the stoop.

"Mr. Miner," she announced, "I think it's best that I stay with Grace for now. I'll take the interurban train back to town later on today. You go ahead. You need to start your search for the men responsible."

More softly, barely audible, she told him, "Sage, you staying around here isn't going to help. Lord knows, maybe I can't either. I just don't want to leave Grace alone." She raised her voice to normal tones and continued, "Tell Ida that, if I'm not back by supper, she's in charge until I return. Ask Matthew to help her."

Sage welcomed the opportunity to escape the weighty grief that seemed to fill every corner of the small house and its yard. He called an unanswered 'goodbye' through the crack in the door to the woman. She sat unmoving in a rocker, staring blankly into the air before her eyes.

Climbing in and turning the buggy, he began the trip back into town, snapping the leather reins to send the horse into a vigorous trot. "Grace," he thought, "so that's her given name." An apt one he suspected.

The night before, Sage had no luck finding Tobias Pratt. Late in the evening, though, he'd got a lead on where he might find the crimp come morning. Dawn the next day had come and gone by the time Sage reached the Couch Street wharf. He stood looking down the length of gray, gouged planks running alongside the tin-roof warehouse and out over the river. Wagons rolled up to deliver the wooden crates and barrels that men were loading onto carts and pushing into the warehouse. Likely readying for the next day's shipment, he guessed, since no ships were tied up to the wharf's iron hawsers. Most likely the morning's ships had sailed before dawn with the receding tide.

About fifty feet off the wharf a small rowboat, crammed to its gunnels with men, was wallowing its way toward a sailing ship anchored about two hundred feet upriver. A rotund old man, nearly dwarfed by an oversized hat with a tall crown, sat in the stern, his face toward the ship. The old man fit Laidlaw's description of Tobias Pratt perfectly. Sage swore. Matthew's skulking around, trailing behind on his bicycle, had prevented Sage from reaching the wharf before Pratt rowed out to the ship. Sage had been forced to duck out of sight down a filthy stairwell and wait until the boy gave up the hunt. Maybe that bicycle wasn't such a good idea.

Behind him a creaky voice spoke, "Don't worry, son. If you're thinking to ship out on the *Mary Jane*, ole Pratt will gladly come back to fetch you."

Sage looked around to see another old man, age hunching his back, perched atop a nearby wooden crate, apparently contemplating the view and enjoying the sun on his face. A smoldering tobacco pipe was resting in a thick-fingered hand that was missing its thumb. At Sage's notice, a toothless grin split the old man's deeply creased face.

Sage laughed. "Nah, I'm not looking to ship out. I was hoping to work with Pratt," he said.

"You be a rowing man?"

"I rowed a fair bit in Frisco. I figure this river's a mite easier than the Bay," Sage lied. He had never rowed on San Francisco Bay. He'd only hung around Frisco's Barbary Coast waterfront a few weeks while he hustled inexpensive passage to Alaska and the Klondike. Still, he was no stranger to rowing. The mine owner insured that he enjoyed all the trappings of an elite education. That meant serving on the University's rowing team. Nowadays, he sometimes rowed the Willamette River for the pleasure of feeling that familiar rhythm in his muscles.

The old man pulled his pipe from his mouth and nodded wisely. "I know that's true. That ole' Bay is a rough one," he said. He gestured with his pipe stem toward the rowboat, now more than halfway to the ship. "Matter of fact, your timing is good.

The feller rowing that boat is shipping out. Ole Pratt's going to have to pull his own oars if he wants to make it back here to the dock. By the time he ties up, he'll be 'dee . . . lighted' to hire a younger man to row him to and fro, heh, heh."

Sage settled himself on a neighboring crate. He gazed around. A ship repair operation was in full swing fifty feet up-river. A small sailing ship lay on its side atop a floating raft, its barnacle-encrusted bottom exposed, its stern afloat in the river. Men were at work on the stern end while standing atop river rafts, some of them using pry bars to strip metal sheathing from the hull. Others floated along behind, scraping the unsheathed surface down to the planking. Hard to believe that such a frail structure withstood crushing ocean waves and battering sea winds. The seagoing life was foreign to him except for luxury passenger travel to Europe and the short sail up the inside passage to Alaska. Mining, stevedoring, farming, gold sluicing and falling trees; those were livelihoods he knew well and, with the exception of mining, he sometimes liked the work's physicality. But the idea of working aboard a collection of tarred-together sticks midst a vast expanse of pitching ocean? No, thank you!

He looked northward, gazing down the river to where it curved slightly west. Summer's low water meant the outflow end of a wooden sewer pipe dangled over exposed boulders, instead of being submerged in the river. A town grew big enough, like Portland, and people started switching from their cesspools, septic tanks and outhouses to indoor plumbing. The switch meant more business for the sewer pipes that dumped into the river. The brown gunk flowed without pause. Funny how some folks thought, just because you flushed a water closet, it meant whatever you flushed disappeared. Good thing the breeze sent the stink the other direction. Wouldn't think the fish liked sewage all that much. Sure wouldn't want to eat a fish that did.

Sage looked the other direction, back toward the whaler.

"Heh, heh," came a spumy cackle at his side.

Sage twisted to look again at the old man on the neighboring crate. Seeing he'd secured Sage's attention, the old man began talking, "That rotten old beached bucket you're looking at is an arctic whaler, name of the *Karluk*. She was heading for Alaska and started taking on water. They couldn't pump her out quick enough. Captain had no choice. It was sail up here or sink. 'Course, the fresh water in the river killed the barnacles on her plates. That was good but that weren't her worst problem. Barnacles just been slowing her down. They wasn't what was sinking her.

"You see where they pulled that copper plate off'n her?" he asked, pointing with his other hand toward the bow of the whaling ship. Sage saw with a start that the old man's other hand also lacked its thumb. How the hell had that happened?

The old man responded to the question on Sage's face. "So you noticed both my thumbs was missing, did you?" He raised his hands side-by-side so the absence was unmistakable. "A son-of-a-bitch captain tied me in the rigging. Wasn't able to keep my toes on the deck for long enough. Ain't seen these thumbs for more than fifty years. I tell you, I miss 'em every day."

"Why'd he do that to you?" Sage asked, recalling stories of devil ships and cruel captains. No way to escape a bastard captain in the middle of the ocean unless you killed him. Even if you succeeded, there'd be no putting the act behind you. Mutiny at sea, no matter how awful the captain, carried a death sentence. Just the thought of being trapped aboard such a ship made his skin crawl up his back. It'd be claustrophobic, only above ground, surrounded by an endless expanse of bottomless water.

The old man was rooting around in his own memory, re-living the loss of his thumbs. "Bastard claimed I was insubordinate because I spoke up. He was too hard on the younger boys in ways that weren't natural." Despite explaining those missing thumbs for more than fifty years, his words carried outrage. The easy geniality on the old man's face was gone. "Next time we hit port, I scarpered. It was hell making my way home from Africa, took a couple years. I didn't care. Heard that later in that same voyage someone stuck a knife between the captain's ribs while he was whoring it up in some Chilean brothel."

The old man shifted atop his box and said, "Them days are long gone for me, my boy, but captains like that are still sailing. Old salts like me, we know all of 'em that comes to port here." He puffed vigorously on his pipe and nodded toward the beached whaling ship.

"So, what was sinking this whaler here?" Sage asked.

"Well, you see the squiggly channels and small holes in the wood? They mean that sea termites honeycomb the planking. Carpenters can tamp new oakum, that's hemp coated with tar, into the seams, plank them over, tar 'em up and sheathe her with metal. But she'll still be barely seaworthy. Old and riddled as she is, I'm willing to bet her inside frame is rotted out. I sure know I wouldn't want to be sailing her into the Arctic."

"She's going back into the Arctic this close to winter?"

"The captain's a crazy drunkard so she might. She'll leave port soon, once she raises a crew. Maybe instead of heading north so late, her captain might decide to hunt humpback whales down around Mexico, then beat across to the Japan grounds for sperm whales. Come April, though, if she's still afloat, she'll for sure head into the Arctic seas, looking for the bowheads. Won't never touch land the whole trip."

"Bowheads?"

"Them bowhead whales carry the most baleen. Whalebone—that is. They grow more of it than any other kind of whale. More oil, too, not that their oil brings much anymore. Nowadays, with that cheap kerosene oil everywhere, fella can't hardly give whale oil away. Still, the baleen is worth something. Women need their corsets. Besides, folks fashion other stuff from whalebone—combs, boot shanks, why, even tongue-scrapers—anything needing some bendability."

"You said 'if' she gets a crew? You mean men don't want to sail on her?"

"Heck, no! Every sailor working the coast knows the *Karluk* is a hell ship. And not just because she's near rotted out. Like I told you, her captain's a drunken bully. And he's reckless. The crew that ships with him ain't any better. No decent man will come out of that trip alive."

He gestured again, "No siree. Looking at that hull, I wouldn't give a chicken's butt on her chances of returning from the Arctic."

"The Arctic's rough sailing?"

"St. Elmos Fire, I thought you said you worked Frisco. That's where most of the Pacific whaling fleet berths. Ain't you heard the stories about ice packs sneaking up on ships and crushing them like they were eggs? Or whales and icebergs stoving them in? Ain't you heard about seas fifty-foot high and ice so thick on the rigging that the ship plum sinks from the weight of it?"

The old man shook his head, lost in the memory, obviously not expecting Sage to answer. "I sailed whalers for 'nigh on to thirty years, and I tell you, sure as I'm sitting here without my thumbs, that any man shipping out on that there *Karluk* is a dead man floating."

A thunk against a wharf piling grabbed Sage's attention. Tobias Pratt had returned. The high crown of the dirty tan Stetson hat slowly rose above the wharf edge as the hat's wearer climbed the ladder, a bow line clutched in his gnarled hand. Sage nodded a quick goodbye to the old whaleman and strode to the top of the ladder, reaching for the line that the wheezing man gratefully released. He clambered up the final rungs as Sage looped the line around the iron hawser.

FIFTEEN

PRATT'S STRUGGLE TO ROW THE boat across the river current and climb the ladder left him gasping for air. He bent over, hands on his knees, so that Sage saw only the top of his soiled hat, his hunched shoulders, and his booted feet. "My Lord, I believe I'm near to having me a heart spasm," the old fellow gasped.

The whaleman's cackle floated to them from his perch atop the crate, "Well now, Toby. Looks like, today, the good Lord is watching after you. This young man's been looking for you. Seems he wants a job rowing your boat."

Pratt stopped his gasping and straightened. His calculating blue eyes traveled over Sage's frame. "You ain't too big in the muscles, are you? Fact is, you look a little scrawny," he said.

Sage smiled slightly, "I'm plenty . . ."

"Don't bother spinning no stories, 'cause I'm not going to believe them anyway. We'll see how you get on soon enough. I don't believe nothin' nobody tells me 'cause every single man I talk to is a damn liar."

The old man perched on the wooden freight box cackled again, "Toby, you keep flapping that miserable yap of yours and you'll be beating your own record and lose this man before he even touches an oar. And here I thought I heard you worrying about a heart attack."

Pratt twisted his lips into a grimace and deliberately sent a brown stream of tobacco juice in the heckler's direction. "Don't be telling me how to run my business, Thimble, you nosy old sod." He turned to face Sage. "I pay a dollar a day starting out plus vittles and a bed at my boardinghouse. I expect you to be ready to work at any time. The tide rules the ships, and I can't be dilly-dallying around while you spark some whore. I say 'hop' I expect you to hop and that's it. If you want, you can give it a try."

"I'll accept your . . ."

"Get your rear in gear. Don't stand there gawping. I ain't gonna pay you for doing nothing." Pratt turned away from Sage and stomped down the wharf on a pair of bowed stumpy legs. His path was straight as an arrow, not deviating an inch to avoid the dangers posed by the men trundling crates to and fro. Instead, it was they who paused to allow him passage. For Sage, it was different. He had to dodge right and left to avoid colliding with the again-speeding hand trucks.

From behind him, the now familiar cackle sounded one last time and Sage heard Thimble call, "Don't be taking Toby personal, he hates everybody equal. Heh, heh, heh."

Well, at least I managed to brighten up ole Thimble's day, Sage thought as he hastened to catch up with the squat man whose rolling gait moved him along at an unexpectedly fast clip.

As Sage overtook Pratt, the crimp shot back over his shoulder, "You watch and keep your yap shut 'cause you don't know nothing and I'm not going to waste my breath explaining things to you until I know whether I'm going to keep you around or not."

Sage followed orders. He kept his yap shut. Pratt never did. Sage was treated to Pratt's life story. "I been working the crimping business for over forty years. Started out in Frisco before moving up here to Portland. Used to be it was a good business. Now, it's dying out. Busybodies are getting laws passed while steamships are making sailing ships and sailing men obsolete. Now, it's the damn unionizing. Those dumb union bastards mobbed up and stoned a boardinghouse, can you believe it? This business is on its last legs, so if you're scheming to snuggle next to this old man and take my business, think again. 'Cause when I'm gone, the crimping business will be gone. So trying to cozy up to me won't get you no more than an empty duffle.

"No more jabbering," Pratt snapped, irritated as if it were Sage who'd been blabbing on for the last two blocks. Pratt, prattle. There's an ironic coincidence. Sage smiled, although Pratt didn't notice. Instead Pratt turned stern, saying, "It's time I sign up some men. I don't want you saying nothing that'll scare them off, so you keep your mouth shut and your mug friendly, you hear?" He fixed an angry glare on Sage.

Sage, taken off guard by the unexpected necessity of replying, managed a quick "I hear you. Keep my mouth shut."

Pratt stomped up to three slightly inebriated men. They stood with their backsides against a building's brick wall, dingy canvas sea bags piled at their feet. The warm smile on Pratt's face was likely meant to convey the idea that unkind words never crossed his lips. The chameleon in Sage admired Pratt's instant transformation. "Well now, men, you look have the look of fine sailing men. Are you wanting a berth?" Pratt asked.

"Shit, Pratt. You signed us out on our last ship and let me tell you . . ." One of the men pushed off from the building to wave a wobbling finger in Pratt's face. Sage stepped forward and the man calmed down, leaning back against the building and continuing with his complaint. "That ship weren't all you cracked it up to be. We ate too much duff. Some days we couldn't tell whether the black bits in that God-awful wheat-paste porridge was raisins or cockroach butts."

Sage tensed for an explosion. None came. Pratt stayed in genial character, his inquiry mild. "What ship was that you sailed on, lad?"

"The *Esther Lynn*, around the Horn."

"Ah, the *Esther Lynn*. Tell me, boys–her officers, they didn't beat you, right? And you weren't marooned or made to freeze from lack of clothes in them Antarctic seas, was you, lad?"

Another man tugged at the feisty one's sleeve. "Leave off, Jack. We'd be lucky to ship out with old Pratt here and well you know it. He don't crew no hell ships, and the duffle bag he gives you, well, it's not full up, but he gives you a damn sight more than most crimps."

At this, the third man piped up. "I know that's right. I shipped out of this port a few years back, and once I'm on board, I see the crimp Mordaunt robbed my duffle. Instead of dungarees and coat, it was stuffed with a woman's old corset and her mismatched shoes. It was the ship's slop chest for me and I still came near to freezing 'round the Horn. Don't ya' know, when I landed in Cape Town, I owed more for them clothes than what I'd earned. At least Pratt here provides a decent duffle and he don't steal from it afore you go." The man nudged the sea bag at his feet with a salt-rimed boot.

Pratt, seeing the tide flowing in his favor, pulled three white cards from his pocket and handed one to each man, saying, "You boys best stay with me. I'll give you room, board, and a little bit of spending money for tobacco and drink while you're ashore here. I'll be paid by your next captain when you sign on." The three men exchanged glances and shrugged. They pushed off from the wall, shook Pratt's hand and promised they'd turn up at the boardinghouse in time for supper.

Pratt turned to Sage, his face stripped of all joviality. "Pick up their bags and haul them to the house where they'll be safe," he ordered. When he again addressed the three sailors, his tone changed. He handed each man a silver dollar as he said with near paternal concern, "Take care, now, and watch what and where you drink. We're experiencing a bit of a sailor shortage in port. Some of my competitors are using the blackjack and the knockout drops. There's been more of that going on . . ."

The three of them turned away to swagger down the sidewalk in their rolling sailors' gait, heading deeper into the North End. There they'd find saloons thick on the ground, loose women and free eats aplenty to accompany the bottomless beer mugs. All of it calculated to empty their pockets. The three seemed like decent fellows. Sage hoped they wouldn't encounter trouble.

Pratt began marching back in the direction of the Couch Street wharf, trailed by Sage straining under all three duffles. "What's your name anyhow, and where are you from? I ain't seen you around the port before," Pratt asked.

"Twig Crowley, from San Francisco . . ."

"Humph. 'Twig Crowley' and my name's 'turkey in the

straw.' No mama ever named her son 'Twig.'" Sage gambled, kept his mouth shut and sure enough, Pratt kept on prattling. "Ain't no never mind. Like I say, if you can pull an oar, I'll keep you. Otherwise, you'll be on down the road. We'll find out soon enough. The *Clarice* will be rounding Swan Island about now. She'll just be anchoring when we reach the river."

Evidently, Pratt was mulling over his exchange with the three sailors because he said, "That's the problem, you see, what those men said. I'm getting squeezed by the law and making less profit while my competitors use every lowdown trick you can imagine, and then some, to get rich. 'Course, you look like you've a bit of the snake in you, so maybe you admire men like that. 'Twig Crowley,' sure you are. Like I was saying, no decent woman ever named her son 'Twig' and a man that ain't proud of his given name can't be trusted. My mother named me 'Tobias', and I've never claimed to be anyone else."

Sage kept his trap shut. He wasn't sure Pratt even noticed. Each block grew longer as the weight Sage carried grew heavier. These duffles must be filled with rocks. Sure can't be gold from the looks of their owners. A few men passing by took a second look, as if bemused at the picture of an empty-handed, yakking Pratt, being trailed by an overloaded, staggering Sage. A few street dwellers, both men and women, called out to Pratt but he merely flipped a friendly hand in greeting without slowing. Nothing slowed the man's rolling gait or his yammering–neither the greetings nor Sage's total lack of response to the questions the old crimp threw out over his shoulder. Sage, when he wasn't shifting the load to lessen his pain, contemplated the probable pleasure of cotton balls stuffed in his ears. Painfully clear now was the meaning of Stuart Franklin's crack that there'd be no choice whether to listen to the old crimp.

"Take me, mine's an honest operation. I don't hold with bribing the port master, and I don't make the police part of my game. And I never ever use the underground. I'm taking a serious risk here. Maybe I feed and house those men back there only to have them ship out for someone else or head off inland looking for gold. That's why I take ahold of their duffles up front." Pratt paused at a curb to scrape horse dung off his shoe sole. Even that activity failed to stop his flow of words. "They take off, I'm out everything I put into them, including the advance money I paid them. By the bye, I don't pay my runner in advance. You'll be paid at the end of the day and not a minute sooner. So don't waste your breath asking."

They reached a quieter street, running westward, up from the river bank. Pratt paused to doff his hat at two soiled doves. They giggled and the raven-haired one called out, "Mr. Pratt, dearie, send a sailor boy or two our way. Us girls needs a favor and a drink."

Pratt nodded agreeably without pausing in his tirade. "Anyway, if you stick around, I'll send you out scouting for men. So listen up, because there's my reputation to uphold, and I don't want any green runner drumming up worthless men. The best men are the professional sailors like those three back there. Next best is soldiers, 'cause they know where to jump when ordered. After that comes the country bumpkins–lumberjacks and farm boys. They're worthless as teats on a boar the first month at sea. Spend most of their time hanging over the railing feeding the fish. Once their guts calm down, they know how to work hard."

Here Pratt stopped on the sidewalk and turned to shake a pudgy finger in Sage's face. "But don't you ever drum up an Indian, because they're trouble."

Curiosity at this unexpected warning spurred Sage to ask, "Why?"

"Boy, you are one ignorant fella, ain't you? An Indian man works real hard and they make good sailors, but the federal government watches over them, and the captains don't like tangling with the federal government. Something bad happens to an Indian aboard ship and everybody's got a problem–starting with the crimp who put him there." Pratt pulled a large brass key ring from his pocket as he mounted three brick steps. "We need to drop off them duffles because, with any luck, you'll be having to carry a few more before the day is out."

Sage let the bags drop to the sidewalk while Pratt unlocked his front door. It was a two-story flat-fronted clapboard house. So, this was home to Pratt and the sailors he collected. There was a pleasing symmetry to it–what with the stoop and door both precisely centered on the ground floor and flanked by two perfectly matched windows to either side. Bright yellow gingham curtains splashed with blue periwinkles added cheer. Has to be a woman somewhere in Pratt's crimping operation. Clearly, Pratt wasn't inclined to spend money on the building itself since it sorely needed paint. A faint mossy color traced the wood grain on the otherwise naked clapboard, making it look like that green-tinged driftwood you sometimes found on the beach. Across the second story, four double-hung windows fronted the street, curtained by dark drapes. No doubt to block the morning light for hung-over sailors.

"Crowley, quit gawping like a country bumpkin. I ain't fixin' to sell the dang building to you," Pratt proclaimed from atop the stoop, aggressively jerking his thumb in the direction of the open front door. "Get yer fanny moving."

Sage staggered across the threshold onto worn linoleum of an indeterminate brown hue. Despite, its scars and wear it looked clean. No black gunk scummed the corners. On the left side tucked behind the front door was a small alcove containing a cot and a single wooden fruit crate. Pratt gestured toward the alcove. "Drop them bags there for now, Crowley. This room here is your flop," he said. Sage dropped his load as instructed and flexed his cramped hands.

"Get a move on, now. We got us a ship to greet," Pratt growled and headed back out the door.

Minutes later they sat in the rowboat. Sage was glad that the river was low, slowing the current. It had been some months since he'd pulled oars. He rowed steadily and straight to the *Clarice* while Pratt kept up a stream of insults and unnecessary instructions until Sage at last tied the boat to the ship's anchor chain. Pratt stood and grabbed hold of the chain, his beatific smile once more on display. Sage sat on the bench catching his breath and idly enjoying the fantasy of flipping the old man over the side into the water.

"Ahoy on board, men of the *Clarice*!" Pratt shouted upward before turning to say in a normal voice to Sage, "Used to be we'd climb the anchor chain. These days, it's a crime to go on board without the captain's permission. Afraid we'll entice the men to desert with alcohol and promises of wild women." While it was doubtful that a man of Pratt's girth and agility could mount that anchor chain, Sage found the vision amusing to contemplate.

Overhead, faces popped up above the railing and eyes buried within webs of sun burnt wrinkles peered down at them.

"Hello there, men! Name's Pratt. I'm offering you a clean boardinghouse, good grub, and I'll make sure any man who comes with me sets sail with a good berth. No leaky buckets, no bad captains, no empty duffle." Pratt fished around in the cloth bag he wore slung over his shoulder and removed a pint of whiskey. He raised the bottle so that the sun glowed within its amber contents. "I brought you a welcoming libation to enjoy while my runner here, 'Twig' (the contempt was there if you were listening for it), rows you to the dock so's you can partake of the frolicking fun offered by the best port city on the West Coast! So, what do you say, men? You coming ashore?"

While he awaited an answer, Pratt cast a nervous glance over his shoulder. When Sage followed that look, he saw another rowboat making way toward the ship. Two men sat in the boat, scowls on their faces. Pratt hissed, "Don't be staring at them, you idjit. Those are Kaspar Mordaunt's men, and they'd sooner cut us loose from this anchor chain and dump us in the river than say 'Howdy do.' You move that belay pin," Pratt pointed at the 12-inch wooden club that had been rolling about the boat's bottom, "closer to your hand and be alert."

Pratt's next shout that sailed upward was tight with anxiety. "We can't be waiting here all day, men. Let me tell you, I'll treat you right, not like some others soon to tie up to your anchor."

A rope ladder dropped down, uncoiling alongside the hull until it hung just a few feet above the rowboat. A pair of feet plunged over the rail followed by blue dungaree legs. Pratt sighed and sat, pulling a dirty white handkerchief from his pocket to dab at the sweat on his brow.

"Once all these men are aboard and you're pulling us back to dock, make dang sure you give wide berth to that other rowboat. They ain't going to be happy we're carrying the first men off the *Clarice*. They think every man jack hitting port belongs under Mordaunt's thumb."

"Mordaunt isn't as kindly as you?" Sage's tone was ironic.

Pratt twisted his lips and the flare in his eyes said Sage's jab hadn't missed. "There ain't no favorable comparisons to make," Pratt said, "He's a cold-blooded shark. Just last week his runners shot it out with a captain right here in port. Ain't no call for that. The captain was just trying to keep his crew from deserting. Mordaunt has all sorts of angles. He forces the captains to hire his watchmen. They're supposed to stop crimps from getting aboard, 'stead they make it easier for 'em. Captain won't take on the watchman, Mordaunt's runner waits for the sailors ashore, gets them drunk and brawlin'. The police arrest them. Captain has two choices: pay bail to Mordaunt's police cronies or buy a whole other crew from Mordaunt. Either way, the shark makes his killing, the sailors be damned."

Outrage stiffened the old man's spine so that he seemed to sit taller in the boat. For the first time, Sage felt a glimmer of respect for the ornery cuss. Pratt was looking at him steadily as he spoke, his tone somber, his voice quiet while the boat rocked with the shifting weight of the first man settling in.

"And Mordaunt ain't choosy about how he gets his crews. He does it all. Gets them drunk, brains them, knockout drops, some talk of even worse goings-on. He's trying to take over all the crimping here in port. I steer clear of his men, 'specially on dark nights."

The boat rocked violently as a second sailor hit the floor-boards. While Sage clung to the anchor chain, steadying the rocking boat, two other sailors quickly descended the rope ladder. The rocking boat was now overloaded to the point it started shipping water. Pratt untied the anchor rope and turned to act the genial host, making a big show of uncorking the whiskey and clapping the sailors' shoulders.

As the last man settled, Pratt with a nervous glance at the approaching boat, shooed Sage into action. Sage allowed the river current to sweep the rowboat alongside the ship to the stern and away from the bow anchor and Mordaunt's runners. The maneuver maybe elicited an approving glance from Pratt. The old man turned away too fast for Sage to be sure. After the rowboat cleared the ship, Sage began pulling toward the shore, the boat wallowing beneath its passengers' weight. Despite his effort, Sage's eyes remained thoughtfully on Mordaunt's men. They tied their boat to the *Clarise*'s bow anchor and craned their necks upward to shout at the few sailors who peered down at them. Before his rowboat nudged the wharf ladder, Sage counted three men slipping over the side to drop into the Mordaunt boat. Pratt followed his gaze and, for once, he made no comment, only shook his head before recommencing his spiel to his customers.

By the end of his second day as Pratt's runner, Sage was desperate for a respite. Rowing the boat and trailing after Pratt on his rounds from ship to bar to boardinghouse and back again wasn't hard work. Stifling his own retorts and shutting his ears to Pratt's incessant insults and gabble was. The old crotchet ceased talking only to gasp for air at ladder tops or to spit a stream of tobacco juice without the least concern for its landing place. Still, Sage had to admit that old Pratt, in his way, was a fairly decent man.

Sage surprised his mother when he stepped into the third-floor hallway above Mozart's early Wednesday morning. "Good Lord, what are you doing here?" she demanded, fright giving bite to the question.

Sage waved a vague hand in her direction. "I'll tell you later. Is Mr. Fong here?"

"No, not right now. He's been sticking close, though. Waiting on Hanke I suspect."

"Good, I'll talk to him in awhile. I need a few minutes of peace."

"Can I get you anything?"

"Right now, what I need most in the world is silence. Just a few minutes of blessed silence." He entered his room and softly shut the door.

SIXTEEN

"I THINK WE HAVE A PROBLEM with Matthew," his mother informed Sage a few hours later when she entered his room carrying a pot of coffee.

Sage looked up from the day's *Journal.* "Why do you say that? He doesn't know I'm here, does he? You told him I went to Seattle, didn't you?"

"That's the problem. He's convinced he spotted you earlier today down near the Couch Street wharf."

"Damn. I guess I didn't duck fast enough."

"Oh, so he did see you?"

"Probably. I saw him riding his bicycle and nipped into a shop but apparently not fast enough. Damn," Sage said again, this time softly to himself. Matthew underfoot could cause serious problems in an already precarious situation.

Just then the door opened and Fong stepped into the room, closing the door behind him. Sage noticed right away that the deep shadows under his friend's eyes had lightened since last he'd seen him.

"Mr. Fong, Mother just told me that Matthew might have spotted me down near the docks. Did he say anything to you?"

Fong narrowed his eyes in thought. "He has said nothing. But that might be reason for Matthew's strange actions."

"What do you mean?"

"Yesterday, I am at river, talking to Chinese men. To learn more about shanghai tunnels. I think I see red-haired Matthew sitting on bicycle in alley. When I go closer to look, he gone."

"Oh, dear," Mae breathed, "It's dangerous for him to be wandering around the North End."

"It looks like the three of us better find something for Matthew to do. If I stumble over him at the wrong time, it could endanger both of us," Sage said, feeling that old familiar tingle beneath his skin. An ignorant mistake by a naive kid could make the crimps wonder about the new man working the port, "Twig Crowley."

Mae's fist hit the table making Sage jump. "I know!" she said, "We can send him out to help Grace Kincaid. She needs wood cut and clothes washed and other things done around the house. Milwaukie is a pretty far piece from the Portland waterfront."

"Good idea, Mother. The sooner the better," Sage said, and meant it, fervently.

That bothersome problem dealt with, the three turned to Fong's discoveries about the underground and the tunnels running underneath the streets.

"Do the Chinese use the tunnels a lot?" asked Sage.

"Not every Chinese. Chinese opium and gambling dens sometimes down in basements. Also, when Chinese men are very sick, they stay in underground so the white men won't deport them. Some people live there because no cheap rooms up top. It not all tunnels. Under each building are openings in basement walls. That is how, people move from under one building to under neighbor building. No tunnels there. Tunnels are only under the streets going from one block to next block."

"So, you enter by going into a building's basement. After that, you can move through the adjacent basements in the block and use the tunnels to go under any street to the next block?" Sage said, beginning to visualize the setup. "Doesn't everyone see what's happening down there—not just those in the opium dens but also storekeepers who keep their goods in their basement?"

Fong shook his head. "Every business has small area below with walls all around where nobody can go into from underground. Door kept locked. Storekeepers, opium users and gamblers usually stay inside walls. Like a little room–a cellar. Most everybody afraid of what might happen if they go out door into the underground. So everybody stay inside walls unless police raid opium den or gambling parlor. Then everybody run away through basements and tunnels. This is why some China men know underground like back of own hand. Not exactly best China men," he added thoughtfully.

"How many tunnels under the streets between buildings are there? How far can you travel underground?" asked Mae Clemens.

"Underground is beneath whole North End and toward the hills as far as West 23rd Street. Also travel two miles south to Lair Hill. But in downtown, here, not so many buildings connected to underground, mostly the old ones."

"Every building in the North End is connected through the tunnels?"

"Most every one, including Mr. Solomon's hotel."

"And the building owners allow this use of their property?" Sage asked. He'd never allow shanghaiing to go on beneath Mozart's. Especially now that he knew its many ugly faces. The thought of men imprisoned in the dark space beneath his building sent a disgusted shudder through his body.

"If building owners try to refuse, crimps cause many problems. Some building owners, they take much money from crimps for use. Sometimes they are even partners."

"So, everybody in the North End knows that shanghaiing is going on right under their feet?" It was hard to believe that so many people knew of the criminal activity and did nothing about it.

The look Fong sent Sage could only be described as indulgent. "Who you think makes tunnels under street? Who you think makes sure there are openings in the walls between buildings?" He saved the most pointed question for last. "Who you think has bars set in walls between basements so crimps can build cells around them?"

Sage sat back, rethinking that heated exchange between Gordon and Laidlaw in the Cabot Club. He remembered Gordon bragging about keeping himself apprised of North End happenings. Gordon likely owned some of those modified buildings and raked in a cut from the very operations Laidlaw wanted to destroy. No wonder Laidlaw had been so angry and his retorts so contemptuous. Given the circumstances, the British consul had been positively restrained.

Sage shook his own head before returning to the task at hand. "Well, I'm thinking that the answer to Kincaid's disappearance is down there in those basements. He might be alive and well, though I doubt that. But there must be other men imprisoned underground right now. That's how the business operates. It requires a steady supply of men. We need to rescue them and kill the practice for good."

"Young Kincaid not alive," Fong said quietly. "My friend in Gee Kung tong sent message by carrier pigeon. He show fisherman, Hong Ah Kay, picture of Kincaid. Hong say for sure it is man he found floating in ocean."

This quiet affirmation of what they'd already concluded brought Sage unexpected pain. No one said anything for some moments, but then Fong continued. "My friend say Hong Ah Kay told him dead man's feet much sliced up, like cut by glass. Wounds many days old . . . almost healed."

"Sliced feet? What would sliced feet have to do with shanghaiing?" Sage asked.

Fong shrugged. "That all pigeon paper say. Not much room."

"Mother, if I write a quick note, will you see that Matthew takes it to Laidlaw's office and waits for an answer? Somehow, I think the sliced feet are significant. Maybe Laidlaw will know, or maybe Stuart Franklin can tell me, if he's in town."

Mae was gone from the room less than an hour before she returned with Laidlaw's terse answer. He read it aloud.

> "Not certain of reason for the cut feet, but Stuart may know. Expecting him tonight. I'll send him to the nine o'clock Floating Society meeting. You can speak to him there."

Laidlaw's letter also confirmed that he, too, knew about Tobias Pratt's most notable personality trait. "Candle tallow in the ears will deaden irritating noises," advised Laidlaw's scrawled postscript.

Pratt was stomping up and down the wharf and fuming under his breath, when Sage finally turned up. The ship Pratt wanted to meet had yet to drop anchor so Sage wasn't late. That fact didn't stop Pratt.

"I've a mind to fire you," the old man growled. "There's a passel of other idjits just like you looking for work all up and down Burnside Street. I told you that I wanted to know where you were at all times. And what happens? Just two days into the job, and you up and disappear."

Sage let Pratt's ranting roll over him. In only a few days he'd become impervious to Pratt's never ending barbs. As they rowed out toward the ship, Sage waited until Pratt paused to spit tobacco chew into the wind. Then he squeezed in a question. "How could a shanghaied man get his feet all cut to pieces?"

To Sage's surprise the question rendered Pratt speechless and blanched his florid face a paler shade of pink. The old man shook his head so violently that his large lips seemed to quiver. "Don't you ask that question of nobody else, do you hear me? That's a real bad question to ask, and you don't want to know the answer," he finally said.

Sage adopted Pratt's ridiculing tone. "And here I've been listening to you telling me, for days on end, that you ain't afraid of nothing and nobody. Hell, you just turned fish-belly white at a simple little question."

Pratt rose to the bait like a starving trout. "Listen here, boy, I've seen more in my lifetime than you'll ever see or hope to see. Times used to be harder, and weak-kneed sisters like you couldn't last a week in this business. Just because I know the answer don't mean I got to tell it."

"So, why's a simple question got you all shook up, then? You seem scared to me."

"That's because it concerns something that is better for you not to know about and for me not to blab about. The crimps who use the glass don't want people talking about their business."

"So what do they do with the glass? That's all I'm asking." Sage continued to push.

Pratt darted a nervous glance around, as if afraid they'd by overheard by others floating in the vicinity. Then he leaned forward and said in a low voice, "It's said that in the underground, men are kept in cells with no light, barely any grub or water. They're kept there sometimes for weeks without any shoes. Broken glass is tossed around outside the cells so the men cut their feet to ribbons if they try to escape. With glass stuck into their feet like that, they can't run."

Sweat sprang out across Sage's forehead at the idea of weeks in the dark, surrounded by glass shards. Disquiet caused him to fluff his oar strokes. Pratt noticed and pounced.

"Hah! You think you're so smart. Cocky just like the rest of them, but I guess you know now that you got it plenty easy. You'll keep your nose in your own business if you know what's good for you."

Pratt settled back onto the bench seat, his arms folded across his chest in satisfaction. "And let's see you put some muscle into those oars. I'm paying you to get me to that ship sometime today."

Sage pulled at the oars, letting Pratt's gabbling wash over him, as his imagination wandered the underground, his mind's eye seeing that square-jawed young face, gaunt with hunger, making a desperate effort to return to his wife and baby. And, failing, as the glass shards stabbed deep into the bottoms of his feet, crippling him, thwarting escape. Sage felt prickling behind his eyelids and bit the inside of his cheek to drive the vision from his mind.

"Which crimp uses the glass?" he asked Pratt, in a voice that sounded steely calm to his own ears.

Pratt spewed another stream of tobacco juice into the wind which, in turn, flung it toward Sage. He managed to duck his head in time, never losing a stroke on the oars.

"Don't know." Pratt said, as his rheumy eyes involuntarily skittered sideways. He was lying. "Wouldn't tell you if I did," the old salt added. This time, his glare at Sage underscored the truth of that particular remark.

Neither the Sallie soldiers' off-key warbling nor the chaplain's answering harangue accompanied Sage's entrance–probably because Sage arrived late. Franklin already sat on the same rear bench. No one in the room stirred at Sage's entrance. Without faltering his exhortations the chaplain, however, momentarily fixed his attention on Sage. Sage dipped his head apologetically and slid onto the bench.

"I see you're looking more like one of us," Franklin said, acknowledging the flared-bottom dungarees and seaman's cap that marked Sage's transformation from the itinerant landlubber John Miner into the itinerant waterman Twig Crowley.

"I'm working on it, though I think Pratt will deafen me before I'm done."

Franklin chortled softly. Obviously, he knew exactly what Sage meant. The old bastard's endless jabber must be notorious on the waterfront.

In a whisper, trying not to move his lips, Sage informed the other man that the body buried in Astoria was that of the missing labor organizer. "The Chinese fisherman also said that the man's feet were sliced all over. Like he'd walked barefoot in broken glass. Pratt tells me that he's heard tell of shoeless men held in underground cells surrounded by broken glass." In the pause that followed that bit of information, both men stared at the floor as if it were possible to see glass shards glinting in the darkness below their boots.

Franklin nodded quickly. "Yep, and when I've boarded ships there at the mouth of the Columbia, men have shown me their cut feet, some of them cut so bad they have to keep their feet bare until they've healed. Not that they have any choice in the matter. They got cut feet, it means they were shanghaied and delivered aboard without their boots."

"Who does that?" Sage asked, feeling an angry knot bunch his jaw.

Franklin's and Sage's exchange seemed to distract the chaplain. For the first time, his flow of words faltered as he stared at them. Franklin smiled apologetically and waited until the chaplain regained his stride before answering, "The men and captains I talk to all claim that Kaspar Mordaunt, our self-proclaimed 'king of the crimps,' favors that particular tactic."

That name again, Kaspar Mordaunt. After what he'd been learning, Sage thought it would be pleasurable to give Mr. Mordaunt a taste of his own medicine. "God help him," Sage muttered aloud.

"Mr. Miner, you best not meet with me again. At leastways not out in the open like this. Somehow, my reports are still getting into the crimps' hands, and we can't discover who is working with them. I think I was followed here tonight."

"What did they look like, the men who followed you?"

"One is big with a smashed nose. The other is smaller, but I didn't see him good enough to describe his face."

"Do you think they're the ones who attacked you the other night?"

"Could have been. They're the right size."

Neither man spoke again. When the service ended, Franklin left first.

When Sage reached the street door, he remembered the problem of Matthew. Feeling silly, he leaned out the entrance to inspect the street. Sure enough, the boy was there. He lounged against a building corner a block away trying to look as if he belonged there. He wasn't succeeding. No one could mistake that red-topped, freckle-faced countenance for anything other than that of an eager, wet-behind-the-ears country bumpkin. Sage retreated. He pushed back into the building, startling Chaplain Robinson where he stood patting the shoulders of departing attendees.

"Forgot something," Sage muttered in explanation. The chaplain nodded.

Once inside the chapel, Sage spotted a door to one side of the dais. Passing through it, he found a large empty kitchen. Across that room another door opened onto the side street. He exited after first peering out to make sure Matthew had not shifted his position to cover that exit.

Tomorrow couldn't come soon enough. He had to get that boy out of his hair. Hopefully, Grace Kincaid had chores enough to keep Matthew busy until a week from Sunday.

SEVENTEEN

BEFORE CALLING IT A NIGHT, Sage needed to accomplish one more thing. It was time to make his first move toward switching employers. Sage mused that the thought of never again hearing Pratt's querulous voice was like imagining a toothache's absence before the tooth got pulled. Certainly, there'd be no missing Pratt. Yet, his short but intensive exposure to the man's personality would be a lasting memory. Not a bad thing, provided he never heard that voice again.

Men wearing a variety of garb and speaking every imaginable language crowded the smokey and raucous Erickson's saloon. Sage scanned the room looking for just two men. At last he spotted them. They sat at a table near the center of the room, looking like successful businessmen. Each wore a gold watch chain draped across his vest, a bow tie snug against his collar, and a spotless derby hat perched atop neatly barbered hair. Their commonplace appearance was fooling no one. Those seated at neighboring tables snicked nervous glances in their direction. As Sage watched, a staggering drunk sobered up enough to make a wide detour around the table where the two men sat. These were Kaspar Mordaunt's runners and everybody seemed to know it. They were also the men in the rowboat whose arrival frightened Pratt away from the *Clarisa's* anchor chain.

When they noticed Sage approaching their table, they stopped talking and leaned back in their chairs. Each man's expression was challenging, his lips compressed into a thin slash that said Sage should just go away if he wanted to avoid being hurt. Ignoring their blatant hostility, Sage slung a chair away from the table and sat. "Hello, gentlemen," he said, trying for a tone that conveyed nervous bravado. " Name's Twig Crowley. I'm just up from Frisco, looking for work."

"We know who you are. And you're lying. You got work. You're rowing that old tub, Pratt, around the harbor," said the one on the left. He sported a long nose that looked sharp as a knife edge.

Sage shook his head in disgust. "That I am, which should tell you why I'm looking for better work. Pratt's doing half the business he could 'cause he's into coddling them." Sage made a face of disgust. "Besides, he talks too damn much."

The sharp nosed one wasn't buying. "Look somewhere else. We don't hire just anybody like that old windbag Pratt does. And we ain't looking for scrawny fellas like you."

"I'm wiry and I'm tough," Sage said, a mulish tone to his response.

"Hah," said the second man. "There's more to this job than pulling oars. Fact is, I bet you can barely do that from the look of you." His voice sounded gravelly, as if someone had once nearly succeeded in cutting his throat.

Sage shoved his chair backward and stood, balling his fists as he did so. "How'd you like to eat those words, mister?"

From the corner of his eye, he saw a saloon bouncer leave his post at the door and lumber in their direction. Sage sat again and leaned across the table, making his voice carry over the drunken babble around them.

"I'm a hard worker and I don't ask questions. I do what I'm told. Anytime you want to see how tough I am, step outside. I'll have some surprises for you."

Neither man changed his contemptuous posture. Sharp Nose spoke again. "It doesn't work like that around here, Crowley. We've got no reason to trust you. Nobody knows you. But I tell you what. You bring us some men we can ship out. Then, maybe we'll be interested in working with you. There's a whaling ship we're trying to man, and nobody is willing to ship on her. She'll be leaving with tomorrow night's tide. She's just been patched up. Bring us a man for the *Karluk*, and well, maybe, there'll be place for you in our organization. Otherwise, don't bother us again." He dropped his crossed arms to lean forward across the table, speaking his next words with unmistakable menace, his eyes narrowed into brittle points. "And keep in mind one thing. We don't like informers. If that's who you are, then you're already a dead man."

"Got a problem here, Mr. Drake?" The sudden voice at his ear jerked Sage upright in his chair. The burly bouncer stood there, meaty fists on his hips.

"Nope, Amos. Mr. Crowley was just leaving," said Sharp Nose.

Sage stood, nodded at both men, and walked straight out of Erickson's. Once outside, he leaned against the brick front, letting the night air evaporate the sheen of sweat raised by the encounter. After a few seconds, he thought to look up and down the street for Matthew. The boy appeared to be nowhere in sight.

He needed to return to Pratt's, but first he wanted to mull over his rebuff by Mordaunt's runners. Apparently, a willingness to associate himself with Mordaunt's operation was insufficient to get him inside it. Mordaunt set high stakes standards: the devil's standards. No way Sage was going to shanghai a man onto a death ship. He'd have to think of some other angle.

Near Pratt's, Sage stepped into a seedy saloon called "Toppers." He wanted a beer and time to think before subjecting himself to Pratt's incessant yammering.

Inside Toppers there were no musicians, shrieking women, or roaring men—only the splash and swish of the bartender rinsing glassware and the quiet murmur of conversation. Sage welcomed the quiet after Erickson's. He stood at the bar, his foot on the rail, staring into the mirror and pondering the difficulty of trying to ingratiate himself into a band of cutthroats. As his beer mug reached half gone, his ear caught the word "Chink" sounding in a conversation at a nearby table. Sage strained to hear more.

"I guess you could say my philosophy is the only good Chink is a dead one," the man continued, "and, heh, heh, I've done my part in that regard. My way of seeing it, the Chinks need to go back to China and keep their mitts off what belongs to decent white men!"

Sage casually shifted position until he could look over toward that table as he swallowed beer, only to start choking when he recognized the man speaking. He looked like in his picture, only older, with lines etched deeper in a face grown more fleshy over the years. It was Homer LaRue.

Sage turned his back to the man and he tried to control his choking while his mind raced. The man who'd murdered Fong's relatives at the bottom of the Snake River canyon sat, like a giant toad, less than six feet away.

"Yeah, I guess he's done his part and then some." Sage muttered. He wanted to swing around, grab the man, and shove his teeth down his throat until he choked. The sudden surge of fury turned his stomach sour. He grimaced and put his mug down on the counter.

"Mister, is something wrong with the beer?"

Sage's eyes jerked to the bartender, who stood in front of him, looking mildly concerned. Sage looked down and saw that he still clutched the mug handle in a white-knuckled grip.

"No, it's fine. Just got took with a sudden bad thought. Fact is, pour me a second one," Sage said, slapping another nickel down on the counter.

As he nursed the second beer, Sage's mind snagged on the thought of Fong and the wading crane. What had Fong said? Oh, yes, something about the crane needing to be ready for whatever the current brings. Sage smiled grimly to himself, thinking, "Just might be some truth to Fong's advice." Here he'd walked into a saloon to wrestle with the problem of how to get close to Mordaunt. He could have picked any saloon in Portland. He could have never seen Homer LaRue. Instead, he was standing within a few feet of the man who'd murdered Fong's uncle and cousins in cold blood. Sage gripped the beer mug until his fingers hurt. He itched to pound the heavy mug into the man's head, forever stilling that ugly hateful voice.

Instead, Sage calmly sipped his beer until LaRue rose to take his leave. Setting down his mug, Sage left twenty-five cents on the counter for the barkeep and followed the man from the saloon. LaRue turned to the west with a slightly drunken stagger. Sage dropped back, staying close to the darkened buildings as he followed. Five blocks farther on, LaRue entered the glass doors of an older but decent hotel frequented by sales drummers. Sage watched as LaRue crossed the lobby and mounted the stairs. Seconds later, a gaslight flared to life behind a second floor corner window. Sage marked its location before turning back toward Pratt's boardinghouse.

He wasn't anticipating a restful night. Pratt made Sage sleep in the tiny alcove tucked behind the front door, on the canvas cot, even though the boardinghouse had bedrooms to spare. This was because, in the hours he wasn't performing as Pratt's rower or bellhop, Sage performed as Pratt's human guard dog. In that role, he vetted the sailors who staggered in and out at all hours of the night. And, like a guard dog, Sage snapped awake every time the door opened or a floorboard creaked, no matter how great his fatigue. The sleeping arrangement was one more thing he would not miss when he departed Pratt's employ.

The distant rumble of wagon traffic on nearby Burnside Street jarred his thoughts back to the mission and the unrelated problem of Homer LaRue. Life's current certainly delivered the unexpected. He needed a way into Mordaunt's organization so that he could find out for sure whether Mordaunt was responsible for Kincaid's death. And, if he was, by God, Sage would bring Mordaunt down. But how? And now, right in the midst of figuring out how to achieve that seeming impossibility, Homer LaRue's hateful self turns up. Darned if Sage knew what to do about him. Something, for absolutely certain sure. But what?

As that querulous question circled his mind, a pale wash of light began flooding the street. The full moon broke free of low-hanging clouds and lit his path. When he reached the corner of Fourth and Couch, a faint rustle on his left caught Sage's ear. Looking in that direction, he saw only a pile of garbage heaped against the side of the building. Then the pile moved and groaned. Wary of a trap, Sage approached cautiously. He used his booted foot to push aside wads of crumpled newsprint, collapsed freight boxes, and empty cans, uncertain whether the form lying underneath the trash was a human being. When he saw a hand, he began flinging aside the garbage, exposing the man's upper torso. Just as he dropped into a crouch, moonlight illuminated the man's face. It was Stuart Franklin.

"Oh, no," Sage breathed, "Oh, no."

Franklin groaned and his eyes fluttered open to focus on Sage's face. "Miner to the rescue again?" Franklin's faint voice carried a tinge of wonder that it was his new friend who crouched over him.

"What happened?"

"Two men," Franklin gasped out, speaking as if the two words wreaked painful havoc on his throat. He swallowed and started again, "Two men, the same ones as before. One big with a pushed-over nose. The other one was skinny, with a funny looking mustache." Franklin began to pant in pain, his eyes squeezing shut.

He reached out to clutch Sage's sleeve. "They were waiting . . . outside the Society. Can't understand. No one could know I'd be there. Chaplain Robinson let me in the back door. Someone . . . on our side must have told them. They thought I was dead, so they congratulated themselves on making the most of the tipoff. That means . . . you're in danger, too." He gasped again, his hand dropped and his head fell sideways.

"Lie still, Franklin. I'm going for help. I'll be right back," Sage told the unconscious man, He jumped up and ran toward the sound of wagon wheels rolling down Burnside, a street away. It was an empty delivery dray rumbling its way west, the driver atop his seat, slouched with weariness. Sage's arm waving and raised voice caused the weary horse to shy between its shafts.

"Mister, I need your help," Sage shouted, "A man's hurt real bad back down that street. I'll pay you to drive him up to the St. Vincent hospital on Westover."

The man straightened and reined in his horse. "Alrighty, sir. Whereabouts is this hurt man?"

"About a block down," Sage said, pointing back down Fourth. The driver gave Sage a searching look, obviously fearing deception. Then he turned the dray north on Fourth to follow Sage's running figure.

When they reached the dark form on the sidewalk, Franklin lay completely motionless. Sage kneeled at Franklin's side. He held his breath, fearing what he might find. A ragged inhalation by the injured man brought relief and spurred Sage back into action.

"We'll need to lift him into the bed of the dray."

"Just a minute, I got some sacking," the teamster said. "I'll spread it out so he'll have some cushioning." The driver ran to the back of the dray and returned to slide his arms under Franklin's legs.

Seconds later they were heading toward St. Vincent's, Portland's largest hospital. It sat above the city in the foothills of the western ridge. To Sage, crouched beside a man he'd come to consider a friend, the twenty-five blocks seemed endless. As the dray pulled up at the hospital entrance, Sage leapt out and ran inside. Within a minute he returned with two husky men, a stretcher, and a stout nun in a white apron who calmly issued orders to all of them.

Once the doctor and nurses were bent over Franklin, Sage rushed back to the driver who waited atop the dray, his tired horse still wheezing from that last uphill pull. When Sage reached paper bills up to the man, the driver waved them away.

"No, sir. I'll not take any money. Your 'thank you' is enough. I'm just grateful that the good Lord first brought you and then me along at the right time. There weren't too many empty wagons this time of night. I hope your friend makes it. He looks awful poorly."

Sage accepted the kindness. As the wagon with its weary horse and driver rumbled away down the dark street, Sage re-entered the hospital, where the new electric fixtures lit the room to an approximation of daylight.

After endless minutes, the doctor stepped from behind the curtain that shielded Franklin. "You a relative?" he asked.

Sage shook his head.

"You know how to reach any of his relatives? They might want to be here."

Sage remembered that Franklin's grandfather and brother were both dead. Wait a minute, weren't there sisters mentioned in the letter from Franklin's brother? If so, he wouldn't know how to find them. He said to the doctor, "Sorry, I just met him a few weeks ago and don't know him all that well."

"Hmm, well, if you can think of any way to find a relative, now would be the time."

"He's that bad?"

"There's a number of severe injuries to his bones and he's concussed. He's unconscious now, and it is anyone's guess if he'll ever come to consciousness again. If he has family, someone better tell them."

Sage said, "I'm pretty certain he has no one in these parts, but there's a man who knows him much better than I do. I'll go to his house and ask him."

"I wouldn't waste any time," the doctor said, his face grim in the unnaturally bright light.

EIGHTEEN

Sage ran five blocks, mounted the long steps and crossed the veranda to pound on the front door. Laidlaw must have been in the adjacent room because the front door opened immediately. The British consul stood there, with shirt collar open, suspenders loosened, a finger serving as placeholder in a leather-bound book.

"Adair! What's happened?"

Sage sucked air into his straining lungs before answering. "It's Franklin. They may have killed him."

"Oh, dear Lord, no. What happened?" Laidlaw asked, his face going flaccid with shock. He pulled the door wide open. "Come in, Adair, come in."

"No! We've got to get back to the hospital. The doctor wants to know if he has any relatives. You seem to know him best."

Laidlaw said nothing, only grabbed a coat and hat from an oak hall tree and headed out, pulling the door shut behind him.

As they hurried toward St. Vincent's, Sage told Laidlaw how he found Franklin and what the injured man said before he passed out.

"So Franklin said positively that the crimps have an informer in our midst?"

"That's what he said. He said the thugs talked about it because they thought he was dead."

Laidlaw said nothing. When he did speak, he changed the topic. "You still intend to find out who is responsible for young Kincaid's death? Even after seeing the consequences of going up against the crimps?"

"I'm more determined than ever." Sage told the consul how the cuts on Kincaid's feet pointed toward Kaspar Mordaunt as the crimp responsible.

"Mordaunt. That doesn't surprise me. He's the most powerful and brutal of the crimps. I heard tell that when he came up short of a man to ship out, he pulled his own son out of the schoolroom to fill the order. Anything for the blood money, that's Mordaunt. I wager he's the one behind the attacks on Franklin."

"Mordaunt will pay for what he's done," Sage vowed.

Laidlaw shook his head and gave Sage a rueful smile. "Oh, you might be able to prove his guilt to your satisfaction, but bringing him to justice–that's an entirely different matter," he said, "Mordaunt and his runners got most of the judges in this city elected. He's one of the ones I told you about, making a big party out of election days, driving drunken sailors from poll to poll in wagons loaded down with whores and kegs of beer. Some of the men vote ten times over."

"There must be some way to stop him," Sage insisted. He rejected the idea that justice couldn't prevail. That didn't fit his picture of how the universe operated. In a flash of insight he saw how the idea of justice related to Fong's repeated references to the need for "balance." Maybe that's it. Maybe, injustice throws the universe out of balance.

"Tell me again, what the doctor said about Stuart," Laidlaw said, prodding Sage out of his silent contemplation. So Sage told about the broken bones and concussion. After that, both men strode the final block to the hospital wrapped in silence. Within sight of its entrance, Laidlaw pulled Sage beneath a fir tree's low-hanging boughs. "Listen, Adair, there may be a way to get Mordaunt. While at the Cabot Club today, I learned that all Portland's judges, except Clarence Berquist, will be attending a statewide meeting down at Seaside. They'll all be absent for five days. And they're leaving Judge Berquist in charge."

"That's good?"

"Very good for our plans. As far as I know, Berquist is the only judge who refuses the crimps' help on election days. And he's found a crimp or two guilty in the past. As a result, those types of cases are now assigned straightaway to other judges. If you can find an honest policeman to make the arrest and believe me, that will be hard to do . . ."

Sage interrupted, "Not for me it won't," he said, immediately thinking of the stolid but reliably honest Hanke.

"Good, good. That's half the battle. If we can get the evidence. And if Mordaunt is arrested and taken before Berquist, there may be a chance. Mind you, it's just a chance, but it's the best one we'll have where Mordaunt's concerned."

Sage gave a confident nod even though he still had no idea how to get accepted into Mordaunt's operation. He couldn't shanghai someone onto the *Karluk* whaling ship. Not when that the old salt, Thimble, predicted it would soon sink. Admittedly there were times, in the course of his work for St. Alban, when Sage found himself being deceptive. But, he'd never strayed so far as to put an innocent man in jeopardy just to achieve some end, no matter how laudatory the goal. That idea stank. It was too much like the disgusting ploys promoted by that Italian philosopher, Machiavelli. Anyway, this was not the time to sort that out. Sage started to step out from beneath the fir tree, intent on reaching Franklin's side but Laidlaw's hand restrained him.

"No, Adair. You can't enter the hospital. They might be watching. If they see you with me and Franklin, you're a dead man for certain."

So Sage stayed beneath the tree, watching Laidlaw mount the hospital steps. Just as he reached the entrance doors, they opened and the Society's chaplain, Robinson, stepped out. The two men conferred, and then both re-entered the hospital.

❀ ❀ ❀

Next morning, when Sage stumbled out of the boarding-house door into bright sunlight, driven forward by Pratt's hec-toring, the street seemed empty. It wasn't until a familiar voice quavered, "Please, mister, a few coins for a hungry old woman," that Sage saw her hunkered down next to the stoop.

He paused, extracted a few coins, and dropped them onto her soiled palm. Pratt saw and started up. "You lazy son-of-a-gun! First you abandon your post at the door until all hours of the night, now you delay us by doting on some filthy hag. Well, I'll be damned!" Pratt pulled back a foot to kick the old woman who'd just spat on his shoe. "I'm not going to stand for that right on my own doorstep!"

Sage jumped between them, shoving Pratt away down the sidewalk as he shot the woman a warning look. She smiled sweetly and called after him, "I hope to see you soon, good sir."

Pratt snapped back an immediate reply, "If you're still here when we get back, I'll see that you do your spitting in the cala-boose, you old cow."

Mae Clemens cackled wildly in response to Pratt's threat.

The old crimp continued to fume as they walked. "Don't you ever let me see you giving beggars money on my front stoop again. You do that, and pretty soon they'll be thicker than the flies on that horse dung," he said, pointing to a steaming manure pile near the curb. "If you have so much extra money that you're giving it away, maybe I'm paying you too much . . ."

The yammering continued, but Sage let it flow around him like creek water around a boulder. Why had his mother shown up at Pratt's door? Sage understood her message. She needed to talk to him and soon. What about Fong? Why hadn't he carried the message? She'd worked the North End once before in pursuit of a murderer, but only something important would have taken her away from Mozart's to squat on the sidewalk in Portland's roughest district.

After a morning of rowing and a free lunch with beer, they returned to the boardinghouse for Pratt's customary afternoon nap. Within minutes of Pratt's first ripsaw snores, Sage strode out the door, up the street, into the tunnel and soon arrived in Mozart's third floor hallway. His mother waited for him in his room. She looked clean and tidy, her hair tightly controlled by its customary bun.

"What's the matter? What's happened?" he asked.

"Sergeant Hanke came by last night. He said that the folks on the east side of the mountains have no interest in capturing that man, LaRue."

"Fong knows?"

"Fong's the one he told. I just happened to be there and heard it."

"Where's Fong? Why did he let you go to the North End?"

"Don't be silly! He didn't know I planned to go down there. I didn't even see him." Tension made her voice sharp. "After Hanke told Fong the bad news, Fong left and stayed gone until just about an hour ago. That's one reason why I rushed out to find you this morning. I didn't know if he'd already done something and needed help."

"Did he say anything to you when he came in?"

"He assured me that he hasn't done anything yet, but there's no question that he intends to, and soon." She was as close to panic as he'd ever seen her. Not surprising. A powerful bond existed between his mother and Fong. Sometimes that bond irritated Sage because they seemed to enjoy ganging up on him, as though he were a befuddled, amusing kid.

"Where is he now?"

"Upstairs again, in the attic. With that damn hatchet." She hunched her shoulders in a shudder.

Sage stepped into the attic but remained just inside the door. He stood in the shadow looking toward the attic's center. There brilliant light streaming from the skylight fell onto the man who moved within its rays. His movements, unfettered by his loose cotton tunic and trousers, were fluid, as effortless as a fish gliding through water. The gleaming hatchet in Fong's right hand, however, belied any poetic flight of fancy. Its slashing blade shone as a blur of silver.

Fong paused, his back to Sage. When he spoke, his words sounded lifeless. "Mister Sage. Your mother told you Hanke's news of LaRue?"

Sage started at Fong's words. He'd thought he'd gone unnoticed. But then Fong always noticed everything—the subtle change in air currents when another entered the room, a bird touching down in the rooftop garden.

Sage pushed past his hesitation, "Yes, she came to the North End to tell me."

Fong nodded, "Put herself in danger. Your lady mother is fine woman and fine friend." He sighed and sat upon the pine floor, the hatchet close at hand.

Sage sat also and sought to lighten the moment by telling Fong of Mae Clemens's unladylike but heartening spit onto Tobias Pratt's boot. Fong didn't laugh, although his smile did reach his eyes for a brief flicker before winking out.

"Mr. Fong, I know I shouldn't ask this of you, but . . ."

Fong didn't allow him to finish, holding up a palm to stop the words. "No, Mr. Sage, do not ask me. Life has brought my uncle's killer to me. There is a purpose to this happening, one I must complete."

"But the law will call it murder. An execution of a white man by a Chinese man. You'll hang if they catch you!" The panic Sage had suppressed earlier when talking to his mother now roared out at full strength.

"I cannot help that." Fong's jaw clenched in a determination that Sage knew he could not change. Still, Sage tried.

"Mr. Fong, we, Mother and I, we can't continue without your help. You are so important to us. For our sakes, please don't do this."

"Lady wife will have a hard time, too, but she understands what I must do. She has given acceptance even though she hides tears," Fong said, his voice mournful.

"Then don't do it! We'll think of something else."

Fong snapped, "You don't think I have tried for many days to think of some other action? There is nothing. Nothing. LaRue must die. It is a matter of family honor. My family honor. You know nothing of that kind of honor, no white man does. Leave me."

"I do know. I want to help."

But Fong's face closed as tight as his fist. "No more talk, Mr. Sage. Leave me. Now." Sage stood. Before leaving the room he took a long look at the man sitting on the polished floor with the hatchet by his side. He wondered if that look would be his last.

NINETEEN

Mae Clemens waited at the bottom of the attic stairs, her long fingers clenched tightly together, deep worry lines around her mouth. Her eyes sought Sage's. He shook his head. Her hand covered her mouth, stifling a cry.

"He's not budging," Sage said, taking her elbow and leading her into his room.

"What are we going to do?"

"I don't know, something. We've got to do something. I saw him, you know. LaRue, I saw him."

"Where?"

"In Topper's saloon. He was bragging about killing Chinese. Afterward, I followed him to his hotel."

"Maybe you could tell LaRue to leave town, warn him that he's in danger. If he leaves, Mr. Fong can't take revenge against him."

Sage emphatically shook his head. "That is the one thing I cannot do, Mother. LaRue killed over thirty innocent human beings, and he brags about it. If I warned him, I doubt he'd go, I'd just put him on alert and make it more dangerous for Fong. But even if LaRue did leave, Fong would never forgive me. A person needs to believe that somehow, someday, there will be justice."

She clutched at his forearm, her strong fingers clamping down, as she said, "At least Fong would be alive. A dead man's friendship is mighty cold comfort."

He saw no point in arguing. He would not warn LaRue no matter what her argument. He'd spent hours debating with himself. He would not warn LaRue and he would not tell her where LaRue stayed so she could do it. Subject closed.

"Please tell me that you sent Matthew off to Milwaukie to help Grace Kincaid," he said to change the subject and because Matthew hanging about only added to his worries.

"Indeed I did. I gave him money and told him to fill her cupboards with food. I also told him to buy and chop at least three cords of wood so she won't have that worry this winter and to do whatever else she needed. He pedaled off on his bicycle this morning. Says he's going to ride it all the way out there. The prospect of a long distance pedal had him excited as all get out."

"Good, he'll be out of my hair. I swear. Everywhere I turn, I see him skulking along behind me. I suppose that he's figured out I wear disguises."

"I know he has, no question about that. Yesterday he asked me why you went around in different clothes. I told him that's how you helped people, like you did him, but to keep that strictly secret. 'Course, that only whetted his interest. He started peppering me with more questions. It forced me to get a mite sharp with him."

"Oh, that must have been real hard for you," Sage said, dodging a flashing hand swipe in his direction. He commented in a more somber tone, "So many people are in on our secret I'm beginning to think we can't call it one anymore."

"That reminds me, what about Lucinda?"

"What about her?" His tone sounded unexpectedly querulous to his own ears. He took a breath. "I mean, did she stop by or something?"

"Yes. In fact, she stopped by the restaurant late yesterday afternoon. We spoke for a bit. I told her you were working on something. But Sage, you need to see her. She seemed very sad."

"She understands."

Mae shook her head, saying, "Being understanding feels much better if you get the opportunity to show you do understand. I think she feels abandoned."

Irritation surged. "Look, I've got to get back before Pratt wakes up from his nap. Every minute of the day and night he's talking my leg off, never letting me out of his sight. The only time I have to investigate is when I can sneak out after he starts snoring,' Sage said, his tone heated. "There's just no time for me to visit Lucinda."

Mae Clemens sighed. "I've said my piece."

"Good." Sage dropped a kiss on her forehead. "Keep Mr. Fong company. And I'll try to figure out what to do. I'm thinking Fong will wait until nighttime to go after LaRue. Create some kind of kitchen crisis and keep him here for the next two days. Buy me some time?"

"To do what?" she asked.

"I wish I knew."

At the opening to Mozart's basement tunnel, Sage paused, a kerosene lamp in hand, studying its dirt floor and the stained bricks that formed its roof and inward-leaning walls. Usually as he sped along its thirty-foot length. He would tell himself that his mouth went dry because of the dust and that his heart thumped faster because of the speed at which he moved.

"This time, I can't play that game of self-delusion," he told himself. "Too much is at stake. It's time to conquer my fear of the dark. The answers are in the underground."

Despite this internal chiding, the entrance into the tunnel immediately triggered the terror that always seized him whenever his surroundings turned dark and musty. "I have to conquer this fear if I'm going to join Mordaunt's gang," he scolded himself, stepping forward, advancing slowly even though beads of sweat jumped onto his forehead in the tunnel's cool air. "I have no choice."

Sage was sitting on the boardinghouse stoop when Pratt woke from his nap and hollered for "Crowley." Within minutes they were heading back toward the docks and into the rowboat. "Now, this time we're meeting with the captain. Pretty good old boy. Treats the sailors fairly well and doesn't try to steal more than a reasonable amount of their earnings. I steer the sailors toward him whenever his ship's at berth."

"Steal their earnings?" Sage had begun speaking in short sentences so that Pratt couldn't interrupt before he finished the question.

"Yes, you idjit. You think all these ship captains are victims or something? Sailors forfeit their wages if they desert while a ship's in port. If the captain wants to keep those wages, he makes a deal. Points the man out to the crimp, pays the crimp a little bit and then that crimp makes darned sure that sailor misses the sailing. That way, the captain splits the wages with the ship owners and the crimp gets himself a man to sell."

Right. Sage remembered Laidlaw telling him of the practice. Worry about Fong was clouding his thinking, Sage realized. "Doesn't the harbormaster . . ."

"Harbor master, hell. He's more like the crimps' handmaid. He gets his cut, too. Makes more from the crimps than he gets from the State for doing his job, is what they tell me."

"But . . ."

Pratt shot a stream of brown tobacco juice into the wind so it blew toward Sage's face. Sage closed his mouth and ducked his head.

"Crowley, you ask too damn many questions. If you'd used that energy of yours for rowing instead of snooping, we'd get there a darn sight faster. I told you when I hired you, I'm not spending time training someone who wants to take my place. So you keep your yap closed and them pencil arms a-rowing."

The solution slid into Sage's thoughts during that dreamy interval between sleep and wakefulness. The canvas cot had long ago stretched into a gripping pouch that prevented him from shifting his position. But it wasn't discomfort that tipped Sage into wakefulness. Weariness prevailed over the pain of being trapped in one position throughout the night. No, it was the milk cart trundling by. The clanging cans signaled the day's beginning, penetrating his sleep. In that dreaming moment of near awakening the solution presented itself like a calmly uttered sentence.

He struggled upright to sit on the edge of his cot and study the solution from every angle. Its practical simplicity withstood wakeful scrutiny. It should work. He should have thought of it sooner. He hadn't because of his pressing need to get next to Mordaunt so he could avenge Amacker, Kincaid and Franklin and prevent further shanghaiing. But now a solution had seized him, full blown and ready for execution. Only his conscience presented an obstacle. Taking a page from Hanke's book, Sage did not lie to himself about the action he was considering. When it came down to it, though, he decided his conscience would just have to learn how to bear this particular burden. After all, to paraphrase Fong, would life have delivered this opportunity to Sage if it did not intend for him to exploit it?

Sage swung his feet onto the floor and reached for his trousers. The night before, Pratt said nothing about an early start. Unless the tide schedule demanded otherwise, the old man favored lying abed. That left a few hours for Sage to put his plan into action. He jumped up, pulled on his clothes and boots. Seconds later, he headed away from the boardinghouse toward the New Elijah Hotel, a few blocks away. Solomon might not appreciate a visitor at such an early hour, but Sage's intuition said that time was running out.

Solomon stood in the hotel kitchen, using a long-handled spoon to stir the savory-smelling contents of a cook pot. When Sage appeared at the kitchen door, Solomon let go the spoon, whipped off his big white apron and tossed it aside. Another man quickly stepped into his place before the stove. Grabbing a few biscuits and two mugs of coffee, Solomon led Sage into his apartment off the hotel lobby.

Once settled into leather arm chairs, Sage related to Solomon, Fong's Snake River story. Throughout the long story, Solomon sat motionless, his long hands steepled before his face, its high cheekbones making his face regal, like that of a tribal chieftain, though whether African or American Indian, Sage could not have said. This Carolina man could claim ancestry from both continents.

Solomon listened without speaking until Sage finished, after which he said, "My poor friend, such an awful tragedy for his heart to bear." His reaction was not surprising. Solomon and Fong had discovered an affinity and forged a friendship based on mutual admiration. The black man was one of the few men Fong quoted with regularity, along with Chinese sages, Confucius and Lao Tse.

When Sage spoke of Kincaid's death in the Columbia River and the organizer's widow and baby, Solomon's dark face softened and he seemed to gaze inward at yet another troubling memory.

"Always the mothers and the children," he said with a deep sigh, "Always the mamas and babies are left behind."

Having given Solomon the story, Sage made his request. "Fong said that the underground runs beneath the New Elijah, right below our feet."

Solomon nodded. "The underground is under most of these buildings in the North End and under some commercial buildings to the south," he affirmed, leaning forward, intent on making a point. "It's not just white men that are shanghaied using the underground. Seems like some captains have a real fondness for Negro cooks, galley hands and servants." Solomon's lips twisted with rueful bitterness. "We black folk have our own Judases who make a tidy living delivering up their brethren to the crimps."

"I understand that the business owners don't have much of a choice about whether to allow it to go on," Sage said. He spoke carefully, afraid of giving offense by sounding judgmental.

Again Solomon nodded and this time, he sighed heavily before saying, "The crimps came to me and offered me money. Somehow, I couldn't see myself, a deacon in my church, taking money so they could make other men slaves."

"The crimps let you refuse?"

"Oh, no. They didn't let me refuse. But I walled off a portion of the hotel's basement and put in a strong door that's bolted from this side. They can't enter the underground through my hotel kitchen. I told them that there were always too many folks about. Anyway, I promised we would stay inside the walls I built. It's a deal with the devil, but it is one I have to live with. I refuse any payment from them."

Sage paused, uncertain after that declaration, about how Solomon would react to his request. Still, the question needed to be asked. He told the man what he planned for LaRue.

Solomon's response came quickly, without hesitation, as if he'd already anticipated and considered Sage's request. "What you want to do makes sense. It seems like the best solution." Solomon stood up and walked to a large desk containing pigeonholes filled with papers. Ledgers were stacked high on its writing surface. Opening a drawer, he removed something and returned to Sage.

"You get into the basement through the kitchen, just inside the door. It's a sharp right turn. Come in through that kitchen door anytime the kitchen's open. I'll tell the kitchen help to keep their eyes to themselves and out of your business. Otherwise, you'll have to come through the lobby and ask for me." Solomon held out a shiny bronze key. "You will need this to get into the rest of the underground. A kerosene lamp hangs by the door this key opens. Take the kerosene lamp with you."

Sage reached out and took the key. The metal felt so icy cold that it stung his hand.

TWENTY

SOLOMON AND SAGE RETURNED to the kitchen. Solomon nodded toward a door that Sage opened. A flight of narrow wooden steps descended into the dark. Just inside, a kerosene lamp hung from a hook and a box of safety matches lay atop the ledge. Sage lit the lamp and started down. The oily smell of burning kerosene brought to mind the old whaleman, Thimble, and his dire predictions about the future of whaling. That turned out to have been a fateful meeting.

Once in the New Elijah's cellar, Sage raised the lamp high. Solomon's basement looked no different from Mozart's: provision boxes neatly stacked, scattered pieces of discarded furniture, and a single cot tucked into one corner, its blankets smooth and neat. A stout door stood midpoint in a wall that was about twelve feet out from the bottom of the stairs. Near it hung another kerosene lantern. Sage set his burning lamp down and crossed the room to unlock and slide open the bolt. As he slipped the key into the brass lock, his mouth went dry. But he lit the second lamp, opened the door and stepped across its threshold, pulling it closed behind him.

The musty smell hit him like a blow. With a shaking arm he lifted the lantern high so that its light pushed back the inky blackness to either side. After taking a final look at his surrounding, Sage twisted the lantern off. Immediately small gray spots seemed to swim into his eyes and he blinked rapidly to clear them. His lungs started heaving as if all the air were sucked away. Struggling to breathe, he felt fine particles of dust coating, then clogging, his throat. He began choking. The lantern handle became slick from his suddenly wet palm. Then his vision blurred red, as though the blood pounding in his heart were flooding his eyes. One thought overpowered all others: "I have to get out of here!" Sage whirled back toward the basement door, his free hand groping blindly for the door handle, terrified it was no longer there.

Once safe inside Solomon's cellar, Sage locked the door, extinguished the lantern with fumbling fingers and returned it to its hook. Snatching up the other lantern, he fled up the stairs as if one of Conan Doyle's hounds was snapping at his heels.

Pratt sat at the kitchen table, shoveling food in as fast as the cook heaped it onto his plate. "Finally hauled those lazy bones of yours out of bed?" he said. "Sit down and eat up. We have a lot to do today."

"Sorry, Mr. Pratt, I have to quit my job with you. I have some personal business I need to take care of," Sage said.

Pratt's matronly cook dropped tinware into the metal dishpan with a loud clatter. As Sage expected, Pratt's outrage was immediate and loud. "Why, you ungrateful whelp, Crowley. After everything I taught you, you're going to leave me high and dry? I could tell right from the beginning that you were a worthless so-and-so. 'Twig Crowley' my foot. Never believed that for a moment. I know the San Francisco Crowleys and you don't look nothing like them."

Pratt raised his voice to follow Sage as he went to collect his few belongings. "Don't you come crying back to me when you run out of money and need work. It'd be a cold day in hell before I'd hire the likes of you again."

Sage answered Pratt's invective under his breath while he stuffed his clothes into a duffle bag, "And it'd be an even colder day in hell, old man, before I'd think of working for the likes of you again."

Sage entered Mozart's through the underground tunnel and climbed the hidden stairway to the third floor. Once there, he began assembling a different kind of wardrobe. He packed a suit, bow ties, and white shirts into a leather-bound drummer's suitcase. Faint noises from overhead arrested his motion. Floor joists creaked as a slight weight moved across them. Fong was in the attic.

Sage hurriedly finished packing and then climbed the stairs to join him. When Fong saw Sage, a brief smile relaxed his otherwise tense face.

"Mr. Sage. I am glad to see you. I apologize for harsh words yesterday. I know you trying to help. I am glad for your friendship."

"Mr. Fong, no apology is necessary. You are confronting a very serious problem and you must have many conflicting thoughts. I would feel the same in your shoes."

Fong sighed aloud but changed the topic. "And you, what do you plan to do about murderer of young Joseph Kincaid?"

Now Sage sighed. "Solomon was good enough to give me access into the underground, but I don't how to use it. I panic the instant I step into the dark."

"Ah," Fong said. "I have been thinking on that problem of yours. I have an idea, but first we practice the form. All right?"

"Sure." Sage kicked off his shoes and pulled his shirt loose from his pants. "I'm ready." They moved through the one hundred and eight positions of the snake and crane, only to have Fong begin the series again as soon as they reached the end. After four repetitions they stopped.

"Tell me, how go your thoughts right now?" Fong asked.

Sage said the first thing that came to mind. "Empty, open, I don't know. Relaxed. No thoughts, really."

"Ah!" Fong smiled, as if Sage's words pleased him greatly. "That empty mind is how to control panic. I have taught you to move through snake and crane in your thoughts. To control panic, go back into underground, breathe through nose, keep lips shut with tongue touching roof of mouth. Do exercise form in mind over and over. Let no thought fix itself. Keep mind empty, like during exercise. This way, you will understand difference between what you fear and what exists. Remind self basement is not cave deep inside mountain."

Fong reached inside his tunic and pulled out a paper. He squatted and spread it open on the polished floor. Sage knelt beside him and saw a map of Portland's North End and commercial district. It showed the names of each street and each building. Here and there were x's. Fong's finger stabbed at one such mark. "Each x is way to escape from underground. See little tubes going from one block to next neighbor block? These are tunnels under street. Try to memorize. Maybe carry compass."

"Mr. Fong, how in the world did you get this?"

"Like I told you before, Chinese everywhere underground. They made this map that I buy from cousin. I wrote English street names on it."

Fong folded up the map and handed it to Sage, who said, "So, you think I should sit in the underground and perform the snake and crane exercise in my mind?"

"Yes, with light out. That is only way you will defeat panic. Every man has something that make him afraid. When fear make man unable to take action, then mind must be made empty so the person can tell difference between what real and what fear."

Sage cringed at the thought of sitting in that musty blackness, but he assented. "I'll do it. I can see how it might work. Anyway, I have no choice. If I can't go into the underground, I'll never get close to that crimp Mordaunt, and that's the only way I'll get proof against him."

"Good," said Fong. Then he hesitated before saying, "Now, Mr. Sage, I must tell you that I will not be here tomorrow night. So, please not take action then."

The words sounded insignificant but Fong's tone sent foreboding scrabbling up Sage's backbone. He faced it head on. "So, tomorrow you're going after LaRue?"

"If I wait any longer, he may leave, taking opportunity with him."

"I don't suppose that there's anything I can say to change your mind?" Sage asked, despite knowing the answer.

Fong shook his head. "We Chinese are strong believers in fate. Life send LaRue to me. I must act."

"You're saying that because Life has brought LaRue to you, you are obliged to take advantage of that turn of events?"

"That is it. You understand. Yes."

"Of course, life also delivers such opportunities to others, doesn't it?"

Puzzlement wrinkled Fong's forehead. "Why, yes, it does Mr. Sage. Has something happened in hunt for murderer of Kincaid fellow?"

Sage spoke lightly, "Nope. Just checking, wanting to make sure that your philosophy applies to us round eyes, as well as to wise men from China."

TWENTY ONE

FACED WITH THE NEED TO take immediate action, Sage, instead, found himself distracted. For the first time in days, Lucinda filled his thoughts. He needed to see her. Dressed in his gray morning suit, Sage strolled up the street, anticipating her keen interest and even keener observations when he told her what had been happening during the two weeks since he'd last seen her. He sniffed the air with pleasure. On late summer days the heat wafted fragrances from the flowers making fall's chill, with its eye-stinging wood smoke, unimaginable.

Sage paused, looking down at the bouquet in his hand, halted by a sudden realization. Lucinda, as madam of the fanciest parlor house in the city, might know a thing or two about shanghaiing. After all, her customers made money from it. "Why didn't I think of talking to her sooner?" he asked himself as he rounded the corner onto her block.

A shiny, black-lacquered open carriage stood at the curb outside her house. From half a block away, Sage saw the bordello's heavy front door swing open and Lucinda emerge, her afternoon dress the sky-blue color of her eyes. She wore a velvet hat of the same color on her gold hair, the hat's red feather curling against her pale face.

The tall, well-dressed man beside her offered her a forearm to hold. When they reached the sidewalk, he opened the carriage door and helped her in with a theatrical flourish. As the man seated himself, they exchanged words and Lucinda's laughter rang out. With a pang Sage realized that it had been too many days since he'd heard that sound. White-hot jealousy stabbed him. He thought she only laughed like that when she was with him. The carriage rolled north, leaving Sage staring after it. Lucinda never looked back.

When Sage arrived at the drummers' hotel, the clerk was effusive in his welcome since it was Saturday and the hotel was nearly empty. After receiving a key and instructions concerning the hotel's supper hour, Sage climbed the staircase. His clean room contained the unadorned factory-produced furniture usually ordered from the Sears catalogue. He didn't linger. Within minutes he was exiting down the rear staircase onto the sidewalk of the North End, garbed in rough clothes. His suit and sales case were left behind, neatly tucked away in the room's serviceable wardrobe.

All around, men leaned on stoops and buildings, ready for a Saturday night that would be followed by Sunday, that one day a week when it was futile to search for work. Sage lacked their anticipation of impending relaxation since his destination was the underground's stygian blackness. His determination to confront the terror that had gripped him ever since he was nine years old made his stride lengthen and quicken. Although the bright sunlight felt hot on his back, he shivered in anticipation of the dark that would soon envelop him.

The kitchen workers in the New Elijah Hotel glanced up when he entered but quickly snapped their eyes back to their work. Good. Solomon had followed through on his promise. Sage descended the stairs, noting that the lantern's fumes seemed to intensify in the stifling air below.

The brass key released the lock as smoothly as before, but the air streaming inward from the darkness smelled more fetid than he remembered. He resisted a nearly overwhelming urge to slam the door shut. Finally he did, but only after he passed through it.

This time, he breathed shallowly through his nose and lifted the lantern so he could study the floor joists and floorboards that formed the underground's ceiling. Openings in stone and brick walls led into unbroken dark. An overturned freight box sat in the dust a few steps away. He took a seat. After one last searching look and with a shaking hand, Sage twisted the valve handle until the lantern's flame fluttered and went out.

Blackness dropped like a heavy choking weight. He sensed that the stone walls were moving closer. His mouth fell open and his breath turned into short shallow gasps that seemed loud in his ears. A sudden prickle of sweat turned his skin into a magnet for the floating dust particles. The smell of decay drifted up from the dirt floor like a living thing.

"Whoa," he said aloud, trying to divert his thinking. "Snake and crane, Sage. Snake and crane." He closed his mouth and then his eyes to the blackness. In his mind he began envisioning the exercise. "First crossed hands, commence form, grasp bird's tail, single whip, raise hands, and step up . . ." As his imagination began to move him through the physical sensations of the exercise, his surroundings seemed to become less intrusive, receding into an amorphous threat that no longer pressed as close. Gradually, discrete aspects of his surroundings inserted themselves into his mind, but he allowed those thoughts to flow through and out, holding on to none of them, focusing only on the next form in the exercise.

He began to notice that not all of his fleeting impressions triggered fright. Overhead, he heard the scrape of a chair and once a woman laughed without restraint. A scuttle in the darkness, the screech of a rodent in mortal terror and the yowl of a cat said life existed here beneath the city's buildings. The distant rumble of carts, drays, wagons, and carriages issued from a tunnel where it burrowed eastward beneath a street. From that direction, a faint breeze brushed against his cheek, carrying the tangy scent of the river. None of these thoughts, nor the darker ones, anchored in his mind. Instead, they came, caught lightly, loosened and passed without breaking his concentration on the exercise.

Finally, something occurred that did abruptly break his concentration. First he heard the scuffling sounds of feet, then a light glimmered in the neighboring basement beyond the arch in the stone wall. As he watched, a man holding a lantern and, talking softly to two other men, moved into view. From his vantage point, cloaked by the dark, Sage experienced a sense of power and control. His already dilated eyes watched the three men as their shadows grew on the walls and floor. They passed in front of him, completely unaware they were being observed. Once they were past and the impenetrable darkness returned, Sage realized that he no longer feared it. Instead, he felt bemusement and a new awareness that the underground offered opportunities and a haven, if he could learn it well.

Fong was right. This murky space beneath the buildings, roofed over by beams and floorboards, was but thinly separated from the life above. These interconnected basements beneath the city were not rock tunnels carved through a mountain's dark, resisting heart. Dirt and dark were the only similarities and those were superficial.

He rose from the freight box and stretched his arms overhead, his body relaxed, his mind empty but filled with expectancy, as if welcome information might arrive at any moment. His fear of this place was gone. He doubted it would return.

On his way back to the sales drummers' hotel, Sage stepped into a pharmacy. He waited until the other customers left before he approached the pharmacist. His request set the man's hands to trembling. A wash of sweat trickled down the creases in his face and his faded blue eyes wouldn't look directly at Sage. Instead, he looked toward the street, his eyes merely twitching in Sage's direction. Initially, he feigned outrage. Sage kept adding to the pile of coins on the counter until the man's protestations dwindled. Finally, greed overcame scruple. Sage left the pharmacy carrying what he'd come for, pleased with his afternoon's successes. So pleased that he never saw the red-haired boy on the blue bicycle, pedaling furiously around the corner the minute Sage stepped out the door.

The drummer hotel's tired mattress folded him in and Sage napped until the late afternoon. Awaking, he unfolded the map of the underground and spent the next hour tracing its lines until he could draw it from memory. He hoped the map would give him the edge he needed. At six o'clock he descended into the dining room, ready to partake of the hotel's complimentary supper, his stomach gurgling that he'd not eaten the entire day.

Since this was a drummer's hotel, food was served boardinghouse style. The single long table could seat thirty, but just eight men clustered in chairs at its farthest end. Heaping platters of food were passing among the guests. Sage slid into a seat just in time to receive a half-empty bowl of mashed potatoes.

Congenial conversation around the table accompanied the meal. Sage and the man next to him found that they shared a number of experiences and attitudes. Both had worked in gold fields, both had traveled extensively and both had the same thoughts about foreigners. So, they chatted affably throughout supper.

"Say," Sage said to the man, "I promised a potential client I'd meet him at a nearby saloon and buy him a few beers in exchange for his having looked at samples of my company's notions. How about you coming along with me? I'm not real confident he's going to show. I'll buy you a drink. We'll talk a bit with him if he does show, and then we can find ourselves something interesting to do after that. What do you say?"

The man didn't hesitate. "That sounds good to me. I'll just go pick up my hat, and then I'm ready to go."

Sage pushed back from the table and stood, saying, "Don't know where my manners are. My name's John Miner."

The other man also stood and extended his large hand. "Pleased to meet you, Mr. Miner. Mine's Homer LaRue."

TWENTY TWO

SAGE AND LARUE STROLLED TOWARD the Heidelberg saloon and Sage's nonexistent customer. The big man, oblivious to Sage's preoccupation, talked on with little prompting. Sage suddenly realized LaRue had hit upon the topic of interest.

"Look, there's another one. A man hates to see those damn celestials. He looks like a scrawny bird, trotting down the street on his skinny legs with those big baskets slung across his shoulders. It's like living in some damn foreign place. Haw! There's another one. That's the other thing. Everywhere you look, there's another one of them, just like cockroaches. Don't you agree, Miner?"

"Well, this town does have an abundance of Chinese," Sage responded. "Not used to seeing that back East, except in New York. I hear tell that, because of the Gold Rush and railroads, there's more Chinese here in Portland than in any other city, except San Francisco."

LaRue hawked, and spat before continuing, "Sure, and they have a whole different viewpoint from any white man. That's the problem. And there's no getting away from them. They don't just stay in the cities. Oh, no. They have to push into everywhere. It makes me sick."

"Oh, you've seen them elsewhere? Outside the cities, I mean?"

"Hell, yes. Fact is, I come across a whole mess of them once. They were crawling around the bottom of a river canyon in the middle of nowhere like a bunch of ants. I like to tell you, I about dropped my teeth when I looked over the edge and saw them, busily stealing our gold."

"They took over your mining claim?"

"Not *my* mining claim, Miner, *our* mining claim. White men's gold. This is white man's country and there they were, stealing our gold. I can't believe the government let them do it!"

"So, did you try to stop them?"

"Try to stop them, hell." LaRue stood stock still, clapping a hand on Sage's arm, forcing him to halt. He leaned close to Sage's face—so close that Sage felt the warmth in the breath accompanying LaRue's next words. "I stopped them in this life and sent them into that celestial kingdom they talk about, if you get my meaning, heh, heh. Fish in a barrel. Fish in a barrel."

Sage allowed his voice to falter. "You killed them?"

LaRue straightened and smiled widely. "Let's just say none of them climbed out of the canyon and none of them floated away in any boat."

"How many?" Despite knowing the answer, Sage's throat constricted, squeezing the question into a whisper.

Evidently believing Sage felt a need for secrecy, LaRue also lowered his voice. "I hear tell they numbered close to fifty. 'Course, I wasn't alone, but I took care of more than my share."

Sage shook his head, which LaRue chose to interpret as a shake of wonder. "It is amazing, ain't it? But that's what a few white men with good rifles can do. I could tell you a few other things I've done that'd make your jaw drop, heh, heh."

"I bet you could, Mr. LaRue," Sage said, hoping he wouldn't hear about those other things. As far as Sage was concerned, the man's perfidy was pretty much established.

Just then, they reached the door to the Heidelberg saloon. A small dog ran up to them, stood on its hind legs and began to twirl, its tiny paws patting the air. LaRue's foot shot out, caught the creature on its belly and flung it at least five feet. The beggar to whom the dog belonged snatched up the whimpering animal and turned to LaRue, his voice a whine. "Why'd you kick little Bucko, mister? He weren't hurting nobody. Just doing his best to make us a little money."

"Keep that mongrel cur away from me," LaRue snarled. He pushed open the saloon doors and disappeared inside without a backward glance.

Sage paused to look at the dog as it frantically licked its master's face, its brown eyes bulging in fright. "He going to be all right, do you think?"

"I guess so." The old man gently prodded the little dog's belly. The dog didn't cry out. Instead its pink tongue kept licking its owner's stubbled chin. The old man looked at Sage, tears in his bloodshot eyes. "Why'd your friend kick little Bucko like that?" he asked.

"He's no friend of mine," Sage said between gritted teeth. He emptied his pockets of silver coins and dropped every one he found into the old man's hands before following LaRue through the swinging doors.

When LaRue began drinking it was as if his leg turned hollow. Of course, only Sage bought the drinks. LaRue claimed to have left his wallet behind. The more LaRue drank, the more voluble he became.

"Let me tell you, Miner, about the time five of us got drunk down in ole Mexico and hijacked a wagonload of pretty senoritas on their way to a convent. Those Mexican jails are hell holes. Skinny guy like you would have a hard time surviving one."

"Food bad?" Sage kept his tone eager and ignorant.

"Food bad, bugs bad, heat bad, dirt bad, but worst of all is your fellow jailbirds. I ended up breaking two of them's legs and another three's arms before they learned to leave me be."

"So, you're pretty tough?"

LaRue pursed his lips as if he'd bitten a lemon. "They don't get no tougher. I learned to be tough to survive, ever since my pa turned me loose at ten years of age. Said he didn't want the bother no more. Sometimes, a boy has to become a man real fast."

The big man leaned forward to say, "Miner, there ain't nothing I can't handle. I can wrestle a mountain lion, punch some cows and please a passel of women, all before breakfast." He leaned back in his chair and drained his glass before plunking it down on the table with a thump and a belch.

"Think you could handle being on a whaling ship?"

"Ha! That'd be a stroll in the park for someone like me. I hear tell a man just lays about till a whale's spotted."

LaRue wobbled to his feet and headed off in the direction of the toilet, his exaggerated swagger sending him against chairs, tables, and patrons who didn't bother looking up.

Sage watched the man disappear, then signaled the bartender for two refills. Once the glasses arrived on the table and the bartender was distracted by a customer, Sage tipped a small brown bottle's contents into one of them. He gently swirled the glass to mix the liquids.

LaRue returned, his brows knit in concentration as he fought to keep his balance. Flopping down onto the chair, he commented, "I expect you're having a hard time taking in all that I've told you. Salesman drummers like you don't meet a man like me too often." His words weren't slurred and the man remained too alert.

Sage watched LaRue drain the glass sitting before him. "That's for sure," he agreed, while thinking, "Thank God, this farce is nearly over." Out loud he asked, "So, LaRue, you figure there isn't anything you can't handle? You ain't afraid of dying?"

"Thass right, my man," LaRue replied, a slur wrapping itself around his tongue for the first time. As if searching for another drink, his head swung around like a stunned bovine's. His fingers grabbed the table's edge to steady himself.

Sage got to his feet. "Say, LaRue, I know a better place, one that attracts the ladies. How about we move on to there? I don't think that customer of mine intends to show."

LaRue belched before saying, "Yeah, sure, thass be fine." His mouth was now slack and his tongue so thick that he mumbled. Sage assisted the bigger man to his feet, draping LaRue's heavy arm across his own shoulders and turning him toward the door. The two stumbled their way out of the saloon and into the street.

The last ten feet to The New Elijah's kitchen door almost proved Sage's undoing. LaRue's legs were collapsing with inconvenient frequency. The two men fell, more than walked through, the hotel's kitchen door and down the cellar stairs. Sage didn't look at any of the New Elijah's kitchen workers.

❀ ❀ ❀

Erickson's saloon pulsed with noise, driving all thought from Sage's head when he entered it an hour later. On the stage, bar girls were high-kicking in a raggedy version of the French can-can dance. Catcalls came from the balcony above, its railing lined with toffs in fancy clothes. The girls, aiming to please, lifted legs and skirts higher.

Amid the noise, Mordaunt's two men sat at the same table where Sage had last seen them. Once again he approached, slinging a chair around to their table and sitting down. They looked away from the scene on the stage, amusement leaving their faces when they saw him.

"Back again, Crowley?" asked the sharp-nosed runner.

"Thought I'd see how things were going with manning that whaler."

"That's none of your business."

"Seems to me that you made it my business last time we met," Sage said before asking again, "So do you have a full crew?"

"Nah, we're short a couple." This reply came from the gravelly voiced runner.

"Maybe I can help you."

Gravel-voice looked interested, "Oh, you thinking of signing on?"

Out of the corner of his eye, Sage watched speculation twitch across the face of the sharp-nosed one.

"No, not me," Sage said, "But last time I spoke with you gentlemen, you indicated that if I were to find you someone for the whaler, there might be a berth for me in your organization."

Sharp Nose took over once again, this time his face expressed disdain. "You telling us that you have someone for the *Karluk*?"

"I don't believe we've been introduced, and since I'm interested in doing business with you, I'd like to know your names. Mine's Twig Crowley." Sage held out his hand.

Sharp Nose reluctantly stretched out his own. "Mine's Drake. And my partner here is Fogel."

"Well, Mr. Drake and Mr. Fogel, I do have a man for you. You just have to pick him up and transport him to the ship. He'll need a little help. He got tangled up with Dr. Baker's Delight.

"Hmm," This time Drake didn't suppress the speculation in his face. "How long ago did he and Dr. Baker meet?"

"Oh, I'd say about an hour ago."

Fogel laughed. "That means he'll be out for at least another four hours. We don't have to rush him to the ship right away."

"A little less is what I figure. He's a mighty big one."

"Wait a minute. He ain't an Indian, is he? Or some cripple or old drunk?"

"I know better than that. This one is big and white. He claims to be strong as an elephant and twice as mean."

"Ha! We've heard that. They ship out and come back singing a different tune after a season fighting the arctic snow pack. Come to think of it, most of them don't come back to sing at all."

Drake's and Fogel's mirthless cackles made Sage want to edge his chair away from the table. "So, what do you say? Think you might be interested?" he asked instead. This was it. They either swallowed the bait and got hooked now, or he'd have to come up with a whole different approach. He caught himself praying but squashed that impulse. His mind's ear could hear his mother's voice chiding him that it wasn't a proper thing to spend prayer on.

Drake twitched his upper lip as if he were trying to itch his nose. "Depends what you're wanting for him."

"Not a cent. I just want a chance to prove myself with your organization."

The two men exchanged a calculating look before Drake nodded.

"All right Crowley. We can't promise nothing. You take us to our new whaling man and we'll introduce you to our boss. If he agrees, we'll take you on."

"Sounds fair . . ."

"Good evening, boys," a voice slurred from somewhere above the table. They'd been so intent on the discussion that they'd failed to notice the young man who now stood over them. He wore a fine broadcloth suit, displayed a large ruby ring on his pinky finger and had his face twisted in a drunken sneer that made him ugly. Clearly this was a toff descended from the balcony to slum on the ground floor.

Drake's eyes narrowed to glittering slits, but the arrogant young man didn't seem to notice as his next words showed. "I got a message for your boss, Mordaunt. You tell him that I really, really, really don't appreciate him sending messages to my family's home demanding money."

"Oh, you afraid your papa might get a little upset to learn that his baby son is a deadbeat?" Drake asked, reaching for his glass of whiskey on the table.

The drunk's hand reached out and swept the glass off the table, sending whiskey splattering across Drake's chest.

Sage slid his chair back, certain that the young man would soon die. He needed to avoid getting tangled up in the impending ruckus.

Drake surprised him. The man's only reaction was to pull a white handkerchief from his coat pocket and dab at his vest.

The young man blinked as if startled sober by what he'd just done. Then he brazened it out. "You show some respect for your betters! And you tell Mordaunt that he'll get his money when and if I feel like it and not before. I'll not have a man of his ilk pushing himself into my family's home, in person, in letters or in the likes of slow-witted lackeys like the two of you!"

Fogel spoke for the first time, his voice a low growl. "Seems to me, if you are too good to be involved with Mordaunt, you shouldn't have borrowed money from him."

"He's damn lucky someone like me is willing to do business with him and pay those damnable interest rates he charges."

"What exactly did you mean, someone of Mordaunt's

'ilk'?" Drake asked, the words spoken with cold precision.

"Everybody knows how Mordaunt gets his dirty money. He's a parasite and a crook."

Drake's lipless gash of a smile would have frozen any sensible man. "Looks like your papa hasn't told you where he gets his money, sonny boy. Where do you think the money came from to buy that fancy suit of yours?"

The young man flushed and his fists clenched. "If you were a gentleman I'd call you out into the street and teach you a lesson. But seeing as how you aren't a gentleman, it'd be a waste of education because you couldn't begin to learn." That said, he turned on his heel and stumbled off through the crowd.

The three men at the table watched him go. Fogel cleared his throat. "Don't think Mordaunt's going to take kindly to young Mr. Gordon's message."

"I sure hope not," said Drake. "I intend to get some kind of satisfaction from this whiskey bath he gave me."

"Did you say 'Gordon'?" Sage asked.

"That's right. That piece of well-dressed manure was Robert Gordon, heir to Earl Gordon' s fortune. His only son, matter of fact. Even worse than his father, when it comes to thinking his crap don't stink. And he's a blowhard to boot. Gets on Mordaunt's nerves he does," finished Drake with a speculative smile.

Sage remembered Gordon's bragging in the Cabot Club, saying he knew everything when it came to North End activities. Sage doubted very much that papa Gordon knew his own son was courting serious trouble down here among the North End's socially inferior "rabble."

TWENTY THREE

Sage met Drake and Fogel in an alley that had a doorway opening off it into the underground. Fong's map, with its x's, had identified the entrance and it was a simple matter for Sage to break the lock and replace it with one of his own.

Like him, the other two were now wearing overalls. Drake carried a kerosene lantern.

"You got him stashed right below here?" Fogel rasped.

"Near here," responded Sage. His muscles still remembered the work of dragging a limp LaRue across a number of basements and then erasing all the drag marks. He'd wanted to make certain there'd be no backtrack to the New Elijah.

When Sage entered the underground with Drake and Fogel, he felt only a sense of comfortable familiarity. He shuffled through the dust toward LaRue, slightly ahead of Drake's light. His only fear came from the threat posed by the two men following his lead. After ducking under the low arches between buildings, following tunnels beneath streets, and making unnecessary turns to confuse their sense of direction, Sage stopped and pointed toward a motionless figure lying against a damp stone wall.

Drake raised his lantern, moving its light along the length of the snoring body. "Well, Crowley, it appears you told us true. He's a big one and seems sound of limb. It will take a block and pulley from the main yardarm to hoist him aboard the *Karluk*. Sure you didn't give him too much of the Doctor's Delight?"

"Given his size, I'm more afraid that I didn't give him enough and he'll wake up before we get him aboard the ship."

"We got ways of dealing with those kind of situations," Drake said, putting his lantern on the dirt floor so that their shadows flowed up the surrounding stone walls. He removed a leather-covered blackjack from his pocket and slapped it in his palm. Sage moved a step outside the pool of light. Drake continued looking at LaRue, but Sage sensed Fogel moving, sandwiching Sage between the two of them so that he could see only one at a time. Drake's eyes flicked from the still form at his feet into the darkness behind Sage. He stepped toward Sage just as Fogel's footsteps scuffled behind him. Sage envisioned a companion to Drake's blackjack in Fogel's raised hand.

Sage's face must have shown his train of thought because Drake's thin lips stretched into his mirthless smile. "Now, Crowley, we told you that the *Karluk*'s short two men. You delivered one. You wouldn't want us to disappoint her captain, would you? Besides, you and your big friend here will have so much to talk about when he wakes up."

Drake's eyes jumped, signaling that he was about to spring forward. Sage dropped onto his hands while his right leg swept out to catch the lantern, dousing its flame and sending it clattering into darkness. Sage dropped further and rolled, following the lantern's path. As he did so, he heard the "humph" sound of two bodies colliding in the dark. Cursing filled the basement. Upright again, Sage snagged the lantern handle as he moved away from the two men and into a niche he'd discovered earlier. He'd already practiced how to use its configuration to throw his voice straight out to bounce against another wall and back to them. He didn't think they would be able to determine his location when he spoke. Just in case, his groping hand found the club he'd hidden there earlier.

"You busted my nose. You lowdown scum, Crowley," whimpered Fogel.

Drake's voice snarled in the dark, "You damn idiot! You ran into me, not Crowley. Shut your trap! I need to hear where he is!"

Sage smiled in the darkness, waiting for them to quiet. Fong once said "tricking enemy into attacking self was fun." It hadn't been intentional, but Fong was right. It felt satisfying to cause them a bloodied nose and a few bruises with so little effort. Resolving to keep the gloat from his voice, he turned away to bounce his words off a nearby wall, "Seems to me that I've won this round, boys. You got my friend here for the *Karluk* and maybe a little embarrassment that your boss doesn't need to know about. You just recommend me for the job and we'll be even. Like I told you, I don't want a cut from this delivery," Sage said.

"Recommend you, hell," came Fogel's rasp accompanied by a shuffling of boots through dust, blundering in a direction away from Sage. "I find you, you're going to be shipped out as a dead man on that damn whaling ship."

"Fogel!" Drake's sharp voice brought the scuffling boots to a halt. "If you don't want to stumble around down here for the rest of the night, you better shut up. Unless you're carrying a lantern or a candle somewhere in your coveralls that I don't know about."

"Nah, I just have a few matches." Fogel sounded subdued.

"So, that's all you want, Crowley?" Drake asked. "You just want us to tell Mordaunt he should take you on? What's to stop us from putting a knife into your ribs, first chance we get?"

Sage had asked himself the same question earlier, while he was thoroughly exploring this section of the underground. He was ready with an answer. "Nothing at all. But I figure that being the new man, I should pay the both of you a little training fee as we go along. Besides, Drake, once you see me work, you will think I'm an asset. You strike me as a smart man who knows how to look out for his own best interests." Sage didn't bother flattering Fogel. Drake was the leader.

Near silence greeted Sage's proposal, the only sound being LaRue's ragged snores from where he lay against the wall. For the first time when Fogel spoke, his words were something other than derisive or threatening. "A training fee? I never heard of no training fee for runners."

Since Drake didn't jump to hush his companion, Sage explained further. "Well, I'm just calling it that. What I'm saying is that whatever Mordaunt pays me, I give you five percent—each."

"Fifteen," said Drake.

"Ten," Sage countered.

"Deal. But you better not give us any cause to think you're up to something or try to cheat us or the deal's off. You got that?"

The menace in Drake's voice made Sage decide that, deal or not, he'd make sure that Drake never got in behind him. He said nothing, though. Instead, he stepped noiselessly out from the niche, moved in the direction of the men and rolled the lantern toward them. "There's the lantern. I'm sure Mr. Fogel's match will light it. You men can haul your new acquisition to the *Karluk* on your own. I'm sure you understand why I can't stay to help. But I'll meet you at ten o'clock tomorrow morning on the Couch Street wharf so you can take me to your boss."

That said, Sage moved swiftly away from them, not waiting for an answer. Despite it being pitch black, his shoulder bones tried to meet each other in the middle of his back. He could imagine one of the men deciding to throw a knife on the chance it would find its target.

Sage arrived at the Couch Street wharf the next morning just before ten o'clock. The sun was already high in the pale summer sky. Drake and Fogel were late, making him wait on the wharf, but he didn't mind. He used the time to ponder. He'd spoken with Fong and his mother the night before but had said nothing of Homer LaRue.

Fong was distracted. Sage was forced to repeatedly say Fong's name just to pull him back into their conversation. Sage's mind had ambled elsewhere, too. Despite knowing the man wasn't worth a canteen of spit–one of Mae Clemens's harshest judgments–Sage still felt a tinge of guilt when he thought of LaRue being doomed to sail into the whaling grounds on a death ship.

This morning, as Sage waited for the two men, he stared into the cold water flowing past on its journey to the ocean. Sage considered whether a difference existed between guilt and remorse. He definitely felt guilty about the fate he'd engineered for LaRue. Yet, given a choice, he'd rather live with that guilt than undo what he'd done. Simply put, he felt no remorse. He would do the same thing again. Why? Because LaRue was a despicable human being. That gloating voice, bragging about killing Fong's friends and relatives, would forever plague Sage's memory. Anyway, the outcome now lay beyond Sage's control. Life had delivered LaRue to Sage and he had acted as best he could to protect a good man. Relief was mostly what he felt. Relief because Fong was safe. Relief because the ultimate decision over LaRue's fate now rested in hands other than his own.

Those and other thoughts chased themselves around and around until the arrival of Drake and Fogel pulled Sage back into the task of surviving the present. Neither man's greeting was friendly. Not surprising. Fogel's eyes sported purple-black shiners on either side of a swollen nose. Drake had a faint bruise in the middle of his forehead.

Drake lit a cigar, spit out a bit of tobacco and said, "Mordaunt says he'll give you a try but you better give us that training fee like you said or we'll make you wish you never met us."

Sage nodded, asking, "How'd you explain Fogel's nose?"

Fogel scowled and Drake answered. "We sure the hell didn't tell him that we ran into each other." He started walking, leaving Fogel and Sage to follow. The three of them set off for Mordaunt's office in the North End. As they reached the office, a big man bustled out of the door, almost knocking the three men off the steps. He neither apologized nor acknowledged their presence. Which was fortunate since the rude man was Earl Gordon, the very man Sage saw while in the company of James Laidlaw at the Cabot Club. Even though it was unlikely Gordon would recognize him in his seaman's duds, Sage turned his face away until the man rounded the corner.

Once indoors, Sage couldn't help but notice that the carpet before the desk was just the right shade of blood red to hide the real thing. Kaspar Mordaunt lounged in a leather chair, his expansive posture a study in satisfaction. That impression was momentary because Mordaunt snapped upright in his chair as they entered. By most standards, he would be called handsome—straight nose, dark eyes, a luxuriant moustache. But a more studied look revealed cruelty in the narrow mouth and in dark eyes that were as lifeless as obsidian.

"Did you round up the two men before the whaler sailed last night?" Mordaunt's voice came out in a low menacing growl.

"Yes, Mr. Mordaunt," Drake quickly replied. "Thanks to help from Crowley, here. The one he got us brought top dollar. 'Cause he was so big, the captain said he could do the work of two men." As he spoke, he jerked his thumb in Sage's direction.

Mordaunt slowly examined Sage, then said, "We'll see." He turned his attention back to Drake. "Captain Hambley of the *Calypso* is looking for a cabin boy. Won't bring much in return for our effort, but it's the first time Hambley's been in this port, and I want him to get the habit of coming to me."

Drake was again quick to respond. "Cabin boy won't be too hard to find. I've already got my eye on a young fella, as a matter of fact."

"See that he's healthy. The *Calypso* is sailing in two days," said Mordaunt.

"Say, wasn't that Mr. Gordon we saw coming out of here, Mr. Mordaunt? Did he come to pay off his son's debts?" Fogel spoke for the first time.

Mordaunt's eyes narrowed and his face twisted with sudden fury. "What do you mean by questioning me or talking about business in front of a stranger?" Mordaunt half-rose out of his chair, reaching for a brass-headed cane leaning against his desk. "You know better than to open your damn yap!" Fogel beat a swift retreat, backing toward the door.

Mordaunt seemed to reconsider his outburst and relaxed back into his chair. "As a matter of fact, boys, that was indeed, Mr. Earl P. Gordon. And no, he didn't come to pay off his son's debts. That's a separate matter we'll take care of ourselves. No, Mr. Gordon came with a special invite for me. You boys are looking at the new precinct captain here in the North End."

Sage barely heard Drake and Fogel's congratulatory murmurings to their boss. The establishment was rewarding this murderer with a plum political position? He bit his lower lip to control his tongue. Then his mind began racing. As a precinct captain, Mordaunt would rub shoulders socially with the very men who patronized Mozart's restaurant. That meant the land shark would visit Mozart's, which in turn meant Sage faced the possibility of Mordaunt noticing a physical resemblance between the crimp's runner Twig Crowley and the urbane restaurateur, John Adair. As Adair, Sage might avoid such a meeting. But for how long?

Mordaunt was smiling at Sage, his lips stretched into a shark's grin. "No congratulations from you?" he asked.

Sage started, then recovered. "Why, I guess it's taking me a minute to find the words. No boss of mine has ever been an important man in town. For sure, I congratulate you."

Mordaunt must have liked Sage's answer because the shark smile widened. Still, Mordaunt's tone remained testy. "We'll see if I'm your boss, Crowley. My boys convinced me that you might be an asset, especially since you managed to plant a good one on Fogel here." Sage felt Fogel bristle behind him. Apparently, Drake had used the fact of Fogel's black eyes and broken nose to obtain Mordaunt's agreement to take Sage on as a runner.

Mordaunt continued, "But then, it might have been just luck. You don't look like you can do much. I'll tell you right now—and you listen good. If I take you on and you don't produce or you pull something tricky, you're going to be sorry that you ever met me or my boys. Do you understand that?"

Sage nodded eagerly, like he desired nothing more than an opportunity to lick Kaspar Mordaunt's boots.

TWENTY FOUR

MORDAUNT STARED AT HIM LONG enough for Sage to shift uncomfortably where he stood. At last, with suspicion still narrowing his eyes, Mordaunt said, "Okay, Crowley, I'll give you a tryout. See that you meet Fogel and Drake around eight tonight at Erickson's saloon. Afterwards, go get your gear and come back here. You'll be staying right here in the boardinghouse. I want to keep you where I can see you."

Sage got out of there, went to his hotel and checked out. He made a flying visit to Mozart's where he dropped off his salesman's garb and picked up the rest of his seaman's duds. He arrived just as the dinner hour ended. When his mother climbed to the third floor, her steps sounded heavier than usual.

"What's wrong?" he asked her when she entered his room.

"With you and Fong gone, it's more work on me," she said without rancor.

"Fong's gone?"

She nodded glumly.

"He's out looking for LaRue," Sage told his mother.

She rolled her eyes. "You think I don't know that? Why do you think I didn't sleep a wink last night?"

"Guess I was stating the obvious," Sage said as he reached across the table to pat her hand. He wanted to reassure her. To tell her that Fong couldn't get into trouble because LaRue was gone, already on his way to the whaling grounds. But Sage held that information back. He wasn't sure whether he kept quiet from shame or from the need to tell Fong about it first.

Noises sounded above their heads and their eyes jerked up toward the ceiling. Someone was in the attic. Fong had returned.

"I'd better go talk to him," Sage said.

❀ ❀ ❀

"Mr. Fong," Sage began, but stopped when he realized Fong was rolling up a scroll that had hung on the wall for two years.

"What are you doing? Why are you taking down the scroll?" he asked. Was Fong preparing for death or for arrest? Putting his possessions in order? "You don't need to do that. If anything goes wrong, I'll make sure your wife . . ."

Fong flung a trunk lid open with such force that it crashed against the wall. It was the first time Sage had ever seen Fong angry.

"Mr. Fong," he began as the trunk lid slammed back down.

Fong whirled toward him, his face suffused with anger. "You interfered, Sage. You put nose where it not supposed to be!"

How could Fong know? He hadn't been seen with LaRue. He was certain of it. "Fong, I don't know what you're talking about."

"Do not lie! You with LaRue and now he disappear! I just watch you go in and out of his hotel. Cousin who scrub floors in drummer hotel say you and LaRue left hotel together after supper yesterday. LaRue never came back to sleep in bed."

Sage raised a placating hand, "You're right. I did get involved, but maybe I've solved your problem."

Fong's face flushed a deeper red. "It not your business to solve my problem! Where is LaRue? You tell me now." He stepped forward, fists clenched.

Sage stepped back out of Fong's reach, saying, "LaRue's heading downriver on a whaling ship. The ship has rotten timbers, a bad captain and it's heading toward the Bering Strait to hunt whales. It's such a leaky old bucket that no one wanted to sail on her."

"What do you mean?"

"I mean I shanghaied LaRue. Used him as bait to get in with the crimps. They dumped him onto an old rotten whaler heading for the Arctic Ocean. People predict that the ship will sink, and if it does, LaRue will sink with it!"

Rather than being pleased or less angry, Fong turned more infuriated. "You should not have stuck your nose in my business. It is my duty to take care of my uncle's murderer, not you. You had no right, you . . . white man," Fong put a snarling emphasis on the second to last word.

"Wait a minute, Fong. You're the one always blathering on about Life pushing opportunity up against that damn bird's legs. You're not the only one Life sends opportunity to." Sage's words were heated and he could feel his face reddening as anger rose in him at Fong's insult. The man didn't even care what risks Sage had taken.

"It is my duty to kill LaRue. You have robbed me!" Fong shouted and hit his own chest with a closed fist.

Enough of this! "Listen to yourself, Fong Kam Tong, you're nothing but a damn hypocrite. You keep telling me that hatred has no place in a warrior's heart. Yet you were planning to kill a man with nothing but hate in your heart! You are nothing more than a murdering boo how doy! You never changed at all!" Now, Sage was shouting, too.

Fong's lightening blow to Sage's breastbone knocked him to the floor and sent him sliding across its polished surface. The Chinese man followed and raised a foot as if to kick Sage. At the last moment, he checked the motion. Without another word, and taking nothing with him, Fong rushed from the room, slamming the stair door as he left.

A few minutes later, when his mother timidly pushed the door open, Sage still lay on the floor, immobilized by the pain of the blow and shock. He had come close to dying at his friend's hand.

She knelt beside him. "Are you all right, Sage?" She touched his arm lightly but he batted it away.

"Fong is nothing but a phony. He says one thing and does another."

She laughed. "And who doesn't do that, Sage?" She moved to sit on the trunk.

He didn't see the humor. He told her about LaRue and about his fight with Fong, saying, "He preaches that I have to be balanced and I am never to act with hate in my heart. He tells me to live the right way and then he doesn't do it himself!"

She waited a beat before saying, her voice gentle, "Surely, you can see that a man might slip a bit when he's faced with Fong's situation? Sage, you need to see this from Fong's point of view, as his friend, not as his student. Fong thought he had a duty, he worked himself up so he could perform that duty, then you jumped in and changed everything."

"He should be grateful to me!"

"Maybe one day he will be. We'll have to wait and see." She slapped her palms on her knees. "Meanwhile, we have another problem. Matthew's gone missing."

"How could he go missing? He's supposed to be in Milwaukie taking care of Grace Kincaid and her baby."

"Nope, not anymore. That telegram I sent to her husband's kin worked. They rode the train out here from the Midwest. They turned up yesterday and Matthew pedaled home in the afternoon. He reported that Grace's in-laws were full of hugs and tears. They insisted on taking care of her from now on. She'll be all right. She and baby Faith won't be alone anymore."

"Good. You say Matthew came home yesterday, and he's gone now?"

"This morning he left to get snap beans for today's dinner and a tire puncture fixed on that bicycle of his. He didn't come back before dinner, and we haven't seen him since. So, he's been missing at least four hours. That's not like Matthew. He's dependable and wouldn't go missing without a reason. Especially, when he knew we were waiting on those beans."

Sage hauled himself up off the floor, groaning as the movement nudged the new pain in his chest.

"I'll go try to track him down," he said.

Rydman's bicycle repair shop occupied a narrow storefront near the vegetable market. The shop was empty when

Sage stepped inside. For a moment the heavy smell of grease combined with a jumble of objects so bewildering that Sage felt as if he'd fallen into a dustbin of machine parts. Then his eye began to sort the items out into areas of tidy arrangement. Two-pronged forks nestled on hooks jutting from the walls. In one corner, looking like a vase of fantastic flowers, seat posts and leather perches sprouted from a large wooden barrel. Tube tires were stacked shoulder high in one corner. Hand pumps, like the ones used to inflate rubberized carriage wheels, sat upon a shelf in the room's center. On another shelf, he saw nickel-plated shapes, and stepping forward, he realized they were carbide gas lanterns, smaller but similar to those mounted on wagons. Chrome wheels–some giant, others small–also hung from wall hooks. Near the front windows, where the light shone the brightest, tools, sprockets, gears, and chains lay scattered across a cluttered workbench.

Amongst that clutter Sage saw a sign propped against a bicycle bell. He leaned closer to read "Ring for Service." He jangled the bell. Moments later a man strode through a curtain at the back of the shop, pulling a napkin from his collar. He was beak-nosed, bright-eyed and smiling. His smile faded when he saw Sage. His first words explained the reason for his disappointment. "Sorry, I guess I expected to see someone else." Then he came further forward, putting out a hand to shake. "May I help you, sir? Name's Helmut Rydman"

"Hello, Mr. Rydman. My name's John Adair. I sure hope you can help," Sage responded as he stepped forward. "A young friend of mine, Matthew, planned to stop by here . . ."

The man interrupted, "That's who I thought it was when the bell rang. Matthew came in here, left me with a sack of green beans to watch and his bicycle tire to patch. But he never came back."

"When did you last see him?"

"Just before ten. He said he'd return in a half hour and here it is, near to four o'clock and he's still not here. I'm worried. He's been coming here a while now and he seems very dependable."

"He is. That is exactly what has his aunt worried. Did you see which direction he headed?" Sage asked.

"Yes, that way." The man pointed north.

"I guess I'd better go looking for him," Sage said, pulling out his wallet. "How much does he owe you for fixing the flat?"

"Not a thing. I was glad to do it. Matthew's a friend of mine. Runs errands for me and helps me out in the shop sometimes, but he never will take a penny. Like I said, I just don't understand. He's so dependable, and then there's these beans." Rydman leaned down to lift a large cloth bag from the floor. He handed it to Sage. "Would you mind delivering them to his aunt? I can't leave the shop and I thought she needed them by noon."

"She did," Sage said and the two men exchanged worried looks. Taking the beans in hand, Sage thanked Rydman, and stepped out onto the sidewalk. There he paused, looking northward. Just a few blocks away he could see the southern boundary of the North End neighborhood.

Sage dropped the beans off in the kitchen and assured Ida that he would find Matthew. Upstairs, he changed back into his Twig Crowley runner's clothes. As he buttoned up his dungarees, Drake's voice sounded in his head. What had Drake said?

The harder Sage tried to grasp the memory, the more it seemed to slither away. Finally, he shrugged. The sooner he stopped trying to grab it, the sooner the memory would return.

It wasn't until he reached the end of the dank tunnel leading to the alley that the elusive memory flooded back. An awful realization hit him so hard that he froze mid-stride, putting a hand on the tunnel wall to steady himself. He thought it through. He'd been in Mordaunt's office. Mordaunt was talking. Every word now sounded clearly in his head.

"Captain Hambley is looking for a cabin boy," Mordaunt had said.

Drake had responded, "Cabin boy won't be too hard to find. My eye's been on a certain young fella, as a matter of fact."

"See that he's healthy." Mordaunt had replied.

Dread washing over him, Sage faced facts. Over the past week, a healthy Matthew had been haunting the North End's streets, snooping into Sage's activities, going places no young boy should go.

TWENTY FIVE

SAGE GOT MOVING, PRODDED into action by a conclusion as inescapable as Oregon's December rains. Matthew was dependable and he was missing. Someone must be keeping him from returning home. Drake, always on the lookout for easy prey, probably noticed the boy. Drake needed to find a cabin boy. An innocent kid from a small coastal village, who knew nothing about shanghaiing, fit the bill perfectly.

What was the name of that ship, anyway? The *Calypso*, that was it. And, Mordaunt said it was sailing soon. Two days, he said. Was that whole days? Part days? What? Sage arms tensed to slam the trap door open without first confirming the coast was clear. But, he stopped himself. Not the time to panic. The underground was enormous. He didn't know where Mordaunt kept his captives. So, he needed to remain calm, to get closer to Mordaunt before the *Calypso* sailed and find out where Matthew was imprisoned. Sage raised the door cautiously, climbing out only after making sure the alley was empty.

Once on the street, Sage dithered, uncertain what to do. If his fear was justified, searching the North End streets wouldn't turn up Matthew. He could start searching the underground–but where? There were blocks and blocks of interconnecting basements, walled-in cellar areas below every basement area. Or, maybe they were holding Matthew above ground–like in a room at Mordaunt's boardinghouse. A frantic search would only draw attention to himself and take him out of the game before he could find Matthew.

It would be hard doing nothing, but Sage concluded he would have to wait until his eight o'clock meeting with Drake and Fogel. What then? He could try beating the truth out of them, but that would put an end to the mission. It meant he'd lose the opportunity to bring Mordaunt to justice for Kincaid's death and for Stuart Franklin's brutal beating. Somehow, there had to be a way to achieve both: rescue Matthew and bring Mordaunt to justice.

How much time did he have? When did the *Calypso* sail? James Laidlaw could answer the last question, so Sage headed to the British consul's office. Laidlaw knew the sailing schedules better than anyone.

The minutes dragged by as he stood in the doorway of a closed shop across from Laidlaw's office. He was waiting for the consul's clerk to go home. Slowly the sun's line traveled up the brick until, at last, shadow covered the building's front and the sky overhead was the darkening blue of twilight. More than once, Sage caught himself twitching with anxiety. He used another of Fong's sayings to calm himself into stillness: "Waiting crane must stand still so fish does not notice." It wasn't all that helpful since the sound of Fong's voice in his inner ear also triggered a feeling of overwhelming loss. His mother was right. Apart from everything else, Fong was first, and foremost, his friend.

At last the clerk exited the consul office, pulled the door shut behind him and set off down the street at a jaunty pace. As soon as the man turned the corner, Sage scuttled from the doorway, slipped into the office and drew the door shade down as he locked the door. Laidlaw, exiting his inner office, hat already on his head, started before breaking into a smile. "Adair! I didn't recognize you at first. Pardon me for saying so, my man, but your attire today is not up to its usual standard. Back into your disguise?"

"Glad to hear it. That's the idea. Meet Twig Crowley, new runner for Kaspar Mordaunt."

Laidlaw grinned and clapped Sage on the shoulder. "Kaspar Mordaunt's operation—I can't believe you did it. This is wonderful." Face sobering, he added, "and extremely dangerous for you."

"Right now, danger is the last thing I'm worried about. We've got a much bigger problem," Sage replied and told Laidlaw of Matthew's disappearance and why he thought Mordaunt had the young boy imprisoned.

Laidlaw's lips twisted ruefully. "If I were a superstitious man, I'd be thinking that the whopper you first told me about looking for Ida's nephew has come back to bite you in the nether regions." Laidlaw said, even as he pawed among the papers on his desk. He found the sailing schedule. Running a finger down the list, he said, "The *Calypso* is scheduled to sail very early Wednesday morning so she can catch the high tide over the Columbia bar. That doesn't give us much time to find the boy, just tonight and tomorrow."

"I'm meeting Drake and Fogel in a few hours at Erickson's saloon. I'll try to find out from them where they keep the men they've kidnapped. Is there some way of making sure that the honest judge is sitting on the bench tonight when we get Mordaunt? I forgot his name."

"Judge Clarence Berquist is the one we want. I've been checking on that and I think we are in luck. Like I told you, the rest of the local judges have already left town to attend that meeting in Seaside. Berquist stayed home. Says all they do is drink, whore, and tell each other lies. So, Berquist is the only judge in town for the next few days."

"Perfect. He sounds like he might just be our best hope," Sage said. "So, if we're going to get Mordaunt indicted, we need to wrap things up. But even if Judge Berquist issues an indictment, how will we be able to make it stick? Won't the rich men behind the crimps just see that the case is transferred to someone else when the other judges return from their conference?"

"I have been thinking about that very problem ever since you decided to launch this scheme, Adair. The way I see it, there's enough interested individuals here in Portland and across the state that a loud public outcry would prevent the death of Kincaid from being swept under the rug. But we still must catch

Mordaunt's men red-handed. I wish I knew how to get the press on our side from the beginning."

"That's the one area where I can definitely help," Sage assured him, thinking of his friend Ben Johnston, publisher of the fledgling *Daily Journal*. "The *Portland Gazette* won't stick its neck out because you tell me too many of the city's wealthy are benefitting from shanghaiing. But I know the *Journal* will jump on the chance to make this a lead story. I'm certain of it."

Sage didn't mention that, as a major investor in the *Journal*, he possessed some pull with the publisher. While he'd come to trust Laidlaw, the information he gave to the British consul remained strictly limited to what Laidlaw needed to know. That was another of St. Alban's rules.

"So, we just have to figure out how to catch them red-handed and then twist an arm or two to get one of them to admit shanghaiing Kincaid," Sage said, thinking that task would be the hardest and most dangerous part of the whole scheme.

As if reading his mind, Laidlaw said, "You make it sound so easy, Adair, but I'm at a loss as to how we go about doing it."

"I've been thinking that we need the help of an honest copper and a few of his like-minded colleagues," Sage said.

Laidlaw gave a bark of derision, "Good luck. I cannot imagine how you will find one without tipping your hand to Mordaunt. Most of them are on the take."

"Actually, I already know an honest policeman. He is also a friend. He's helped me out before. I'll get a message to him and get him to meet us."

Both were silent until Sage gave voice to his biggest fear. "The question is, can we find out where Matthew is and get everything in place so that we can bring this whole matter to a head by tomorrow night–before the *Calypso* sails?"

"Doesn't look like we have much choice. We will have to make plans and move quickly," Laidlaw said, his mouth a grim line.

Sage hesitated to ask his next question because he feared the answer. He asked anyway, "Is Stuart Franklin still alive?"

Laidlaw's mouth turned down, his face grave. Sage stiffened against the answer. But when it came, it wasn't the worst.

"Just barely. He remains unconscious, so they don't know if his mind functions. One thing for certain, his sailing days are over. He'll be lucky if he can walk."

On that disheartening note, they parted, agreeing to meet at Laidlaw's house early the next morning. Sage slipped out Laidlaw's rear door and hurried back to Mozart's, where he threw on enough appropriate clothes so he could summon his mother from Mozart's dining room and tell her the plan. She agreed to find Hanke and bring him to Laidlaw's house for the meeting.

"Any word from Fong?" he asked.

"Nothing at all," she responded, her eyes softening with compassion.

As he left, she said nothing about being careful, though the hug she gave him was firm enough for his ribs to remember it for some minutes afterward. The news that Fong remained absent expanded the hollowness Sage'd been feeling until he forced himself not to think about it. "There is too much to do and too much at stake," he muttered to himself as he headed back down the tunnel. In just minutes he was to meet up with Drake and Fogel. Maybe he could learn where they were holding Matthew.

As usual, the tobacco smoke lay thick in the air when Sage entered Erickson's saloon. This time, the band's vigorous playing, the women's shrill laughter, and the men's hearty guffaws sounded muted. Sage's intense fixation on Drake and Fogel, as they sat at their customary table, had maybe stopped up his ears. As he made his way toward them, the proverbial butterflies turned so riotous in his stomach that he thought of detouring to the toilet first. But he resisted and stayed on course. Reaching the table, his hearing returned and he felt himself smiling with unexpected ease at the two men. Their faces were unsmiling.

"Gentlemen," he acknowledged as he pulled out a chair and sat.

"Evening, Crowley," Drake said, while Fogel narrowed his small eyes, each of which now sported a shiner turning purple-green.

Sage spoke quickly. "Thanks for talking Mordaunt into hiring me. Especially you, Fogel, for letting me take the credit for your shiners. Mordaunt knows it isn't easy to buffalo you two. Letting him think I did it, instead of dumb luck, is what did the trick. Tell you what, let me buy you both drinks." Sage gestured to a hovering waiter. "Bring us a bottle of your best whiskey," he commanded and Fogel's scowl softened.

"That's decent of you to say," Fogel said in his low growl. "'Course, we're getting something out of you getting hired, remember. Don't be thinking we did it for charity."

"Don't worry, I haven't forgot my promise about the training money," Sage replied, thinking that, with luck, they'd both be in jail before any such payoff came due.

Drake spoke. "We can take it easy tonight, boys. We filled all our orders so we don't have nothing to do but load the cargo aboard just before the ship sails, and that won't be until late tomorrow night."

"You talking about the *Calypso*?" Sage asked.

"Yup, she's the ship that needed men. She sails real early Wednesday morning, day after tomorrow."

"How many does she need?"

"We rounded up five and the cabin boy," Drake said as he reached, without asking, for the whiskey bottle the waiter sat on the table.

"So you found a cabin boy?"

"Just like plucking a baby rooster from the chicken pen," Drake bragged.

Fogel gave a rasping laugh at the image and Sage looked at him inquiringly.

"Drake here made that rooster joke 'cause the new cabin boy's got red hair." Fogel offered in explanation.

Sage's gut tightened as his fears were confirmed. Matthew's red hair was his most noticeable feature. It did call to mind a rooster's comb. Sage cast frantically about in his mind for a way to find out where they were holding the boy. Suddenly he became aware of two strangers standing, too close for comfort, on either side of him.

"Crowley, these are two associates of ours, just come

down from Grays Harbor," Drake said, gesturing for the two men to sit.

The strangers snagged two chairs from a neighboring table without bothering to ask the occupants' permission. Sage could see why they felt no need to be polite. Their faces said they were mean. The big one's nose was mashed to one side, his small eyes almost lost in his round, pig-like face. The razor thin man wore a pencil mustache. His dead, pale blue eyes reminded Sage of the Yukon's winter sky. No doubt about it. These were the men who'd beaten Stuart Franklin nearly to death, he was sure of it. They also fit the description of the two men who'd visited the Millmen's saloon on the night Joseph Kincaid disappeared.

TWENTY SIX

SAGE NODDED WHEN DRAKE raised a questioning eyebrow. Once he'd signaled for two additional glasses, Drake poured whiskey for the strangers and said, "Men, this is Twig Crowley. He's our new man, just hired today. Worked down in Frisco for a while. Crowley, this big fellow here is Mister Bendt." Here he jerked a thumb toward the big man, "and this other one is Mister Krupps."

Krupps spoke, his voice as reedy and thin as the moustache above his lip. "Crowley, huh? I worked as a runner down in Frisco a few years ago. Thought I knew every one of the Crowleys who worked the trade."

Sage fumbled for a response. "Few years back, you say? I wasn't in Frisco then. About that time, I was in the Yukon trying to strike it rich. Too damn cold, so I went back to crimping in Frisco and then awhile ago I decided to see a bit of the countryside. Things got a little too hot around the Bay, if you know what I mean."

"Hmm. Didn't hear no talk of a Crowley being up in the Yukon," Krupps continued to push.

"I'm a distant cousin. There's a bit of bad blood between my ma and the rest of the Crowleys."

"Don't worry about it, Krupps," Drake said. "Me and Fogel will vouch for him. He's been working a few weeks around here and seems to know how to handle a boat and that's all that we need him to do for us."

Krupps dropped the subject, but Sage soon caught the man squinting at him over the rim of the whiskey glass. Sage doubted the man was squinting to keep drifting tobacco smoke from his eyes.

Their gathering broke up once they'd emptied the whiskey bottle. Krupps' suspicious scrutiny made Sage too nervous to probe for additional information about Matthew. As he tried to think of a way to ask where the six prisoners were being kept, Drake signaled the waiter. "Bring me six sausages and hunks of bread wrapped up in paper and a jug of plain water," he ordered.

"Aw, Drake, why you feeding them?" Fogel whined. "Food just cuts into our profits, and they'll be gone tomorrow night anyway."

"You heard Mordaunt. He wants them looking healthy. They haven't eaten for two or three days. Besides, we need them to swallow the water, and by now, some of them have figured out that water has a dose of the dog that bit them in it. They eat the sausage, they'll be thirsty."

After the waiter delivered the food and water, the five men moved to stand outside on the boardwalk. Sage waited to see where they were heading next. He heard a gasp and turned to see the wide eyes and small o-shaped mouth of a man who'd come up behind them. It was Chaplain Robinson, the preacher from the Floating Society meetings. The look on his face showed he'd recognized Sage. Still, his reaction seemed overwrought. Sage had taken no vow of abstinence nor made any promises to the man. The chaplain recovered himself, mumbled something unintelligible and hurriedly moved past, leaving all five men staring after him.

"Wonder what's got into him?" Drake said. He turned to Sage, "Crowley, you go ahead on. We don't need you anymore tonight. Meet us, say, around eleven o'clock tomorrow night, right here at Erickson's. We'll need you to help us load the men and row them out to the *Calypso*. It will take at least three trips since they won't have their legs under them. We have to make sure they stay peaceable until the *Calypso* crosses the bar. Can't have the fools jumping overboard thinking they can swim to the riverbank. Our deal with the captain is to deliver them sleeping like babies."

No excuse to stay with them came to mind, so Sage bade them a goodnight and headed off. He rounded the corner only to turn back and peek around it. The four headed south. He followed from the other side of the street, stepping lightly on the sidewalk planks, trying not to scrape his boots when he hit paving stones. Here and there, from darkened doorways, women's suggestive voices called, but he silently shook his head and kept moving. Sweat soaked his hatband as he strained to keep Drake and the other men in sight. He stayed far back because Bendt kept swiveling to look behind, as if sensing they were being followed.

After a few blocks, the four men halted before a three-story stone-block building. To reach the front entrance of the building, one would have to climb stairways on either side of a broad porch some ten feet above the street level. Between and below these two stairs, an arch provided entry to a stairway that led down to the building's basement. The four talked for a while and then the Gray's Harbor men lifted their hats and departed.

Drake and Fogel descended the steps beneath the arch, the wrapped sausages and water jug in Drake's hands. Sage waited until all four men were out of sight before crossing the street. He stepped down the stairs to the basement door. It was locked. He noted the location. He hoped the runners had taken the shortest route through the underground to visit their captives. It was all he could do. At this stage, he didn't want them to catch him breaking into the underground. He'd have to wait for the best chance to find and rescue Matthew. One misstep could doom the boy and the other shanghaied men imprisoned somewhere in the dark below.

Next morning, Sage stood in Laidlaw's front parlor watching his mother and Hanke come up the street and listening as Laidlaw gave the day's instructions to his clerk over the telephone. The instrument held a place of honor on the small table in Laidlaw's front hall. Might not be a bad idea to get one for Mozart's, save time and all the message carrying. Then he dismissed the idea. The exchange operator would learn too much about their business. Besides, he'd just purchased a bicycle for the ostensible reason of message carrying. That recollection summoned Matthew's freckled face to mind, the vision jerking Sage's thoughts back to the task at hand.

As Mae and Hanke reached the stairs, she took Hanke's sturdy forearm for balance. The morning sunlight caught her hair and it seemed more silvered than he remembered. Dark circles lay under her eyes, and her shoulders stooped. Her night had been as restless as his. Mordaunt's boardinghouse was a hell hole compared to Pratt's. Raucous drunks—men and women both—sang, laughed and fought throughout the night. Mordaunt, himself, lived elsewhere.

Once they were seated, Laidlaw told them of his activities. "I went around to every one of our supporters and told them to be ready to act fast first thing tomorrow morning." Seeing alarm in Sage's face, he hastened to add, "Do not worry yourself. I gave no hint as to our planned activity. Some speculated that we intend to parade around the mayor's house with signboards. I let them think that."

When it came Sage's turn to talk, he spread Fong's map of the underground across a polished table. "This is the entrance they used," he said, putting a finger down on the map. "Sergeant Hanke, any chance you and a few men can trail them from Erickson's to make sure they go to the same place and then follow them in?"

Hanke shook his head. "Don't think that'd be a good idea, Mr. Adair. Me and my men are too well known down there in the North End. They'd spot us."

"I'm just as well known to them," Laidlaw said, "and I don't have your gift of disguise, Adair."

In the pause that followed, Mae Clemens spoke up, "Won't be any trouble for me to hunker down in a doorway near the saloon and trail them when they come out. None of those rascals know me."

When Hanke and Laidlaw looked shocked, Sage laughed. He recalled the picture she'd made when she "hunkered down" beside old Pratt's doorstep. "That would work," he said with a grin that she returned, "and once you meet with up Hanke you can confirm where we entered the underground."

"Now, wait a minute. I'm not sure I can agree that we should put Miz Clemens . . ." Hanke got no further because Mae interrupted.

"It's not up to you to agree, Sergeant Hanke. Besides, I've been in scarier situations than that. Nobody's going to bother a crazy old woman. They'll give me wide berth." Her adamant tone signaled she would tolerate no opposition. Hanke wisely held his tongue.

"So we're set. Mrs. Clemens will follow me and Mordaunt's runners when we leave Erickson's to see where we enter the underground and then she'll tell you, Sergeant. Once you and your men enter the underground, she can keep a lookout for problems on the street."

"What should I do if I see trouble coming?" she asked.

Hanke pulled a silver whistle from his belt and gave it to her. "Get into the underground, if you can, and blow this whistle loud. Not sure what we'll do when we hear it, but at least we'll know trouble is heading our way."

Their plans laid, the meeting broke up. Laidlaw planned to prepare a few more people for action and Hanke needed to enlist the aid of three policemen he trusted. Just four police officers didn't seem enough to Sage. In any potential fight they'd could be evenly matched. They would have to count on surprise and hope that Mordaunt's manpower totaled no more than the four runners Sage had already met.

The four of them left Laidlaw's house together. Sage touched his mother's arm to hold her back from starting down the front steps with Hanke. Seeing that Sage wanted a private word, Hanke continued to the sidewalk while Sage and his mother remained at the top of the stairs. Once Hanke and Laidlaw were conversing and looking away from them, Sage voiced his newest worry.

"You'll be careful, won't you?" he asked her. He figured he could handle just about anything except losing her. They'd just gotten to know each other again, after all those years of separation.

"Sage, my boy, you're the one at greatest risk. Like I said, my part's safe. I'll be so crazy looking people will be crossing the street to get away from me." She mugged a manic roll of her eyes.

"I wish Hanke could round up more police officers," he said. "I don't like the numbers."

"I don't either," she agreed. Then her gaze seemed to sharpen and fix on a thought in the far distance. "Hmm," she said after a moment of silence.

"Hmm what?" Sage asked, his voice sharp. He didn't like it when she got that faraway look in her eyes. In the past, his mother's "hmm" schemes had delivered more scares than he liked to remember.

She reached up to pat his cheek. "Nothing to worry about, son. Take care—you mean everything to me."

Sage's eyes stung, as he realized they'd both been thinking the same thing. "You, too," he said, wishing he could enfold her in his arms and squeeze her tight. But Laidlaw and Hanke would find an action that intimate most peculiar. Always, she and he were to maintain their employer-employee pretense. Yet another precaution upon which St. Alban had insisted. It was a precaution that had likely saved her life a few months back.

Her gentle smile told him that his expression revealed his yearning. "No regrets about this mission, Sage?" she asked softly.

Sage thought about Grace Kincaid's wan face and the fierce determination in Stuart Franklin's weathered one. And then there was awkward, eager Matthew, somewhere underground in the dark, alone and fearful. "Not a single one," he told her firmly. "How about you?"

She didn't hesitate. "I'm happier today than I've been in years. We're doing the right thing, Sage. And in the end, when all is said and done, that is the most a body can hope for in this life—no matter what the cost." With that, she patted his arm and turned down the steps, her back ramrod straight. Taking Hanke's proffered arm she gave a little wave before she and the big policeman strolled east toward Mozart's.

One piece of their plan called for Sage to meet with Ben Johnston, editor of the *Daily Journal*. Fortunately, this was arranged with relative ease given Laidlaw's house telephone and the fact that the *Journal's* newsroom also possessed a recently installed instrument. That was so the newspaper could "get scoops before the competition," according to Johnston's explanation when he reported the need for the additional expense.

A few hand cranks and Sage had arranged to meet the newsman at their customary place—a coffee stand tucked away between two vegetable stalls in the farmers' market. Sage wound his way through the four blocks of stalls lining both sides of Yamhill Street. As usual, the flower blooms momentarily distracted him. So did the sellers who shouted for him to examine chickens in net-covered cages, bricks of churned butter and piles of summer squash, tomatoes, cucumbers and other produce. It being the height of the growing season, the small stalls overflowed. The market was the result of combined consumer and farmer agitation. It effectively cut out the middlemen, allowing the two parties to deal directly with each other. As a consequence, the participating farmers realized higher profits while the consumers enjoyed lower prices. It had been a hard fight but, after unrelenting public demand, the city council finally gave in and issued the street market a license to operate.

Ben Johnston waited at a small table tucked between a fish stall and a vegetable stand— both operated by Chinese men who were yet more of Fong's "cousins." Sage nodded at them and they merely nodded back, used to seeing this strange white man in his ever-changing apparel. All they needed to know was that he was someone Fong called "friend" and they would watch over him as if he were one of their own. Today, he could detect no difference in their reaction to seeing him. Evidently, Fong hadn't informed them of his recent falling out with Sage.

Johnston had departed his office in a hurry. Ink blotches spotted the detachable shirt cuffs he hadn't bothered to switch out. Johnston's haste was typical for him. He was a newsman first and foremost, and Sage had offered him a front-page story.

"My God, Adair. I don't know if I would have recognized you if I passed you on the street," Johnston declared when he caught sight of Sage. "What did you do with that white blaze in your hair?

"That's the idea, Johnston. As for the blaze, lamp black does the trick unless a man is looking up close. The way I smell, nobody's going to want to step that near," Sage said.

"Something tells me this story is going to be damn good." Johnston appeared to quiver like a race horse at the starting gate.

He wasn't disappointed. Beginning with the death of Kincaid—with Sage being deliberately fuzzy about how he got involved—the story unfolded. By its end, Johnston was hunched forward so far that it looked as if he was using his shoulders to hug his ears.

"Boy, oh boy! If you can put Kaspar Mordaunt in jail, it will blacken all their eyes!" he chortled. No need to explain whose eyes would be blackened. Johnston made no secret of his prejudice against the establishment types running the city.

"Think of it. They just crowned Mordaunt 'precinct captain.'" Johnston chortled. "Fact is, they're having one of their little gatherings at the Portland Hotel this very evening, and he's sure to be there! By golly, what a story!"

"Does your enthusiasm mean that if we pull it off and Mordaunt's arrested, you'll make sure they can't sweep it under the rug?"

"Will I ever. By gosh, we can make it the front-page story for five days running. Interview the Kincaid widow, Reverend Quackenbush, Laidlaw and Franklin's doctor. I'll make it so darn public that when those judges come back from Seaside, they won't want to touch it with the proverbial ten-foot pole!"

"Okay, then," Sage said standing up and putting out his hand to shake. "Stay by your telephone and be ready to send a reporter with his flash camera when you get the call." He turned to leave and then turned back. "Promise me one thing, though."

"Anything, anything," Johnston said fervently.

"Nothing goes in the story about me or anyone else being involved except the police. You have to tell it like Hanke and his fellow officers pulled it off by themselves."

Johnston raised a quizzical eyebrow but promised, "It's a deal," he said.

Cautious elation filled Sage as he walked away toward Mordaunt's boardinghouse where he intended to keep his ears open for news about the kidnapped men. The mission was nearing its end. The players were all lined up and success seemed possible. He passed a bin overflowing with green beans and sobered. Their mission to destroy Mordaunt's operation remained secondary to rescuing Matthew from a future career as cabin boy, or worse. Sage paused when a stab of doubt hit him, then he pushed on. He felt like something was missing. Then he realized what it was. This would be the first time in two years that he would be going into battle without Fong at his side.

TWENTY SEVEN

A TATTERED BUNDLE SPRAWLED in an entryway across from Erickson's. Her scuffed boots strayed onto the sidewalk and forced passersby to step around them. Sage did, too, but not before giving her foot a nudge with his own.

They were waiting inside Erickson's at the same table. All four of them. Not just Drake and Fogel but also the two runners from Gray's Harbor, Krupps and Bendt. Sage slid into the only empty seat. Drake was talking and didn't pause. The others only glanced at Sage, except for Fogel, who spread his lips in a smile so wide that his scummy teeth showed. It was the first smile Sage had ever seen on Fogel's face and so unexpected that Sage smiled back without thinking and then felt awkward, as if he'd bumbled into a tea party where he didn't belong.

"Like I said, the boss ain't worried about the nosy do-goods stirring up trouble down at the state house or picketing the mayor's house–whatever it is that they're planning. We've built the business up to where we're the biggest crimp operation in town. Won't be long before we take over all the crimping business. Now that you boys, and Crowley here," Drake paused to nod in Sage's direction, "are on board, we'll be running the whole shebang in no time at all. The sea captains will be scared to deal with anybody but us. And we've got people looking out for our interests. Fact is, the boss is becoming an important man about town, thanks to us. We've delivered the votes in the last three elections!"

"Ah, well, I don't know," came Krupps' reedy voice, a little slurred with drink, "there's always someone who thinks he can bring you down." Bendt, the uncommunicative one, bestirred himself to nod in agreement, his small eyes gleaming in the folds of his porcine face.

Fogel leaned forward across the table toward the Gray's Harbor men, tossing another grin sideways at Sage, catching him off guard. "Me and Drake, we know how to take care of those that try to mess in our business, ain't that right, Drake?" Fogel's face and voice were unnaturally gleeful. That marked change in personality, more than the words, started alarm bells clanging inside Sage's head.

Irritation seemed to flit across Drake's face, but Sage thought he must have imagined the expression because Drake, too, grinned and his voice was easy as he answered. "That we do Fogel, that we do. Anybody tries to get crosswise of us, and our business, will find himself a hundred fathoms down, crabs stripping his toe bones and snacking on his eyeballs." The four guffawed and Sage joined in, only to have them stop laughing so abruptly that only his laughter continued on. Sage shifted uneasily in his chair. What was going on here?

Abruptly, Drake stood, "Now that Crowley's arrived we might as well get a move on." They all pushed back their chairs and stood, Sage turning toward the door they usually exited. Drake grasped Sage's arm. "Not tonight, Crowley. We'll be leaving here a different way tonight." He led them at a quick pace through the swinging kitchen doors. The five trailed past dirty-aproned cooks stirring pots on hot stoves and rows of squatting Chinese men rinsing beer mugs in buckets of grimy water.

"Remind me never to eat here," Sage muttered to himself. The unease he'd been feeling grew stronger. How long it would take his mother to realize he wasn't coming out? "Why we going this way?" he asked Drake's back.

Before Drake could speak, Fogel answered, "We go through Erickson's cellar whenever we got business we want kept especially private." His hand cuffed the back of Sage's shoulder like a weighty bear paw. Fogel's touch caused Sage to twitch in alarm. What had got into Fogel tonight? Just yesterday he wouldn't have extended a short stick to Sage if he'd seen him drowning. Now he'd turned all grins and pats on the back.

Sage fought the urge to whirl, push past the men on his heels and run out Erickson's doors. He could see himself doing it. There'd be witnesses in the crowded saloon.

Then the opportunity passed. Drake opened a door, grabbed a lantern that hung just inside and lit it. He passed the lantern back to Krupps, who was behind Sage and lit a second one. Raising his lantern high, Drake led them down wooden stairs into the saloon's cellar. Krupps followed so close behind that Sage could smell the man's lavender face tonic. Without pausing, Drake led them through a tangle of wooden boxes, full flour sacks, and broken furniture to a heavy wooden door set into the wall. Sage felt Krupp's stare on the back of his neck the entire way.

Taking a key from his pocket, Drake unlocked the door, gestured them through and locked it behind them. The five of them stood in the underground.

Dust began to clog Sage's nose. The inky blackness beyond the lanterns pushed inward and he felt an inner shriek of fear building. Quickly he looked up and counted the wooden floorboards, listening for the thumping boots and the drunken life taking place overhead. He heard all those sounds and more. This was no mine shaft buried deep in a mountain, he reminded himself, and was gratified to feel his heartbeat slow and his fear subside.

"What'sa matter?" This question came from behind him, from the heretofore silent Bendt. "'Fraid of the dark?" A sneer laced the man's low voice, and Sage twisted to see if there was a sneer on his face, too. But Bendt stood just beyond the circle of Krupps's light, his face an indistinct pale moon gleaming in the dark.

Sage again felt a sudden urge to move away from the four of them, but he kept his boots planted. Stepping away from them would look strange and it would be unsuccessful since they could grab him easily. Besides, without a light, how far could he get?

"Hey, now, don't be teasing the new man, Bendt. He's still getting used to our little underground operation here. They do it different down there in Frisco, don't they, Crowley?" Drake asked.

Krupps chimed in before Sage could respond. "That's right, Crowley, Frisco doesn't have the same kind of arrangements, do they? Tell them how it's different."

"Ah," Sage searched his mind for the stories he'd heard when he'd hung around San Francisco's Barbary Coast waterfront. "We'd fish the men out of the water right after the saloon trapdoors dropped them into the Bay. We'd tie our Whitehall boat to a piling near the trapdoor, wait for them to drop through, drag them aboard and row straight to the ships. Got to be quick so they don't drown, since they're pretty woozy from the knockout drops." Sage hoped he'd gotten the name of the boat right. "So, are we going to stand here all night?" he asked, wanting the subject to change.

"This way men," Drake responded and began shuffling in a direction that seemed southerly to Sage. Good, that meant they were heading in the direction of the entrance he'd seen them enter the night before. The fallback plan was that if his mother lost him, Sergeant Hanke and his men would use that entrance to enter the underground. How long would she wait before she gave up and told Hanke to go ahead with the alternative? Would their timing work or would Hanke be too late?

They kept moving south, passing under Burnside Street and through a series of basements. His companions were silent but, once, when Sage stumbled over a water pipe, Fogel caught his arm to prevent him from falling. When Sage said, "Thanks," Fogel rasped, "Wouldn't want you to hurt yourself." Somehow, his tone belied the kindness of the words.

Warning bells began a steady clang in Sage's head. These men are all in a strangely vicious mood, he thought. Maybe it's how they prepare themselves to do their evil deeds. A dim glow a few basements ahead stopped Sage's musings. Drake didn't hesitate, just kept moving toward it.

A scuttling sounded off to the side, probably rodents disturbed by their passage. Drake must have heard the noise, because he lifted his lantern, casting its light around the basement. The light showed nothing but discarded wood crates and lumber. The smell of joss sticks and opium began scenting the air. The heart of Chinatown must be somewhere close overhead.

Drake lowered his lantern and moved toward the distant glow. Just what was that light? Maybe they didn't leave their captives in absolute darkness, like Franklin said. Or maybe someone stood guard there. Or, maybe other men were waiting to help move the drugged men. If so, they would outnumber him and Hanke's group for sure.

Sage was wrong. The glowing light was not for the captive's benefit. Nor were there reinforcements. A solitary man who was neither guard nor extra helper was holding the lantern aloft. It was Kaspar Mordaunt himself, incongruously dressed in top hat, black dress coat, silk waistcoat, white cravat, and thin patent leather shoes.

Sage felt a spurt of satisfaction at the sight. Mordaunt would be here for the raid. Hanke would catch him red-handed. Things were turning out better than Sage could have hoped.

As they came within the circle of Mordaunt's light, Sage saw that the man's eyes blazed with hatred. Even as he took this in, Fogel and Krupps grabbed Sage's arms. At the same time, Bendt's meaty forearm clamped across Sage's throat so that his windpipe felt like it was being crushed.

Mordaunt's thin lips spread in his shark's grin. "Step forward, Chaplain," he said over his shoulder into the darkness beyond his lamp. "Is this the man you saw meeting with Stuart Franklin?"

Robinson stepped into the weak light to squint at Sage. "It sure is. I watched him scheme with Stuart Franklin the whole time I was preaching the Word." His chin appeared to quiver at the remembered affront.

"Okay, Robinson. Get your ass end out of here. Drake will stop by tomorrow with a donation for you," Mordaunt didn't suppress the contempt in his voice. Without a word, the Friend's Society chaplain shuffled off, carrying Drake's lantern.

No one spoke while the man moved beyond earshot. In the relative silence, snores penetrated the panic roaring in Sage's ears. He glanced to the left, seeing a wooden wall and iron slat gate. It was a holding pen. The snores were coming from inside the pen.

Mordaunt caught his look. "Ah. So that's what you were looking for? The location of the cell? Congratulations, Crowley, or whoever you are, you've found it. You can die a happy man. You're not a very smart man, though. Besides the preacher, Krupps here also tumbled to your game. He'd worked for the Crowleys and he'd never heard of no 'Twig.' We telegraphed down to Frisco, and sure enough, nobody's ever heard of a Twig Crowley working the Bay."

"We get to kill him, boss?" Fogel rasped, as he gave Sage's arm a vicious twist.

"Yes, Fogel. He's not to leave this underground alive."

"But, boss, if we ship him, we can make some money." Drake said.

"Not this time." Mordaunt's voice was sharp. "We want to get rid of someone permanent, we ship him dead, like we did that first union troublemaker from the plywood mill. I let you talk me into sending the kid organizer, Kincaid, out alive and now I get a telegram from Frisco saying the captain wants his money back. Said Kincaid wasn't drugged enough and jumped overboard and drowned himself before the ship ever made the ocean." He shook his head. "That was one loose end that never should have happened. And you did a shitty job with Franklin, too. He's still alive and in the hospital."

Bendt's arm tightened so that just breathing became a struggle.

"How you want it done, boss?" Drake's tone was chilling because it carried no more emotion than if he were asking which horse Mordaunt wanted saddled.

Krupp's excited piping erupted before Mordaunt could answer. "How about I stick him a few times?

Bendt's fetid breath came blasting over Sage's shoulder as he said, "Heck, we might as well all take a turn at him. Like you said, Drake, he'll be a hundred fathoms down by this time tomorrow. The captain will be happy to drop his body overboard since we're making sure he's shipping out with a full crew."

"You keep talking and that stinking breath of yours will do the job all by itself," Sage managed to croak before Bendt's arm squeezed so tight that red spots popped up before Sage's eyes.

Mordaunt lifted his brass-headed cane from where it leaned against a support column and tucked it beneath his arm. "I'm off to an important event," he informed them. "You boys have your fun. Just see that he doesn't leave here alive. Tell the captain we'll charge him twenty dollars less for each live one if he'll dump the body once the ship clears the river bar. If he's the man I think he is, he'll jump at the offer." That said, Mordaunt picked up his lantern and strode off.

Would Mordaunt encounter Hanke and the other policemen? Was a cry of alarm in the offing? Sage tensed, waiting for any opportunity. Nothing happened. Silence reigned in the aftermath of Mordaunt's departure. It was so quiet that he could hear street noises: the rumble of drays, the carousing of people still abroad in the night. His ears strained for the sound of shuffling feet moving through dust. Instead, there was only the scuttle of rodents and the heavy breathing of the men who held him. Even the snores of the imprisoned men had quieted. The only noise coming from the pen was the soft rustle of clothing as they turned in their drugged stupor.

TWENTY EIGHT

"I GET FIRST CRACK AT HIM," Fogel said as he bounced on his toes in front of Sage. "Before he dies, I want to feel his nose break." Sage waited, immobilized by the combined grip of Bendt, Krupps, and now Drake, who'd taken Fogel's place holding Sage's left arm. Fogel balled his fist, making ready to let fly. Sage tried to twist in the men's grip, but Bendt's arm, an iron bar across his throat, held him in place. Sage thought of Fong then, but none of his friend's pithy advice came to mind. So, Sage focused his attention on his belly, following Fong's instructions and hoped that the effort would lessen the shock of Fogel's punch and give Sage an opening to act unexpectedly.

As Fogel drew back his arm, Sage squeezed his eyes shut to protect his eye sockets. But the punch never came. Instead, a shrill whistle sounded and Sage's eyes flew open to see a hard object bounce off Fogel's forehead. Fogel staggered back a step, arms flailing as he fought to keep his balance. At the same time, the barred door on the holding pen slammed open and the hulking frame of Sergeant Hanke crashed into the basement, followed by three equally large policemen. Sage had barely grasped what he was seeing before Bendt grunted and released Sage's neck.

Sage did not hesitate. His foot flashed out in a kick to Fogel's chest, hitting the man so hard that he thought he felt

Fogel's breastbone snap. Fogel was falling to the ground as Sage whirled to face Bendt. But, the heavy man no longer stood there. Instead, he writhed on the ground at the feet of two Chinese men. Behind them, a serene Fong stood at the front of even more black-clad Chinese men.

Fong bowed, nodded toward the four policemen who were bringing Drake and Krupps under control, and then he and Sage's other black-clad saviors melted into the black underground so fast that Sage wasn't certain but what his imagination had conjured them up.

"Looks like we done it! Got every one of the villains," boomed a panting Hanke.

"You were inside the holding cell?" Sage asked.

"You bet. Been there so long I could draw you every mark on the planks some poor souls have scratched."

"But how . . . ?"

Hanke cut him off, stepping close and saying softly, "It was Mr. Fong and your mother, but nobody's supposed to know. They changed the plan this afternoon."

Sage nodded. Keeping his voice low, he said, "I understand." He raised his voice and continued, "Did you and your men hear what Mordaunt said?"

"Better than that." Laidlaw's voice came from the darkness on the far side of the basement. Britain's consul stepped into the light. "I was back there behind a packing box. I took down every word and so did our young friend here." Laidlaw jerked a thumb toward the man beside him. It was one of the *Journal*'s reporters. "We heard him admit to killing that first organizer and being responsible for Kincaid's death as well. He also made it clear that he gave the order to kill Stuart Franklin. And we also heard him order his runners to kill you. Wrote down every word of it."

Hanke came up, holding a moaning Fogel in his grip. The reporter whipped out his camera and snapped the two, lighting up the underground with its flash. Fogel tried to lunge at the reporter only to be jerked back to Hanke's side.

The policeman blinked a moment before saying, "We best get to the courthouse. Judge Berquist has been waiting some hours now for us to bring him these criminals. We'll drop these four off, get them arraigned. After that, we'll go round up Mordaunt and that so-called chaplain, Robinson."

"He's attending some kind of fancy do," Sage said.

"Portland Hotel," Hanke said, "where all the rest of the city's so-called 'finest' are whooping it up right now. Come on," he said, jerking Fogel along beside him, "time's a-wasting."

When they saw who Hanke held in custody, jaws dropped on the two additional policemen summoned from the precinct station to open the courthouse in the middle of the night. They couldn't spread the alarm, however, because Judge Berquist, being nobody's fool, ordered everyone confined to the courtroom. He ordered one of Hanke's men to station himself outside the door to prevent anyone sneaking out or in.

The proceedings were short. Hanke told his story and left with one of his men to arrest Kaspar Mordaunt in the Portland Hotel's ballroom just blocks away. The reporter and Laidlaw gave their evidence.

Berquist, a tall scrawny man with gray wisps fringing a freckled dome, presided from a lofty bench. His lowered brows met together on his forehead, letting all present know that he did not tolerate nonsense. "How about the six men who were in the holding pen? They willing to testify about who put them there?" he asked.

Sage and his mother sat on the rearmost bench, slouched down so that, in the dim gaslight, their faces were indistinct. But at this question Sage straightened up, intent on hearing the answer.

Laidlaw responded without hesitation. "Actually, these rascals were holding five men and a boy. I know the lad. He works in a local restaurant. All six have given their word that they'll point their fingers straight at Mordaunt and his men. Tonight, though, we told them it would be acceptable for them to spend time reuniting with their families and friends."

Judge Berquist wasted no time. Slapping his gavel down with a resounding bang, he addressed the four men who stood before his bench, heads hanging, policemen at their elbows, "The four of you are bound over for trial, without bail, on a multitude of charges including kidnapping, murder, and attempted murder. I'll let the district attorney sort it out." He aimed his gavel at the four who stood before him with faces either sullen or dumbfounded. "You best cooperate with the district attorney. These are damn serious charges. And if they are proven true, I will see you feel the full power of the law around your filthy necks." He smacked the gavel down for emphasis.

With that, Berquist ordered the two policeman and Hanke's remaining man to transport the prisoners to the city jail. He spoke sternly to the policemen just as they reached the door with their prisoners, "See that they get there, too, or I'll have you arrested! Report back to me when you're done and don't be talking to nobody. You do, and I'll jail you for contempt so you can share a cell with those rascals!" He looked toward Hanke's man, who winked back. Obviously, Berquist knew how the land lay when it came to collusion between Portland's crimps and the police.

Not long afterward, Mordaunt's outraged protestations echoed in from the courthouse's marble hallway. "I'll have your damn job. I'm a precinct man. You embarrassed me in front of my friends. I'll have all your jobs, by God. Just see if I don't!"

When he entered the courtroom and saw those assembled, Mordaunt's ranting stopped abruptly. Catching sight of James Laidlaw, Mordaunt allowed his lip to curl and he hissed, "This time, Laidlaw, you've gone too far." A rustle coming from the rear bench caught Mordaunt's ear, and turning, he saw Sage. Although Mordaunt's face paled, he still shot a venomous look toward Sage before he turned to face the judge.

"I trust that you are through with your tirade, Mordaunt?" The judge spoke in a chilly but mild tone. Mordaunt clamped his mouth shut.

The judge continued, "Mr. Mordaunt, we have witnesses who will testify under oath that you ordered five men and a boy shanghaied and delivered onto the deep-water vessel *Calypso* this very night. They will also testify that you admitted you were responsible for the death of Mr. Joseph Kincaid and another man named Amacker. You further admitted in their presence that you ordered the beating death of a man named Stuart Franklin. Finally, if it becomes necessary, they will also testify that you personally authorized and ordered the death of one," here Judge Berquist looked down at a paper before him, "Twig Crowley. What do you say to these charges, Mr. Mordaunt?"

Mordaunt stood mute, a stunned look on his face as he struggled to reconcile what he believed should have happened with what must have actually taken place. Finally, in a choked voice, he asked, "Where are my men?"

"Your men," Judge Berquist told him, grimness deepening his voice, "await you in jail." Minutes later, Hanke grabbed Mordaunt's elbow and led him out. Hanke looked so proud that Sage feared the sergeant's chest might pop the brass buttons off his uniform. Sage waited until the sounds of their exit died away, then he and his mother slid from the back bench and left the building. Once outside, Sage sucked in the fresh air, placed his mother's hand on his forearm and set off toward Mozart's.

Late the next morning, Sage climbed the granite steps to Lucinda's door, a bouquet of yellow roses in one hand. He'd decided it was time to repair the damage his absence had probably caused their relationship. Regret filled Elmira's face when she swung the door wide and saw who stood on the step. "Oh, Mr. Adair," she said, her brown eyes softening with sympathy, "Miz Lucinda's not here. She's been gone a few days now."

"Gone? Gone where?"

Elmira looked distressed. "She's traveling on the train to Chicago with a friend."

"A friend? A woman friend, you mean?"

Elmira slowly shook her head from side to side, "No, Mr. Adair."

Sage looked across the street into the yellowing leaves of the park, feeling a flick of autumn's cooler air hit his face. He turned back to Elmira and asked softly, "Well, Miz Elmira, when is it that you expect to see Miz Lucinda back from her trip?"

"I'm sorry, Mr. Adair, but when they left, she didn't say

when they'd be coming back. Miz Clara's running the house until then. If Miz Lucinda comes back at all."

As Sage descended the steps, the door behind him clicked shut softly, as if Elmira wanted not to let the sound of the closing door increase his pain. He walked up the street, flowers dangling bloom-end down from his hand, painful emotion grabbing hold of his thoughts with a brutality that caused his step to falter. So he'd gone and done it. He'd let someone special, someone he needed, slip through his fingers. He couldn't blame Lucinda. His mother had warned him. If you care about someone, if you love someone, you have to show it. Now, in his arrogant conceit, he'd lost Lucinda. His fault, no one else's.

He dropped the flowers into the lap of a homeless woman, who sat on the sidewalk with her back against the wall, her face upturned to the sun. He didn't pause to see her reaction.

TWENTY NINE

WHEN HE TOLD HIS MOTHER about Lucinda's departure from the city, she neither chastised him nor said she'd warned him. She merely squeezed his shoulder and left him to brood alone. Fong resumed his place in their lives, acting as though nothing had happened. Sage, still miserable over losing Lucinda, spent his time alone, readying his rooftop garden for winter by trimming branches, clipping rose hips and filling the planter boxes with a thick layer of hay.

A week later Mae Clemens held an intimate dinner party, closing Mozart's for the occasion. Fong spoke for the first time about how he came to be in the underground in time to aid Sage and Sergeant Hanke. In front of everyone–Ben Johnston, Angus Solomon, James Laidlaw, Sergeant Hanke, and a heavily-bandaged, stiffly-moving Stuart Franklin–Fong said, "Mrs. Clemens is very determined lady. She came to provision store and told me Mr. Adair need help. So, I have a talk with my pride. I think Mr. Adair a very good friend, and it would be wrong to turn my back."

Puzzlement wrinkled the face of everyone except Mae Clemens and Sage. Fong saw the puzzlement and hurried on, saying nothing whatsoever about LaRue and Sage's role in the man's departure from Portland.

"She tell me of plan to trap the shanghai men. We decide it would be better if we find holding pen in afternoon and already be there. I meet with Mr. Laidlaw and he agree. He also thinks that someone needs to be there writing down what people say. He talked to Mr. Johnston and to Sergeant Hanke, so in the end the underground was full of people. It was hard to keep them all quiet when we are waiting. This time Sergeant Hanke," Fong tilted his head toward the big policeman, who blushed, "finally got a hiding job where he could make plenty of noise."

The others laughed. They had either heard, or heard tell of, the deafening snores coming from the supposedly drugged men inside the holding pen, snores that covered up the advance of Fong and his men.

"It looks like Mordaunt and his men will either hang or spend the rest of their lives in prison, with much credit due to Mr. Johnston." Laidlaw said. "His newspaper has made the entire town sit up and take notice. No way they can sweep the whole affair under the table." Laidlaw raised a glass of wine to Johnston, who returned the gesture, displaying to one and all the ink stains on his cuff.

Hanke gave his information next. "The plywood factory's manager hasn't escaped. He's going to spend time in court trying to explain his role in the kidnapping of Amacker and Kincaid. Those Gray's Harbor runners, Krupps and Bendt, have loyalty toward no one but themselves. Ten minutes of questioning and they were telling how they met with the factory manager for the job and went back later to get paid off once they'd delivered Kincaid aboard ship.

"That manager was stupid. He conducted the transaction right in his office. The office clerk remembers the two shanghai-ers coming in. He's more than happy to testify. He liked Kincaid, spoke a piece at his memorial service and didn't like the man-ager at all. The entire factory shut down for Kincaid's memorial service. The factory owner paid for it, gave Ms. Kincaid money and fired the manager. We haven't been able to pin anything on the owner. But then, you always got to wonder. After all, he hired the man. Must have liked how the manager thought to keep him on."

Sage knew about the factory shutting down for the memorial service. He and his mother drove to Milwaukie to attend the event. They'd wanted to pay their respects and to take one last look at Kincaid's wife and child before they left with her in-laws. It had been a gratifying experience. The heartfelt tributes from Kincaid's coworkers sent tears running down the faces of his parents. They stood flanking Grace Kincaid, their arms holding her tightly throughout the entire service.

As for Grace, she'd taken Sage's hand and said, "Mr. Miner, I will be forever in your debt. You said Joey hadn't left Faith and me and then you proved it. She'll never know her daddy but she'll always know he never wanted to leave her. That he died trying to get back to her and to me."

"The real crooks in this," Johnston's voice interrupted Sage's thoughts, "Mordaunt's financial backers, are slinking about town, trying to act as if they knew nothing of his doings."

"So that means Earl Gordon is going to escape responsibility for his part in Mordaunt's land shark operation?" Sage asked.

Laidlaw raised an eyebrow and cleared his throat. "What was it that you told me Mr. Fong here likes to say, Adair? Something about how floating in life's current can turn up unexpected things?" Sage nodded, despite the inaccuracy of the paraphrase.

Laidlaw didn't keep them waiting. "You told me that Earl Gordon's son owed Mordaunt money. It turns out Mordaunt wasn't the only crimp the boy owed. The night of Mordaunt's arrest, Gordon's son disappeared from Erickson's. Gordon hired Dickensen detectives, but they couldn't find him. Word around the harbor is that the boy is now somewhere out in the Pacific Ocean, on the *Calypso* no less, hauling lines and lifting sails. I must admit that the idea tickles my ironic funny bone. He was well on his way to becoming a blowhard like his father."

The thought crossed Sage's mind that if the pampered Gordon heir survived, the hard work might mold him into a better man than his father. "Does Gordon know they shanghaied his son?" Sage asked.

The Scotsman's watery blue eyes held a subdued twinkle. "Let us just say that the information was conveyed to him—so he knows. I suspect this is the first time in Gordon's life that money can't soothe his discomfiture or relieve whatever guilt he is capable of feeling. He is looking pretty bleak these days—lost quite a few pounds. Not the same man at all." Laidlaw did not try to suppress the satisfaction in his voice.

Sage thought of Grace Kincaid and of little Faith who would grow to womanhood never knowing her father. But still, she would hear stories about the loving, brave, unselfish man he'd been. There was satisfying irony in the fact that one of the men ultimately responsible for the continued existence of the shanghaiing business, Earl Gordon, was now feeling a measure of the torment Grace Kincaid had suffered. For a brief moment, Sage sensed that there was a pattern to Life's currents. A pattern that surfaced, rippled and changed things before vanishing as if it had never existed. He hoped so.

At the evening's end Sage watched out the window as Matthew darted around the corner to waylay the departing Hanke. The boy looked at Hanke in the same way he had once looked at Sage.

At the touch of a warm hand on his shoulder, Sage turned to see his mother. "I guess you know that Matthew's switched his hero-worship to our Sergeant Hanke since you didn't want the boy to know the role you played in his rescue," she said.

"Thank God," Sage said fervently. "Being someone's hero is a real burden because there always comes that day when they discover you are somewhat short of perfect." Sage looked around the dining room. "Where's Mr. Fong?"

"Upstairs, in the attic, I think," she answered, understanding.

Fong sat cross-legged on the floor. The hatchet lay before him, its steel edge glinting in the candlelight, its wooden handle satin smooth from those years of use that Sage didn't want to think about.

For some minutes Sage said nothing and merely sat beside the other man, gazing at the weapon, wondering how to begin this conversation. Eventually he cleared his throat to say, "You know, Mr. Fong, LaRue may survive his whaling trip and turn up here again–he's ornery enough. You might get another chance at him."

"Ah," Fong said, his tone mildly resigned, "If LaRue does return, I will not be the same man I was a few weeks ago." Sage turned his head to look at the other's profile. He saw nothing there to explain what Fong meant. He saw only that serenity that he'd never be able to emulate.

Fong spoke again, "Sometimes a man is lucky. He has friend who is like calm pond is to crane. Smooth water of pond is sometimes mirror of crane's truth and sky in which he flies."

Fong reached out a hand to clasp Sage's wrist. "You are such a friend. You make me see that my actions do not match my words, my Way. I almost step away from promise I made to my uncle's spirit that day in the desert when I thought LaRue was dead. You save me from mistake. I am most grateful," he said.

Sage covered Fong's hand with his own. Then, when the intensity of the moment became overwhelming, he retreated into the familiar, "Which wise and illustrious Chinese sage blessed us mortals with that pond saying?"

Fong turned to look at him. A smile slowly spread across his face, "Fong Kam Tong," he said, tapping his chest with two fingers and lowering his eyes modestly.

THE END

Historical Notes

Although this is a work of fiction, it relies on a number of historical facts, a few of which include the following:

1. In 1887, thirty-one Chinese gold miners were murdered on a sandbar beside the Snake River. Their bodies were hacked into pieces and tossed into the water. There were six white murderers. The stories about what really happened vary. One version names Homer LaRue as one of the ringleaders, asserting he absconded with the gold and was never brought to justice. Out of the remaining five men arrested for the crime, one never went to trial, two escaped jail and the other three were found innocent by a white jury although they had confessed to the crime.

2. The story of Fong's San Francisco days was somewhat inspired by the tong highbinder life of Eng Ying Gong. Boo how doys who survived their days of violence with gun and hatchet were allowed to "retire" from their respective tongs and live in peace. Hong Ah Kay was, in fact, a Chinese poet living in the United States during this time period.

3. For many years the British consul, James Laidlaw, collaborated with the Norwegian and other foreign consuls to put Portland's crimps out of business. The powerful of Portland opposed their efforts for the reasons stated in the preceding fictionalized story. In the end it was the steamships, with their need for fewer but more highly skilled men, along with the unionization of the sailors, that finally put an end to the practice.

4. The Seaman's Friend Society did work in tandem with the foreign consuls to get laws passed that would outlaw crimping and its darker companion, shanghaiing. One of their members, R. M. Stuart, kept notes of the interviews he conducted after rowing out to intercept ship captains whose ships were waiting to cross the Columbia River bar. Contemporaneous writings of the Society record the suspicion that the chaplain of the Society might have been supplying information to the crimps.

5. The letter attributed to Stuart Franklin's younger brother is a verbatim excerpt of one actually written by Frank B. Richardson to his grandfather in 1888. Shortly after writing the letter, young Richardson's ship sank to the bottom of the South Atlantic with all hands reported lost.

6. Bunco Kelly was a Portland crimp. He did deliver a number of dying men on board a departing ship. The men had drunk what they thought was alcohol, only to die of formaldehyde poisoning. There was also a crimp named Kaspar Mordaunt although he operated out of San Francisco. Finally, strange as it may sound, one of Portland's crimps shipped out his own son when he came up one man short of providing a full crew.

7. Researchers believe that the worst crimps, also known as land sharks, used the interconnected basements and tunnels beneath Portland for both jailing and then transporting men to the waterfront. The Chinese, however, were even more familiar with the underground. In addition to operating opium and gambling dens there, its dusty darkness was also where they nursed their sick and dying. They were forced to do so out of the very real fear that reports of Chinese deaths from disease would touch off wholesale deportations. Lastly, as their numbers in Portland grew to being the second largest in the country, some Chinese were forced to live in the underground because those few buildings in which they were allowed to reside became excessively overcrowded.

8. Much of the Columbia River cannery work was divvied up among the various Chinese tongs. Only the members of the designated tong could work in the canneries controlled by that tong. Chinese working in the canneries generally refrained from talking to white men except through their English-speaking "China boss." This was true even though some spoke English as well or better than their China boss. They did this because the European-Americans in the surrounding communities, along with the police force, tended toward periodic and violent anti-Chinese sentiment. This threat led the Chinese cannery workers to adopt the tactic of limiting their interactions with whites.

9. When the exclusive Portland Hotel opened for business, one of its drawing cards was that its dining room service was supplied by exceptionally well-trained African Americans imported from the Carolinas. One of these men did, in fact, establish a hotel for black railroad porters. Many of the Portland Hotel's skilled, hardworking men, started other side

businesses. In time, their families became the nucleus of Portland's black middle class.

10.   Sage's boss in the labor movement, Vincent St. Alban, is modeled after Vincent St. John whom many workers called "the Saint" because of his kindliness and bravery. He eventually became one of the founders of the Industrial Workers of the World organization, its members known as the Wobblies.

11.   Countless men and women died in the United States because they spoke up for the right to have unions and engaged in a sixty-year-long fight for an eight hour work day.

About the Author

S. L. Stoner is a native of the Pacific Northwest who has worked as a citizen activist and as a labor union and civil rights attorney for many years.

Acknowledgments

I want to start by thanking the readers of *Timber Beasts*. Their enthusiasm and support for this series encouraged Sage to keep adventuring and fighting the good fight.

To the extent this series accurately reflects history, that is due to those who have done their best to preserve the past. In particular, I want to thank the staff of the Oregon Historical Society, the Portland City Archives, the Multnomah County Library, the Cascade Geographic Society, the Mt. Angel Abbey Library and the San Francisco Maritime Library. These organizations deserve our gratitude and our support. Special thanks also to Ross Reiter of the Pacific Northwest Labor History Association for his untiring efforts to preserve and share labor history. In Oregon, Jim Strassmaier, through the Oregon Historical Society, has pulled together a squad of oral historians who are trying to preserve the people's narrative. It is not only that ignorance of history dooms us to repeating it; there is also the fact that our ignorance robs us of the opportunity to celebrate the lives and victories of those who came before us. Working Americans are the continuation of a proud tradition, one that created those American characteristics best loved by the world.

This book in the series received special assistance from Sally Frese, Joel Rosenblit, Helen Nickum and Denise Collins. Many heartfelt thanks to each of them, particularly Helen and Denise who read every single word with care. And, special thanks are due Debra Murphy, of Pearland, Texas, for her willing and able assistance in the final stretch. Any remaining errors are solely my own.

Family members and friends, both old and new, are the loving foundation of this series. Fortunately, they number too many to name here without forgetting someone. I hope as they read this and other books in the series, they see themselves in the characters: their own beauty, intelligence and humanity mirrored back to them.

Last and most important, the greatest credit goes to George Slanina, whose unwavering support, kindness, and pithy observations make this series possible.

Other Mystery Novels in the Sage Adair Historical Mystery Series
by S. L. Stoner

Timber Beasts

A secret operative in America's 1902 labor movement, leading a double life that balance precariously on the knife-edge of
discovery, finds his mission entangled with the fate of a young
man accused of murder.

Sage Adair Mysteries coming soon . . .

Dry Rot

A losing labor strike, a dead construction boss, a union leader
framed for murder, a ragpicker poet, and collapsing city
bridges, all compete for Sage Adair's attention as he sloughs
through the Pacific Northwest's rain and mud to find answers
before someone else dies.

Black Drop

Crisis always arrives in twos. Assassins plan to kill President
Theodore Roosevelt and blame the labor movement. Young
boys are slated for an appalling fate. If Sage Adair missteps,
people will die. Panic becomes the most dangerous enemy of all
in this adventure.

Request for Pre-Publication Notice

If you would like to receive notice of the publication dates of the third and fourth Sage Adair historical mystery novels, Dry Rot and Black Drop, please complete and return the form below or contact Yamhill Press at www.yamhillpress.net.

Your Name: _____

Street Address: _____

City: _____ State: _____ Zip: _____

E-mail Address: _____

Yamhill Press, P.O. Box 42348, Portland, OR 97242
www.yamhillpress.net

Author Contact: slstoner@yamhillpress.net